BLOOD SECRETS

A gripping crime thriller full of suspense

GRETTA MULROONEY

Published 2016 by Joffe Books, London.

www.joffebooks.com

ISBN- 978-1-911021-57-5

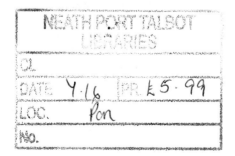

For Lesley, my personal forensics expert.

Chapter 1

I've had enough of all this crap. I've had it with misery and suffering. And secrets. No one cares about anyone else. Everyone's in it for themselves. They're all just using other people and it stinks. The innocent suffer or just get left behind. I'm leaving it all. I'm setting out to free my spirit. I'm going to travel to the Otherworld, to embrace the place of transformation and peace. I want the deep calm of the shining stars.

Tyrone Swift scanned the handwritten lines several times. They read like a despairing suicide note. The words suggested someone who found the idea of death powerfully seductive. Romantic, almost. Someone young, he thought. There was a drawing of a bird at the top of the note. It was darkly shaded and looked like a raven. He recalled a girl he had known at school who had drowned herself, filling her pockets with stones and walking into the sea at midnight in Brighton. She had become mournful during the year prior to her suicide, introspective and immersed in the melancholy poetry of Christina Rossetti and Robert Frost. He couldn't remember her name now.

The note was attached in an email sent to his business, *swiftinvestigations.com*. He scrolled back to the body of the email, sent just ten minutes ago at eleven p.m. and read the message from a Rowan Bartlett:

> *Dear Mr Swift,*
> *I have scanned the attached note for you to see. It was found in my son's room on the day he disappeared from home and it seems to suggest that he intended to commit suicide. He was found the day after the note was discovered. He had been brutally beaten about the head and left for dead. He was blinded, sustained severe brain damage and was paralysed. Whoever did this terrible thing to my son has not been found. I will ring you tomorrow to discuss further.*

It was an odd way to establish contact with a private detective. The message was somehow clinical yet melodramatic at the same time. But Swift was used to all sorts, and grief made people act strangely. He decided not to reply. He would leave the initiative with Bartlett. He switched off his laptop, stretched and headed for bed. The anguish expressed in the note played on his mind for some time.

* * *

A thundering on his front door woke Swift in the early hours. He lay for a moment, muzzy-headed. The sound, like an erupting sky, was repeated, followed by a prolonged ringing of the doorbell. He looked at the clock: three a.m. He dragged himself from bed, threw on a dressing gown and ran downstairs, twisting his ankle on the last step. He yanked the door open and was confronted by two large firefighters, framed against a fire engine complete with flashing lights.

'We had a call from this address. Do you have a fire?'

Even as the tallest one spoke, they were shouldering past him into the hallway, jackets rustling. The two of them filled the space with their urgent bulk.

'Hang on. I haven't phoned you. There's no fire here.'

They looked at each other and the tallest one consulted a phone.

'We definitely have this address. You're a Mr Swift and this is your address?' He read it out.

'Yes, that's my name and this is my address but I didn't ring you. You just woke me up.'

'We'll check anyway. Are you alone in the house?'

'No, I have a tenant upstairs in the top flat, Mr Cedric Sheridan.' The knot was coming loose on Swift's dressing gown and he pulled it tight. There was a certain disadvantage in being naked under a thin layer of towelling in front of these well-padded men. 'Cedric's in his eighties, let me wake him. You're welcome to look in my place and my office in the basement. I'll get you the basement keys.'

One of the firefighters went out to speak to the rest of the crew while Swift fetched his office keys. As he handed them over, he saw that several of the neighbours had their lights on or were looking out of their windows. He was going to be popular. He headed up to Cedric's flat, letting himself in with the spare key. Cedric disproved the commonly held view that old people were light sleepers. He was lying on his back snoring, the earpiece of his radio trailing across the pillow. Swift shook him gently, sitting on the side of the bed to avoid looming over him.

'What is it, dear boy?' Cedric sat up, resting on his hands. He always wore gaudy pyjamas and his top was patterned with pink and yellow butterflies.

Swift explained about the fire brigade. He handed Cedric his dressing gown, glad that he wasn't the kind of man to get into a flap. He took a quick look in Cedric's kitchen and bathroom and headed back down to find the firefighters, who were trudging around his flat looking grumpy.

'I've been to the top flat and can assure you there's no fire, but I know that you have to check anyway. Presumably you haven't found anything here or in the basement?'

The one in charge folded his arms. 'Nothing. You do know that it's a criminal offence to waste the fire brigade's precious time?'

'Yes, I do know that and as I've already told you, I didn't phone you. Two weeks ago an ambulance arrived here in the early hours because I had apparently reported a heart attack. A month ago the police came to an alleged break-in just after midnight. We're talking malicious calls.'

'Got enemies, have you?' The firefighter who had been up to Cedric's was eyeing him curiously.

'It seems so. I'll let the police know about this, to add to the other two false call-outs.'

'What do you do for a living?'

'I'm a private detective.' He braced himself for the inevitable witticism.

The tall one laughed, throwing his head back. 'Hopefully you can solve it for yourself, then. Okay lads, let's be on our way.'

Swift flinched as the man bellowed at the crew, oblivious to the hour and the neighbours. His unwanted visitors strode away into the night, slamming doors. He watched as the fire engine revved and drove off. The neighbours had vanished and lights were being switched off. He stood for a few minutes, looking up at the pale full moon sliding between banks of dark, fast-moving cloud. The chill breeze bore the marshy night scent of the nearby Thames. He breathed it in. It was early September and the days already carried the edge of autumn, the wind streaming from the north.

Upstairs, he accepted a cup of cocoa from a wide-awake Cedric, who maintained that it had kept him going during the war.

'Your hoaxer again, then, Ty?' Cedric asked.

'Looks like it.' Swift didn't care much for cocoa but made an effort.

'Still no idea who it is?'

'There are a couple of possibilities. I gave the names to the police. I'm sure they'll tell me that this call is like the first two, made from a public phone box in London. Sorry about the disturbance.'

'Don't worry, dear boy. It's far more annoying for you.'

Back in his flat, Swift drank a glass of water to get rid of the milky coating on his tongue. These hoax calls were more than annoying, he sensed a cumulative malice behind them. The police had asked him to listen to the first two recorded calls to the emergency services but the sexless, muffled voice gave no clues. He had also looked at some grainy CCTV images from around the phone boxes but could see no one he recognised. He lay in bed, thinking about the names he had given the police. Vincent Lomar was a nasty piece of work he had come across when investigating a missing woman, but Lomar was still serving a jail sentence. Peter Carmichael was a slave trafficker Swift had uncovered, but he had fled London and had last been heard of in Amsterdam. Swift himself had verified this with an old colleague in Interpol. He had wondered about Cedric's abusive son, Oliver. Swift had almost broken his arm when ejecting him from Cedric's flat, but Oliver had disappeared for six months to an artists' colony up a remote mountain in Andalucía with no Wi-Fi or phone signal. Swift could think of no one else from the recent past who was vicious enough to employ these methods, focusing on his home. He knew that such hoaxes carried a threat and it was Cedric he worried for, rather than himself. As he drifted into sleep he thought that he had better do an apologetic round-robin note to the neighbours.

* * *

Swift finished breakfast and threw breadcrumbs out for the birds. He had noticed that the hanging nut container was almost empty and refilled it. The swallows were still around, not yet ready to migrate and he liked to think he was helping them prepare for their journey. Cedric had cleaned out the two nesting boxes that hung on the sycamore tree at the bottom of the small, rectangular garden. He was a treasure of a sitting tenant. He had been an old friend of Swift's Aunt Lily and Swift had acquired Cedric with the house in Hammersmith which she had left to him. As well as cutting the lawn, providing Swift with jams and chutneys and occasional hot meals, he was an inspiring and kindly presence in the house and Swift was deeply fond of him. If only Cedric could find the strength to refuse access to his son, Oliver, who visited in order to hassle his father for money and sometimes physically abuse him. Swift was entertaining the unlikely hope that Oliver might get lost in mists up the far-flung Spanish mountain and never be found, when his phone rang.

'Swift Investigations,' he answered.

'Ah, yes, good. Good morning, that is. You're the detective?' A man's voice, mild and hesitant with a slight accent he couldn't place.

'A private detective, yes.'

'Good. Well . . . oh dear, now I've rung you I don't know where to start . . .'

'How about your name?'

A robin had appeared and was pecking at the breadcrumbs. Swift stayed very still.

'My name is Rowan Bartlett. I emailed you last night.'

'Yes, I read your email and the attachment.'

'I thought . . . that is I felt I needed to do something. I simply can't accept that the police never found the person who attacked my eldest son and left him blinded and beaten within an inch of his life. I don't know why he left that note or what it meant and he can't tell me. He can't communicate. I can't rest, you see, until I find out.'

'When did this attack take place?'

There was a pause and a sound like a sigh. 'Fifteen years ago.'

Swift was taken aback. The email had suggested a recent event. 'That's a significantly long time ago.'

'Yes, I'm afraid it is.'

'The police found no trace of the perpetrator?'

'They found nothing except the rock that was used to beat him.'

Bartlett's voice was becoming quieter as the conversation progressed. The robin hopped sideways, selecting a larger breadcrumb.

'So if this happened fifteen years ago, why are you asking questions now?'

'I retired recently and came back to London. I suppose . . . I suppose I have time to think, time to grieve for the man my son is now and the man he should have grown into. This is complicated, you see and not easy to speak about. Is it possible for you to come and talk to me? I have arthritic hips and I'd rather not travel across London. I saw on your website that you used to be in the police, so it seemed you would be well-suited to such an investigation.'

'I might be able to help. I can come to your home. When would be convenient?'

They agreed eleven a.m. the following morning and Swift made a mental note of the address in Tufnell Park.

'What is your son's name?'

'Edward Bartlett. We call him Teddy.'

Swift recorded the address on his phone, shifting slightly. The robin glared at him and flew away with a final crumb. He folded his long limbs on to the dew-dampened cushions of the garden swing and googled Teddy Bartlett. Several newspapers had carried the story. A paragraph in a north London paper dated August 29, 2000, recorded that he had been reported as missing by his sister, Sheila Bartlett:

> *Mr Bartlett left a note indicating that he might be intending suicide. He was found the following day near Low Copsley in Epping Forest by a woman walking her dog. He had been badly beaten and is in a critical condition in intensive care. The police are appealing for anyone who might have seen him in the area.*

Swift looked at his watch. Nine thirty. He was due to meet Ruth, his ex-fiancée, for lunch at one o'clock. Today, at last, he was determined to tell her that he couldn't go on seeing her. His chest felt heavy at the thought and he pressed his hands across his heart momentarily, as if to secure his courage. He headed down to his office to write a brief letter of apology to the neighbours. As he was printing off a dozen copies, his phone rang. The call was from PC Simons, who was liaising with him about his hoaxer. Simons had discovered that Swift had worked for the Metropolitan police and Interpol and had subsequently started addressing him with exaggerated respect.

'Ah, Mr Swift, good morning. How are you, sir?'

'Fine, thanks. Any news?'

'I'm ringing to let you know that last night's 999 call was traced to a phone box at Paddington station.'

The previous two had been from Euston and Charing Cross.

'Seems like our hoaxer might be a traveller or a train lover, or just using large public areas to ensure anonymity.'

'Exactly, sir.'

'PC Simons, please cut out the "sirs." They make me nervous.'

'Of course, s . . . of course, Mr Swift. I've listened to the call and it does seem to be the same voice. Our computer program thinks it's probably a male but it's only seventy per cent sure. We'll look at CCTV from around the station, but as you know, we've found nothing helpful at the other locations.'

He knew too that these incidents would be low on the police radar and that he was only getting this contact because of his ex-Met status.

'I think it's clear that whoever is doing this is canny enough to work their way around cameras.'

'That's right.'

'I see. Well, thanks for letting me know.'

'Just to remind you to look out for your personal safety in this situation.'

'Thanks, yes.'

'I'll be in touch if there are any developments.'

Swift thought the only development likely would be the next hostile contact, which would be in a few weeks if the current pattern was maintained. All the emergency services had been used. What next? He had told Cedric to ensure the front door and his own door were securely locked at all times, but he had the feeling that whoever was behind this was unlikely to show their hand in person.

* * *

Swift caught a bus to Sloane Square from Hammersmith, then walked to the Evergreen, the small pub in a side street near Victoria where he and Ruth had been meeting for more than a year. They had been engaged when she left him five years ago for Emlyn Taylor, a barrister. She married her new man speedily, moving to Brighton. Swift had taken a long time to recover from the blow, immersing himself in work and spending hours rowing on the Thames, trying to drown his sadness in the deep waters. They had met again a couple of years later at a friend's engagement party. Ruth's husband had developed MS and she had become subdued, unlike the carefree woman Swift had lived with. They had started to meet for lunch once a month when she came to London to teach. Swift had been about to tell her that he had to stop seeing her when she'd had a miscarriage. She turned to him for help, phoning him frequently. Swift knew that while he carried on seeing Ruth he was blocking his path to any new relationship. He was filled with guilt and self-disgust at the covert nature of their meetings. He had told no one about them, not even his cousin Mary, who he was close to. Yet, when Ruth was on a two day course in London several weeks back and stayed overnight at a hotel near Holborn, he had slept with her. Or rather, he had not slept. Lying awake in the airless hotel room as she slumbered, he had gazed at her beauty, which was no longer his, thinking of her husband in the wheelchair in Brighton, whose breakfast would be prepared by a paid carer. Earlier in the night, lying in the crook of his arm, she had whispered, *I'm so fond of Emlyn and I can't leave him, but the longer I'm with him the more I understand how much I love you and always will.*

That night had perhaps been a necessary final betrayal. Swift knew that whatever happened to Ruth in the future, she had to deal with it within her marriage.

Today was their first meeting since that night in the hotel. He saw her walking towards him as he reached the Evergreen, striding with her easy step, her coat flying open, long butterscotch hair glinting in the sun. He felt a terrible sadness as he smiled, stooping to kiss her cheek. The pub had been redecorated in a greyish white paint with photos of cypress, spruce and holly trees on the walls; all evergreens, Ruth pointed out. They said hello to Krystyna, the waitress who had been serving them every Monday since they started meeting and who assumed they were husband and wife. They ordered wine and looked at the menu, which rarely changed except for the soup of the day. It was so familiar, their browsing was a mere formality and provided a bridge into their meeting.

'You look well with your nut brown tan,' Ruth told him. 'Have you been rowing a lot?'

'Every other day the last couple of weeks. The weather's been so good, it was hard to resist.'

She smiled. 'You're an addict.'

'You're right, it is a kind of addiction. I definitely get restless and cranky if I miss out for longer than a couple of days. I suppose there are worse cravings.' Like seeing you, he thought. Seeing you is a terrible, destructive yearning.

Her eyes seemed to cloud, as if she had read his thoughts. As their food arrived she started talking about her class and he listened, eating without appetite, his stomach clenching when he thought of what he was going to say to her. He swallowed his wine, not really wanting alcohol but needing Dutch courage.

'How's Emlyn?' he asked after a while.

She studied her plate. 'Up and down. He's been getting these bouts of sudden anger recently. It's not uncommon in people with MS but I've found it hard to adjust to. Emlyn has always had such an even temperament, yet some days now he's full of a sort of bitter rage. Shouting at me, at himself. Cursing life and the hand he's been played.'

'I'm sorry. How do you handle it?'

'I just listen. Sometimes I walk away, come back when he's calmer, and talk to him. He's always apologetic — well, for a while. Then he'll turn on me without warning. Anyway, I don't want to dwell on it now. Did you have lunch with Joyce?'

11

'I did, yes. I got away reasonably unscathed although I had to work my way through heaps of food. She's immersed in her golf club these days.'

Joyce was Swift's stepmother, a well-meaning but overwhelming woman. Swift had lunch with her each year on the anniversary of his father's death. He would have preferred to spend the day quietly, remembering both his father and mother, attending vespers in Westminster cathedral and lighting candles for them. Swift was no longer a Catholic. His parents had shared a solid, enduring faith and the only time he entered a church these days was when he wanted to recall and converse with them. Yet Joyce deserved his presence and attention. She had loved his father, even if Swift couldn't bring himself to love her. She had cooked a huge roast for lunch. It was far too much food for the two of them, but Swift had manfully made his way through as much as he could. Over the dense, sherry-laced trifle he had fielded the usual questions about his single status and lack of romance . . . *I don't understand, Ty. You've got your own business, you're tall and good-looking and you keep yourself so fit. Women should be falling at your feet.* Swift had laughed, imagining himself stepping over swooning women laid out like a domino rally and changed the subject.

After lunch, he had helped Joyce plant a new rose in the garden. Whenever he looked at the apple tree, he could picture his mother sitting beneath it, wearing her linen sun hat and reading. Joyce had returned to the subject of his love life as he wielded the spade, commenting that lots of people used the Internet to find partners these days and maybe he should give it a try. *You can get too fond of your own company, you know, and you do tend to be rather private and remote.*

He had nodded and changed the subject, annoyed with her prying but acknowledging that there was a core of truth in what she said about his apparent aloofness.

'Sometimes you just have to do your duty in life, don't you?' Ruth smiled wanly as he described Joyce's dogged questioning, and asked Krystyna for coffees.

He guessed she was thinking about her marriage. Krystyna brought their coffee with a tiny shortbread biscuit in each saucer and cleared the table next to them. Edith Piaf was singing quietly in the background. *The Autumn Leaves*. Swift watched Ruth twisting open a sachet of sugar, tipping it onto a spoon and then slowly immersing it in the cup. It was the way she always did it, and it was the last time he would watch her do it.

'Ruth,' he said. 'Ruth . . .'

'It's okay, Ty, I know.' She stirred her coffee, not looking at him. 'I know what you're going to say.'

'Let me say it. We can't go on meeting. It's hopeless and wrong. This has to be the last time.'

She raised her cup and sipped, finally looking at him, her eyes misted. 'Yes, I know. We've said it all before. I've been selfish continuing to see you, taking up your time, your life.' She closed her eyes for a moment, took a breath. 'I'm glad we had that night in the hotel. I'm glad, that's all. It meant a great deal to me.'

'And to me.'

'I heard the door closing though.'

'Yes.'

She drained her cup, tipping her head back, then nodded. 'Tell you what, Ty. I'm going to go now, just head off.' She picked up her coat and bag, touched his hand gently. Her fingers were cool and dry. She pushed her cup aside, flicking the biscuit with a nail. 'Neither of us like shortbread, we never eat it.'

Then she was gone, just a trace of her perfume on the air as the door closed. He cradled his coffee and stared ahead, numb. She was a brave woman and generous, letting him go with such aplomb. It had to be done and that was the way to do it. He drank, looked at the shortbread and ate one, deliberately. It was cloying and unpleasant. From now on it would be the taste of sadness. He swallowed and asked for the bill.

'Everything okay for you today?' Krystyna asked.

'Yes, fine thanks.'

'Your wife had to dash off? She looked a bit upset, I thought.' Krystyna had witnessed Ruth's morning sickness one lunch time and had been told of the subsequent miscarriage when she enquired about the pregnancy.

'She's okay. There's somewhere she needed to be.'

Krystyna brought him his change, gliding towards him in the black plimsolls that always made a slight squeak on the wooden floor. He stood and made a decision, trying out his new status of honest man.

'Ruth isn't my wife, by the way. She's someone else's wife.'

Krystyna put her head on one side and crossed her arms over her crisp white shirt, clutching her elbows. 'She's gone home to her husband?'

'Yes. For good.'

'That's probably for the best.'

'I think so.'

Another customer was signalling impatiently for service. Krystyna flipped her notebook from her back pocket.

'Take care, make sure you come back. I have to confess I always eat the shortbread you leave!'

She squeaked away and he smiled, leaving a generous tip on his way out.

14

Chapter 2

Blackhorse Close in Tufnell Park was a fifteen minute walk from the tube station. Swift disliked the confined spaces of the underground but the morning had brought heavy rain and it was the quickest route. He zipped his leather jacket as he walked, keeping to the nearside of the pavements to avoid the spray from passing vehicles. Number sixty-five was a detached, double-fronted house of yellowing brick with traditional sash windows and iron railings at the front. There was no gate but two white columns topped with stone pineapples flanked a short mosaic-patterned path to an oak front door. He tapped with the heavy iron knocker, watching as the rain lashed dusky pink late roses.

A pallid man in his sixties opened the door. He was of medium height, and looked up at Swift.

'Mr Swift. Exactly on time. I like that in a man. Do come in out of the rain. Appalling day, quite a shock after the weeks of Indian summer.'

Swift followed him through a door on the right, into a comfortably furnished but down-at-heel sitting room with dulled parquet flooring and a large open fireplace. There was a high log fire burning in it, although the day wasn't cold. Rowan Bartlett sat in the well-worn velvet-covered easy chair drawn up beside it, motioning Swift into a large leather armchair opposite.

'That chair should be comfy for you, with your long legs. Forgive me for sitting almost in the fire. I lived in Sydney until quite recently and I haven't yet adjusted to the climate. Do move your chair back if you want.'

'Yes, I will, thanks, and I'll take off my jacket.'

Bartlett picked up a poker and turned one of the logs so that it blazed higher. He was slightly built with sloping shoulders and a generally faded air. His jeans and shirt seemed too big for him. When he spoke he held his head to one side, a little like the robin in Swift's garden as he contemplated crumbs.

'May I offer you tea or coffee?'

'No thanks, I'm fine.'

'Well . . . let's see. Before we begin, may I ask you to tell me a little about yourself in terms of your previous career? I read the summary on your website. I hope you don't mind. It's just for reassurance.'

Swift crossed his legs and gave him a level look. 'It's a reasonable question. I worked in the Metropolitan police for eight years. During that time I was seconded to Interpol and I liked it so I took a permanent post. I worked there for five years, then decided I would like to run my own detective business. If we agree that I am going to work with you, I can provide further references if you want.' He didn't add that his other reasons for leaving Interpol were that he was sickened by the sex trafficking investigations and that he had been stabbed in the thigh during a case, leaving him with a serious injury. He bore a rigid scar as a life-long reminder.

'I don't think that will be necessary. Now that I've met you, you inspire a certain confidence.'

Bartlett had a habit of half closing his eyes when he spoke and Swift wondered if this was a mannerism or an indication that he was feeling troubled and uncomfortable.

He was still holding the poker, rubbing the domed top between his fingers.

'You must think it odd, that I've waited all this time before initiating a private investigation into what happened to my son.'

'I expect you have your reasons but it would be helpful if you tell me.'

There was a silence which Swift didn't interrupt. He was comfortable with silences and often employed them. Many people found them difficult and rushed to fill them with chatter that could be useful. He could see that Bartlett was struggling with his emotions. He watched the fire flickering and spitting. Its background hiss punctuated the stillness. Bartlett replaced the poker, reached for a piece of paper on the mantelpiece, and held it out.

'This is the note Teddy left, the one I scanned to you. I assumed you would want to see the original.'

Swift took the few lines. They were written in a fluid hand in black biro on a piece of lined perforated paper torn from a notepad. The letters were rounded and even. He read again the mixture of distress and romantic hope of something better.

'Where was this found?'

'Teddy left it on his pillow. His sister found it when she came home.'

'Was Teddy suffering? Depressed?'

'Not as far as I know. He was a quiet, thoughtful boy, doing well at school. But I wasn't here, you see. I was in Australia when this occurred. I came back for a month but I had to return to my life there, my work.' He flinched visibly. 'When Teddy referred to abandonment and people looking out for themselves I believe he was talking about me, at least in part.'

'What makes you think that?'

Bartlett sighed, folding his hands in his lap. He cleared his throat, his voice becoming even quieter. 'I left the family, this house, when Teddy was eleven. I had formed a

17

new relationship. It was with my wife's sister, Annabelle. She had emigrated to Sydney and we met for the first time when she came back to visit. The rest, as they say, is history. I found employment there — I am a retired surgeon — and went to live with her. We married eventually.'

'When you say family, who else lived here?'

'My first wife, Tessa. My daughter, Sheila, the eldest. And my sons, Teddy and Tim. Sheila was fourteen when I left, Tim was five.'

Quite something, running off with your sister-in-law, Swift thought. 'So there must have been quite a lot of angst in the household.'

Bartlett's eyes were almost closed. 'Yes, my actions caused upset. Tessa never really accepted that I had gone and she slipped into depression. You must understand that my wife was already a hypochondriac, a very demanding, clinging woman. I found life with her a terrible trial. I had a challenging job and every evening I came home to tears and recriminations. Nothing I did was right. I used to dread opening the front door. Annabelle was a breath of fresh air, a true companion and support to me, someone I could share my life with fully — at least so it seemed.' His voice had developed a whining inflection as he spoke of his relationships. 'I wrote regularly after I left and sent money and occasional photographs. Sheila was the only one who ever wrote back. She sent a letter every couple of months, telling me how they were getting on. Sometimes she enclosed photos.'

'How old was Teddy when this attack happened?'

'Just turned sixteen.'

'Why does he say "Otherworld?" It's an unusual expression.'

'I'm not sure. He read a good deal of poetry and I believe he had taken an interest in mystical subjects. What do you make of the note?'

'It's tormented, sorrowful, and full of pain. It's also confusing. It can be read in different ways.'

Bartlett turned to the fire again, adding another log. The room was already uncomfortably warm. Swift watched him fussing with the poker, thinking that he didn't seem to know much about his son. Major changes could happen in adolescence and Bartlett had been on the other side of the world. And he hadn't stayed around long when this terrible incident had occurred. Looking at his bowed frame he appeared a defeated, if not a broken, man.

'Have you come back to London permanently?'

'Yes. My marriage to Annabelle ultimately proved unsuccessful and we separated recently. I had to retire because of my arthritic hips. Tessa died of a brain tumour five years ago. Sheila urged me to come back and it seemed the right thing to do. I have no other children and there was nothing else to keep me in Sydney. I have been thinking about Teddy and decided to take some action. I suppose as one grows older and there is no longer employment to occupy the day, one grows reflective. Sheila tried to dissuade me. She thinks I will just revive bad memories, but I feel I owe it to him to do this. Tessa, you must understand, objected to me seeing Teddy after the attack, even when he was in intensive care. She made a dreadful fuss at the hospital and I backed off as it was causing the staff so much difficulty. For two weeks we didn't know if he would live and I only managed to spend an hour with him.'

'Where is Teddy now?'

'He lives in Mayfields, a care facility in Hendon. He has to have help with all his bodily needs, twenty-four hours a day. He can't speak or communicate in any way. It's a miracle that he survived. I've been to see him there recently. He doesn't remember anyone or anything and hasn't since the attack.'

'What about your youngest son? Does he live here?'

'No. Tim lives in Battersea. We're not in contact, I'm afraid. I've tried since I came back but . . .' He waved a hand.

There was the sound of a key in the door, then a thud. Bartlett looked up with an anxious glance.

'Ah, that's my daughter, Sheila. She hoped to get back in time to see you.'

'She lives here with you?'

'Yes, the two of us rattle around in this large house.'

A hefty woman in a straining navy blue nurse's uniform came through the door, hands in her pockets. She had frizzy hair pulled back at the sides with barrettes, her father's pallid complexion and a long face with a pronounced jaw and double chin. Bartlett half rose from his chair.

'Sheila, this is Mr Swift. I've been giving him some basic details about Teddy.'

She nodded at Swift, speaking in a rush. 'Dad, I've told you not to sit so near the fire, it's not good for you, you know it makes you sit still for too long. Come on, move that chair back a bit.'

She made him stand and pulled the chair away from the fire. She wasn't much taller than her father and had the same sloping shoulders but because of her bulk she appeared to tower over him. Her legs were slim and shapely in dark tights and Swift reckoned that she was a woman who had hidden a petite frame in layers of surplus flesh. He was interested in why someone should choose such a form of disguise.

Sheila drew a chair up near her father and planted her legs apart, her feet, in black lace-up shoes, turned outwards.

'I have an hour for lunch,' she said to Swift, looking at him with blank, muddy-coloured eyes. 'I'm a district nurse, for my sins.' Her voice was loud and breathy, accompanied by a slight wheeze. She gulped and swallowed now and again as she spoke. 'I'm not keen on Dad employing you. I don't think it will do any good, raking over the past but he's determined, so . . .' She pulled a face and folded her arms.

'I understand you found your brother's note. Could you tell me about what happened? I know it's some time ago but as much detail as possible would be helpful.'

'Oh, I told the police so many times, I think I know it all by heart. It was August 27, 2000. I came home from the hospital about five o'clock — I had just started my nursing training. Mum was lying down as usual and I expected to find Teddy working on his summer reading. He was due to go into the sixth form. Teddy usually timetabled that part of the day for study. When I couldn't find him, I looked in his room and found the note on his pillow.' She coughed, holding her chest.

'What happened next?'

'Obviously I was very worried. I woke Mum up. We searched the house and garden, twice. We were frantic. Then I called the police.'

'It was school holidays when this happened. Had Teddy been at home that day?'

'He was still in bed when I left at eight a.m., Mum had no idea what Teddy had done that day. Mum wasn't well, she took medication for depression. She slept a good deal, in the day and night.'

Bartlett had covered his face with one hand as his daughter talked. Swift added to his notes while Sheila cleared her throat, took a sweet from her pocket and popped it in her mouth.

'What did you make of his note?'

'Well, it was terrible, shocking. He sounded so upset. The police asked if Teddy had been depressed in any way but we didn't know of anything that might make him want to take his own life. I'd been anaemic for a couple of months that summer so I hadn't been as on the ball as usual, but I hadn't noticed any problems.'

'And this Otherworld he referred to in the note and the drawing of the bird?'

'Otherworld means the next life, after death. Teddy had been studying Druids in connection with Roman Britain and started reading about Celtic mythology. That's where he found out about the Otherworld. The bird he drew on the note is a raven. It has special meaning for Druids. Teddy was imaginative, you see, always had his head in the clouds.' She smiled for the first time.

Bartlett shifted in his chair and she turned to look at him, taking his hand and patting it.

'Are you okay, Dad? This must be hard for you.'

He shook his head and ran his free hand through his thinning hair. He seemed to have faded even more in his daughter's presence. Sheila pulled up the cushion behind his back. Bartlett wasn't an invalid but her solicitous tone made him seem like one. Swift watched, thinking how much her stoutness aged her, despite her unlined skin.

'Teddy was found the next day?'

'That's right, the twenty-eighth. A woman found him and called the police. It was in Epping Forest, a place called Low Copsley, near Chingford. That's where he had been attacked. We were told about two o'clock that afternoon and we went straight to the hospital. We were informed immediately that Teddy had major brain injuries.'

'Why would Teddy have been in Epping Forest?'

Sheila shook her head. 'We never knew. The circle of trees where he was found is called The Yew Grove. It's meant to be a sacred place to Druids, so all we could think was that he had gone there to take part in something to do with those beliefs.'

'What about friends or girlfriends?' Swift asked. 'Did none of his friends or other students from his school know anything?'

Sheila transferred her sweet from one side of her mouth to the other, hamster-like.

'Teddy didn't have a girlfriend. He was young for his age, a bit of a nerd. He didn't have many friends, at school or outside. He wasn't much of a joiner. If he wasn't studying or drawing he spent time with Mum or doing the garden. He loved nature.'

He wasn't much like an average sixteen-year-old, Swift thought.

'Given his interest in Druids, did he have connections with any groups with those beliefs?'

'No, nothing like that.'

'What about your brother Tim? Did he know anything about what Teddy had been doing that day?'

'Tim wasn't here. He was staying with our Aunty Barbara in Dorchester. That's our mum's sister. He went to her in the middle of July and came back for the start of school in September. He had a cousin about the same age to play with there, so it was a good arrangement.'

'Did the police give you any results from their investigation?'

Sheila pinched the bridge of her nose and swallowed. 'Not much, to be honest. They visited Teddy's school, talked to the neighbours and looked through his room and all his things. They didn't find anyone who'd seen him that day. The last time I saw anyone was when a Detective Inspector Peterson came round and said they had no evidence of who had been with Teddy. The rock used to attack him only had his blood on it. That was about eight months later. We knew by then that Teddy would never be able to tell us what had happened. In the end the police seemed to think it had been a random attack.'

A phone rang and Sheila pulled her mobile from her pocket. She stood up and stepped towards the window where she conducted a low conversation about an order for drug supplies. She was clearly issuing instructions. Bartlett stood also, grimacing and rubbing his right hip. He indicated that he was going to get a glass of water and Swift nodded that he would have one. The dry air had made his throat rough. He read quickly through his notes, writing down a few more questions. Then he watched Sheila, who was rubbing the window pane with a finger as she insisted that someone check details on a database.

'Sorry about that,' she said, sitting again. 'I head up two teams and it seems no one else can ever make a decision. I don't know what they'd do if I broke my leg or decided to go away for a couple of months. They even rang me when I had flu!'

Swift smiled. There was a self-importance to her boasting. He imagined she liked to rule the roost.

'Was there anything missing from Teddy's room when he left home that day? Did he take anything with him?'

Sheila shook her head. 'Nothing apart from his leather rucksack. That would have had his wallet in. The rucksack was found near him but the wallet had gone.'

'Mobile phone?'

'He didn't have one, none of us did in those days. The only other thing the police said was that he had bits of whitethorn in the left pocket of his jacket and bits of blackthorn in his right pocket. That's Druid stuff again.'

'Do you have anything of Teddy's I could look at — old school books, diaries, personal things?'

'I'm afraid not. Mum burned all his stuff on what would have been his seventeenth birthday. I came home and found a bonfire at the bottom of the garden. She did the same with anything Dad left behind after he went to Australia. Mum used to say — this will sound terrible — she used to say it would have been better for Teddy if he'd died, instead of being left a vegetable.' She looked down at her hands. 'I'm afraid to say that I've found myself thinking like that at times. I go to see Teddy and talk to him but there's not much point. He gives no sign of knowing anyone, or any understanding. That probably sounds terrible, coming from a nurse.'

She dropped her voice and coughed as Bartlett came in carrying a jug of water and three glasses on a tray. Sheila leapt up to take it from him and busied herself pouring. Bartlett stood by the fire and took a couple of painkillers from a packet on the mantelpiece.

'Did you never want your children to visit you in Australia?' Swift asked him, taking a glass of water and drinking. It was tepid.

Bartlett looked down, then at Sheila. 'I did ask once, about a year after I emigrated, offered to send the tickets . . '

'Mum wouldn't let us go,' Sheila said. 'Dad sent me a letter asking and she got hysterical. She made us promise never to go there.'

'So, you hadn't seen Teddy since you left, when he was eleven. You didn't ever visit London?' Swift looked straight into Bartlett's eyes, determined that this time he wouldn't be allowed to let the lids drop.

'No . . . Tessa said she would refuse to let me see the family, so it seemed best to stay away. I didn't want to cause any more distress to them all. I hope you don't think too badly of me, Mr Swift.' The whining note had come back into his voice. He sat down and once again, Sheila reached for his hand.

'I wasn't asking from a moral standpoint,' Swift said neutrally. He looked at the two of them, hands entwined. It was an interesting scenario and he wondered how chaotic the abandoned family had been. 'I am happy to take a look at this. I'll need you to sign a contract and give me a deposit. I need a few more details as well, the name of Teddy's school and any friends he had, however casual, your Aunt Barbara's details and Tim's address. Does he know you're asking me to investigate?'

'Sheila has emailed him,' Bartlett said. 'And you'll need to know that he calls himself Tim Christie these days. It was his mother's name. He decided he didn't want to keep mine.'

'I tried to persuade him not to but . . . we don't really have much contact anymore.' Sheila gave a despondent sigh.

'Okay. I'd like a photo of Teddy as well, please, as near to the time of the attack as possible.'

'I have a couple ready, the police used them too. There's a school photo from the previous November and a family one that Aunty Barbara took when she visited for New Year in 2000. We weren't big on photos so they're the most recent before Teddy was attacked.'

Sheila went to a bookcase and found an A4 envelope. Swift decided to open it later.

'Do you think you can find out who did this?' Sheila had gone to stand behind her father, one hand on his shoulder.

'I can try. If I can't find anything significant, I'll tell you that there's not much point in continuing. I must add that if I am successful in identifying Teddy's attacker, you'll be opening yourselves up to a lot of new pain.'

Bartlett rubbed at his face and covered his eyes for a moment. Sheila looked grim. Swift thought he saw a flicker of something like annoyance in her expression.

Bartlett spoke first. 'At least we would know something instead of always wondering why and who. We would have some sense of justice being done.'

Sheila nodded. 'I miss him so much, Mr Swift. I miss my Teddy every day. I still make a birthday cake for him every year, strawberries and vanilla with a teddy bear piped in chocolate icing. His favourite. I take it to him in Mayfields. They mash some up for him.' She put a hand to her heart as she spoke emphatically. 'This has been a terrible wound in our family.'

Swift wondered if Sheila had heard those words spoken in a TV drama or police appeal. They sounded scripted.

'You and Teddy were close, then,' he said.

'We were, yes. We did everything together, really. Mum used to say I was a mother hen, the way I was with Teddy. I used to iron his uniform, make his packed lunch, organise the dentist, and remind him to take his vitamins. I suppose because Mum wasn't well, I had to step up.'

She cast a wary glance at her father but Swift could see that the memory gave her satisfaction.

'And Tim? Presumably you had to do a lot for him as well.'

'Yes, of course, but Mum was better with him. In fact she focused mainly on Tim. He was her favourite. She called him "my little man." I suppose that's often the way with mothers and youngest children, especially boys.'

Swift would have liked to be a fly on the wall in the household she was describing. He leaned forward.

'Sheila, you were here with Teddy. As his big sister, almost a second mother to him, you knew him as well as anyone. Have you ever had any ideas about the reason for Teddy's note, or recalled anyone Teddy had got mixed up with who might have wanted to harm him?'

She shook her head slowly, clasping her hands together dramatically. Her father motioned her to sit down. She took a breath, her mouth twisting in distress.

'The police asked me all that. I didn't know then and I don't know now. I just don't know and I blame myself. I've lain awake so many nights, wondering what was going on with Teddy and why he couldn't tell me. It hurt as well, you know, that he wrote that terrible note and couldn't turn to me. I asked myself over and over what I missed, what on earth he was doing out in Epping Forest. There hasn't been a day gone by since when I haven't woken up hoping it was all a bad dream.' There were tears in her eyes.

Bartlett handed her a hanky, patting her shoulder. She dabbed at her eyes, her gulps for air mingling with sobs. Swift waited, then told her calmly that he would do what he could to establish what had happened. He made sure he had all the details he needed, secured the deposit and signed contract and said he'd be in touch. As he left, he heard Sheila urging her father to have a hot lunch, reminding him she'd left soup in the fridge. He had reached the end of the road, hunching his shoulders against the persistent drizzle, when his phone rang.

'Mr Swift, I just wanted to thank you again for coming.' It was Sheila, sounding breathy.

'That's okay.'

'I wondered . . . if you do find out anything, could you contact me first? Dad's quite frail, you know, physically and emotionally. I'd like to be able to break any news to him.'

'My contract is with Mr Bartlett. I understand that you feel protective towards your father but I'm obliged to inform him as he's my primary client. If you like, I can make sure I tell you at the same time.'

'Oh. I just thought that it would be for the best, given Dad's situation.'

He could hear her irritation. 'Maybe your father is stronger than you think. I'll be in touch.'

There was something about the woman that he found disturbing and it wasn't just her bossiness. Her fussing over her father seemed unnecessary and a little ridiculous. He sat on the dank tube train, thinking that being the oldest child left in charge of a depressive mother and two younger siblings couldn't have been a picnic. Perhaps now she had her long lost father back she couldn't help but focus on him. There was no ring on her finger and there had been no hint of a partner.

He opened the envelope and drew out the two photographs. The first was the family group taken by their aunt. They were sitting on a sofa by a Christmas tree in the room he had just visited. Tessa Bartlett sat at one end, staring with glazed, unfocused eyes at the camera. She was a plump, long-faced woman in a drab navy tracksuit, lank hair scraped back in a ponytail. Her daughter looked very like her. She had her arm around Tim, drawing him into her. He was pulling a funny face, a thumb held up, a half-opened present on his lap. Teddy was next to Tim, thin like his father and with a sweet expression. He was a good-looking boy with neat features, dressed in a greyish white sweatshirt and jeans, his short dark hair like a cap. Sheila was beside him, an arm around his shoulders, not as hefty as she was now but already tending that way. She looked frumpy. She was squeezed into a roll-neck jumper and her face was impassive as she looked towards her brother. The school photo of Teddy was the usual head-and-shoulders shot. It showed him with a hesitant smile. His face, with its narrow bones and pale grey eyes emphasised his wistful, slightly elfin look.

Back at Hammersmith, Swift glanced in the window of a hair salon, ran a hand through his thick dark hair and decided it was time to brave a trim of his unruly curls. He was having dinner that night with his cousin Mary Adair, and last time they'd met she had asked innocently if he was deliberately cultivating the eighties perm look. He resisted the hairdresser's suggestion that he should have a warm wax conditioning treatment and sat watching the scissors dance. Then he closed his eyes, puzzling as to why a quiet, studious sixteen-year-old would leave a harrowing note before coming to terrible harm.

Chapter 3

Mary Adair had been Swift's close companion since childhood. She had supported him when his mother died just as he turned fifteen and when Ruth left him, a quiet, unobtrusive presence. He in turn had held her hand after a couple of failed love affairs. She bore a marked resemblance to his deceased mother and every time he saw her handsome face and wavy brunette hair he felt a jolt of welcome and fond recognition. They had both joined the Met after graduating and Mary was now an assistant commissioner. She had met her partner, Simone, the previous year and they were living together in Clerkenwell. Their apartment was one of six converted from a four-storey Victorian workhouse. It was the largest, on the top floor, with a wide balcony that ran the length of the building.

When Swift arrived, Simone told him that Mary was running late. The rain had stopped and the evening was just warm enough to sit outside, where Simone had put out plates of antipasti and bread. As always, she was dressed in a linen dress in pastel tones that complimented her café au lait skin. They drank wine and talked while a chicken roasted in the oven — or, rather, Simone talked in her lilting Geordie accent. As usual, she was like a tap turned on full, her conversation flowing unrelentingly. Her heavy, auburn-tinted hair formed a curtain around her face as she described a lecture she had recently attended on the usefulness of insects in determining time of death. She was a forensic pathologist and sliced the bread with the kind of deft strokes Swift thought she must use on the autopsy table. He was pleased to see how happy Mary was with Simone. They were a close couple. They had bought a state-of-the-art tandem on which they cycled at weekends, touring parts of Surrey and Essex, and spent evenings planning routes for their adventures. Yet he was never quite at ease with Simone. He thought that this was to do with her barrage of words and her overwhelming opinions on every subject that came up in conversation. It seemed to him that, despite her keen intellect, she was judgemental and too quick to pronounce on people and situations. He realised that this discomfort was partly due to a difference in temperament. He approached the world with a cool, dispassionate eye that sometimes resulted in others finding him standoffish. These were useful talents in the private detective but not always so advantageous in the man.

He drank his wine and ate an artichoke, listening as Simone, in quick succession, took issue with her managers, funding from the government, the local hospital and the US response to events in the Middle East. He disliked being lectured as well as her assumption that he agreed with her. A kind of boredom settled over him and he made few responses. Simone didn't notice as she moved on to the topic of rail improvements and the resultant chaos when travelling around parts of the city. Swift heard Mary's footsteps with relief and rose to greet her. She was tall, reaching almost to his shoulder and as he kissed her, she smelled of something light and deliciously peachy.

'Ah,' she laughed, 'there's been a hair incident since we last met!'

'You cut me to the quick,' he said, 'gave me a style trauma. I had it trimmed this afternoon. I think I've managed to wash all the mousse out.'

Mary hugged Simone and went to change while Swift laid the table. Simone was a talented cook and the chicken and roast vegetables followed by fruit compote were delicious. Simone continued to hold court throughout most of the meal, tapping her knife on the table when she wanted to emphasise a point. She shared her views on the Ukraine, the treatment of Ebola and the efficacy of winter flu vaccine, with Mary and Swift making occasional comments that were frequently interrupted. Swift observed his cousin, who was an articulate, independent-minded woman, wondering if home life was always like this and how she could tolerate the stream of consciousness from her partner. Mary smiled happily, her eyes gleaming with their usual vitality, nodding as Simone spoke, regarding her as if she was some kind of oracle. Perhaps that was the working balance of the relationship, Swift thought, there was a talker and a listener.

They moved back to the balcony for coffee, watching as lights came on in the surrounding dwellings. A few conker-coloured leaves drifted on the light breeze and rustled on the stone floor. For a moment Swift was back in the Evergreen with Edith Piaf singing and Ruth sitting opposite with sorrow in her eyes. He quickly suppressed the memory. Mary opened the chocolates Swift had brought. He saw her exchange a glance with Simone as he bit into one.

'Ty,' she said, sipping her coffee, 'there's something we wanted to ask you.'

'Oh yes?'

'Hmm. Simone and I have been discussing having a child. We'd like to be parents and now would be a good time. We're both in our mid-thirties so it's time to make decisions about such things.'

'Well, that sounds good. Are you thinking of adopting?'

Simone answered. 'No, not adoption. We'd like a child who is related to us biologically and I very much want to carry a baby and give birth, which is another reason for getting on with it.'

Swift reached for his coffee. 'There's no reason why you can't do that, presumably, via a donor clinic.' He was a little hazy on the subject but he knew that some gay women used donated sperm.

Mary was dipping her spoon in and out of the jug of cream, making swirling patterns. She looked at Swift and laid a hand on his. He smiled at her, turning his palm up to give her a gentle squeeze.

'I think it's great, Mary. You'd be a terrific mum.'

'Well, I hope so.'

'Can I make first claim to be godfather?'

Mary was blushing now. Simone leaned in and put an arm around her shoulders. She started to speak but Mary put a finger on her lips and turned to him.

'The thing is, Ty, we wondered if you'd be the donor.'

They were both looking at him encouragingly. Taken aback, he took a gulp of coffee.

'You want me to be your child's father?'

Simone nodded. 'Yes. It's not an uncommon arrangement. It makes a lot of sense really, especially now we know so much about DNA and hereditary conditions. With a family connection it means you know about the baby's genetic inheritance, unlike with an unknown donor.' She mentioned a celebrity gay couple who had recently given birth to a child fathered by one of the partner's brothers.

'I'm a bit gobsmacked.'

Mary refilled his cup for him. 'You'll need to think about it, Ty, we know that.'

'But not for too long,' Simone added. 'I'm not getting any younger! It would be quite easy to arrange. You just make your sperm donation and a clinic does the rest.'

Swift resented the assumption in her words. He had a bizarre mental image of the baby criticising the midwife's technique as it emerged.

'Hang on, Simone. This wouldn't just be about a "donation," as if I'm giving to charity. You're asking me to be a father, to enter into a relationship with a child. It's a huge responsibility and not something that's been on my agenda.'

Mary bit her lip. 'We know it's a big decision, Ty. If you did decide you could, it would mean a lot to me, to us. Will you think about it?'

He looked at her face. She'd always had his back but this was something different. He wished she'd asked him on her own but knew she couldn't have, that her partner had to be involved.

'I'll think about it. There are so many questions. What exactly would be my relationship with this child? Would it know I'm its father? Would you expect me to look after it as well?'

'Well, obviously you'd have access . . .' Simone began.

Swift pushed his chair back. 'Access! Sounds like I'm divorced without ever being married.'

'Ty, we can talk this all through.' Mary sounded upset.

'Possibly, but not just now. This has been rather left field. I completely understand you wanting to be parents and the time factor. It's an enormous issue to consider. I'm not sure I'm your man, so don't bank on me agreeing and do please look seriously at your other options.' He stood. 'That was a lovely meal.'

Mary saw him to the door and he put his arms around her. She seemed vulnerable in a way he'd never known.

'I know Simone can come on a bit too strong,' she said softly. 'She means well and of course she's anxious to get on with things.'

'I understand. Any baby will be lucky to have you as a mum.' He told her he'd talk to her soon and gave her a close squeeze.

He walked to St Paul's, glad of the lifting breeze. He tried to get his head around the request they had made of him. His relationship with Mary would be utterly changed, for starters, and if he agreed he would be bound in a strange intimacy with Simone. He had never seriously considered having a child. He and Ruth had talked about the possibility in some remote future but since she left him he'd had no thoughts on the subject. He wasn't sure he would ever want the responsibility or that he would be suited to fatherhood. He stood for a few minutes, looking up at the illuminated cathedral before heading to the bus stop for Hammersmith. He acknowledged to himself that if he felt more warmly towards Simone, he might be reacting differently. Upstairs on the crowded bus, the woman in front of him was holding a toddler who was fast asleep, head lolling on her shoulder. Swift studied the trusting child, then moved further down the bus, where he sent an email to Tim Christie, explaining that he was looking into what had happened to Teddy and asking if he could visit the next day.

* * *

Swift slept badly, waking often and thinking about Mary and Simone. Four a.m. found him staring at the ceiling, reflecting that he had just finally parted with the only woman he had ever considered parenthood with. He knew that he couldn't agree to their proposal, that it would complicate his life in a way he wasn't prepared to allow. He hoped that Mary wouldn't be too dejected by his refusal and decided that he would tell her on her own.

At six he abandoned trying to sleep. He checked the river tides, had a quick shower and a coffee, put fruit and a water bottle in a waterproof bag and headed for Tamesas, his rowing club. It was only a ten minute walk and he was on the Tideway by seven, sculling steadily towards Chiswick. There was a strong current after the rain and he was travelling against the tide so he stayed close to the bank. Swift rowed because it was as necessary to him as breathing. He also rowed both to forget and to remember. On this morning, he rowed to clear his mind. He focused on his breathing, blinking the slight drizzle from his eyes. The demands and challenges of the Thames allowed no other thoughts or anxieties. He concentrated on the rhythm of the oars slicing through the deep water, the other sparse river traffic, the direction of the breeze and the stream. He was now in the blissful state of being at one with the river that he craved. It was a heightened awareness and sense of profound peace that he had first discovered as a teenager and that brought him to his boat so often. A group of mallards were swimming near Putney Bridge and further on, he spotted some pied wagtails on the river bank. Just above Chiswick he ate a banana and an apple, drank some water, then headed back, waving to a runner who was pounding along the path.

* * *

Tim Christie said he would be home at four that afternoon. He lived in a first floor flat near Battersea Park. Swift arrived at four fifteen, noting the battered-looking cherry-red transit van outside. It bore an uninspiring logo with damaged lettering:

> *Christie Home Improvements*
> *Big enoug to cope*
> *Smal enough to care.*

Christie answered the bell promptly, saying he'd just got in and was making a cuppa if Swift wanted one. Swift accepted, following him down a narrow hallway into a spartan galley kitchen.

'Haven't any biscuits, I'm afraid,' Christie said, pouring boiling water. His voice was light and he hesitated slightly as he spoke, with just a hint of a stammer. He had a chesty, hollow-sounding cough. He was wearing grubby jeans and a short-sleeved T-shirt that exposed tattoos on either forearm. Both appeared to be flowers, amber-coloured and surrounded by dark green foliage.

'That's okay, just tea is fine.'

They sat in a poky living room at the front of the house, furnished with two battered sofas that looked as if they had been left there by an old person. There were small piles of things scattered around on all the surfaces: balls of string, half-burned candles, numerous boxes of matches, spanners, playing cards, used lighters, coins, electrical leads, a few socks, several torches, tubes of glue and lots of painkillers. A battered bicycle wheel was propped against a wall, well-thumbed magazines stacked in tall towers on the floor. Christie still looked very like the boy in the photograph, with open features and spiky, sandy-coloured hair. His eyebrows were thick and high arching, so that his expression had an air of permanent surprise. His right heel tapped the floor and he rubbed at a mark on his jeans.

'Haven't had time to change. I spent the day renovating a patio.'

'I saw your van. You have your own business?'

'Yeah, all kinds of home and garden maintenance. Work's not all that reliable but I get by.'

Swift wondered about Christie's reliability. He could detect the unmistakable scent of marijuana lingering in the air and he had spotted a glass pipe on the kitchen counter. That and the cough strongly suggested heroin use.

'Thanks for meeting me. You father has asked me to see if I can find out anything about what happened to your brother.'

'Yeah, Sheila emailed me. I didn't reply. I steer clear of her. Bit late for questions about Teddy, isn't it?'

'Perhaps. Sheila has doubts about it but your father has decided to go ahead.'

'Well, I suppose they haven't much else to talk about, those two. He's scurried back from Oz, tail between his legs after another failed marriage and she's got someone to dominate. You could say they suit each other.' He reached out and switched on a lamp. It was light outside but the sun had moved to the back of the house.

'Sheila has told me what she knows about what happened around that time and how she found Teddy's note. I understand you were in Dorchester.'

'That's right, with my aunt. It was the third summer I'd been sent there. Apparently I got on well with my cousin.'

'You didn't, then?'

Christie's heel tapped again. He didn't have his father's habit of dropping his eyelids but he made almost no eye contact, looking over Swift's shoulder.

'Luke? He's okay but we never had that much in common. He was the only boy, with an older sister, so Barbara, my aunt, liked to get me there as a companion. I missed my mum. I'd rather have been at home.' He glanced at Swift. 'Kids get passed around like parcels, don't they? Or abandoned.'

Swift avoided replying. 'How was Teddy when you last saw him?'

'Fine. He spent a lot of time in his room, reading and doing essays. He never seemed to notice me much, just ruffled my hair now and again or got me to help him shift stuff in the garden. I saw him the morning Barbara came to pick me up. It was early and he was still in his pyjamas, so he waved goodbye from his bedroom window.'

'You didn't notice if he seemed upset at all?'

He shook his head. 'No. Like I said, we didn't spend much time with each other.'

'So you don't know of any reason why Teddy might have written a despairing note or why he went to Epping Forest?'

Christie flinched. 'No.'

He placed a hand on his knee to stop the tapping and straightened his leg. The tattoos were catching the lamplight and Swift looked at them. He recalled reading somewhere that they could be read as a creative impulse or as an expression of anger. He wondered if Christie had self-harmed as a boy.

'Sheila and Teddy were close, though?'

'Like conjoined twins, those two. Sheila was always fussing around him, bossing him about, and calling him her teddy bear. She controlled all of us in fact. Mum didn't function and stayed in her bedroom most of the time, so Sheila was able to establish her own little Tufnell Park fiefdom. She's one of those people who likes to control everything and everyone around her. Yes, top dog, that's what Sheila likes to be. She got used to being able to run the house when Dad left. I wouldn't fancy being one of those nurses who work with her. I bet she's the Stalin of the surgery.' His face grew pinched as he spoke.

Swift heard the pain and spite of a bewildered child and this time he decided to follow it.

'You certainly don't seem to care much for your sister.'

'You're right. She's a bully, likes to manipulate people. I never liked her and I avoid her.'

'It must have been hard for you all, after your father left.'

Christie folded his arms. His words were bitter and the stutter had become more noticeable as he started to speak.

'Excuse for a father, more like. How does a man do that, leave his family and bugger off halfway across the planet with his wife's sister?'

'I think you'd have to ask your father that.'

'Not bloody likely!' He stared at the floor, then straightened and spoke louder as if energised by memory and anger. 'One minute he was calling me his little mole — I used to burrow under the duvet into their bed when I woke up in the morning — the next he'd vanished. He's emailed me and left me phone messages since he got back but I'll never speak to him again. I'll spit on his grave. He sent photos you know, from Sydney. Mum used to throw the unopened envelopes in the bin but sometimes I'd ferret around in the rubbish and look at them. All these pictures of him smiling in the sunshine, looking carefree. Him and blonde, glamorous Annabelle hanging out at the beach under blue skies while we lived a kind of half-life with a miserable mother who rarely got dressed. And this looking for Teddy's attacker. What does he care? My mum never got over him abandoning us. I had a shell of a mother, that's what I had once he'd buggered off. She was always necking pills and boozing brandy and coke. She was either ignoring me or hugging me close, breathing fumes on me and saying I was the only man in her life. She was asleep or half asleep a lot of the time. I loved her but I was frightened of her because she was lost, somehow. The house felt like a ship where the rudder has broken and the crew are stumbling around the decks.' He glanced at Swift, his eyes reddening and shook his head violently. 'Sorry. Sorry about this. I'll be back in a minute.'

Swift took a breath as Christie shot out of the room. He stood and examined the books on the shelves by the window. They were mainly about DIY, home maintenance and gardening. There were no photographs in the room and apart from a calendar, no pictures except for a small framed painting above the lamp. It was of a white animal, like a deer, in a green forest glade framed by tall oak trees heavy with acorns. The deer had large eyes and was holding up one hoof, as if beckoning. It had a Disneyesque quality that Swift found unappealing and the style of the painting seemed at odds with the plainness of the furnishings. He gestured to it as Christie came back in.

'This is an interesting picture,' he lied.

'Teddy did it. He gave it to me for my eighth birthday.' Christie had composed himself and now he straightened the frame. 'It's a white hind. Supposed to be a symbol of happiness to come. That's what Teddy said, anyway. He was into Druid and Celtic stuff.' He sat down again. 'Sorry about that outburst. I've no idea where that came from. I haven't talked about any of this for a long time.'

Swift sat. 'Are you okay to talk a bit longer?'

'Yeah, no problem.' He sipped his cooling tea.

'Your father and Sheila mentioned Teddy's interest in mythologies. Did you see the note he left that day?'

'Yeah, that thing about the Otherworld.'

'What did you think he meant?'

'I'm not sure. He often talked about stuff I didn't understand — airy-fairy, you know. All about healing and the significance of the elements, animals and plants.' He managed a faint smile, remembering. 'One of my friends' dads came round to collect him once and Teddy was wafting about holding a holly branch and talking about tree lore and the salmon of wisdom. I was embarrassed at having this nutty brother and my friend's Dad winked at me and said, *teenagers, eh?* That was nice of him. Do you have siblings?'

'No. I'm an only child. I think a lot of teenagers go through strange phases, though. Any idea what Teddy meant when he said in his note that everyone was using other people?'

Christie shook his head. 'No idea.'

'What about friends? Did Teddy have any particular mates?'

Both of Christie's heels were tapping now and Swift thought he had better not stay much longer. On the other hand, Christie still seemed keen to talk about his childhood.

'People didn't come to our house much. That time a friend came to play with me was unusual. I suppose Teddy must have had friends at school but he never mentioned any.'

'Your family was very insular.'

'I see that now. I don't really know why. I suppose it's usually the mums who help with social stuff and mine was . . . well . . .' He rubbed his forehead and eyes. 'My mum used to keep me off school, you know, when she felt lonely and wanted company. We'd sit in her bedroom playing cards or dominoes. I spent a lot of time in her room with her. She had a TV, a radio and a kettle and microwave in there. She'd heat herself soup or baked beans and eat them in bed.'

'Your mother established her own bedsit within the family home.'

'Exactly, yes. I've never thought of it like that but you're right. It smelled like a burrow, stale and fuggy. I remember when I read The Hobbit I thought of my mum's room, except hers wasn't clean and tidy. In some ways I didn't mind being in there so much because Sheila hardly ever talked to my mum, so it meant I could avoid her. I must have missed loads of school. It all added up, odd days here and there. Probably explains why I left at sixteen with two GCSEs.'

'So what about Sheila? She must have had friends.' Swift thought he could guess the answer.

'No, she didn't socialise at all. She was either cooking huge meals and cakes or lying on the sofa, reading magazines. She snacked on chocolate and biscuits all the time, getting fatter by the year. That summer Teddy left us she was ill and taking tablets, but it didn't stop her piling weight on. I remember she used to pull me and Teddy against her — she had a strong grip — and hold us with her hands locked behind our backs. I used to find it

42

suffocating. She'd say we had each other and that was all we needed.' He yawned, shaking his head, his face now drained of colour.

Swift put his notebook away. 'Thanks for your help. If you think of anything else, do contact me.' He placed a card on the coffee table.

Christie read it. 'Okay, thanks. I suppose you must hear a lot of family crap.'

'All families have their share, so I get to listen to some.'

'Right, yeah. Okay, see you, then. Sorry again for being a pain.'

At the door, Swift turned. 'It might be an idea to get the missing letters on your van replaced. It doesn't look too reassuring for potential customers.'

'Oh, yeah. I've been meaning to get round to that.'

Swift walked through Battersea Park, bought coffee from a kiosk and headed for the Thames Path towards Chelsea Bridge. Being with Christie had troubled and saddened him. It said a lot that a surgeon's child had left school at sixteen and was working as an odd job man, using drugs. He pondered the deterioration and claustrophobia of the Bartlett household after their father left. No wonder Teddy had escaped into mythologies. Sheila's controlling behaviour struck him as a needy, violent love. Perhaps Teddy had been desperate to get away from her.

He watched a police marine boat race upriver and rang DI Nora Morrow. He had met Nora while working on a previous case and felt a mutual attraction. Ruth's miscarriage and her need for his help had stopped anything progressing between them and Nora had backed off, clearly sensing that his life was complex. Now, hearing her cheery Dublin accent, he smiled. He said he needed a favour regarding information about a new case and asked if she could look up the old records for Teddy Bartlett.

'Okay, Ty. Email me the details and I'll see what there is. Been out on the river today?'

'This morning. How about you?'

'Not since we went out that time, months back. Work getting in the way, as usual.'

'Can I buy you a drink as thanks for the favour?'

There was a slight hesitation, then she said sure, that would be great. He took a deep breath after the call. That was the first time in years he had been able to ask a woman out with a clear and easy conscience.

* * *

Swift opened his front door just after six o'clock and was assaulted by a nauseating smell. Lying on the doormat and the surrounding tiles was a large pile of bloody offal. He almost stepped in it but managed to jump as his foot lifted. He looked down at the glistening, twisted shapes of livers, hearts, kidneys and what he thought was tripe. Blood had spattered up the walls and dripped onto the skirting board. He gagged and turned away to the doorway to breathe, bending and holding his jacket collar across his face. He looked up and down the street, in case the perpetrator was waiting to see his response. It was quiet, just a woman walking with two children and a suited man with a briefcase entering his house a couple of doors away. He could hear the sound of jazz from Cedric's flat and moved quickly to clear the stinking pile away before his tenant knew about it.

He left the front door open and took several photos of the entrails. Then he donned rubber gloves and found large bin bags, bleach, a scrubbing brush left by his aunt and a pack of cleaning cloths. It took him a good half hour to clear the mess. He put the door mat in a separate bag. Luckily it was bin collection the following day and the weather was cool. He scrubbed the tiles and washed down the skirting board, the paintwork and the back of the door. Even after he had rinsed the floor three times with hot water and bleach, he was convinced he could smell the feral, cloying aroma of the organs. He found some Jo Malone men's cologne his stepmother had bought him a couple of Christmases ago. He disliked most aftershaves and had never worn it. He sprayed the hallway liberally, glad that he had finally found a use for it. It certainly helped obliterate any lingering traces. He emailed PC Simons, attaching the photos he had taken, then put his clothes in the washing machine and took a long, scalding shower. He used handfuls of shower gel, washing his hair twice.

Whoever was doing this was becoming bolder, acting in daylight, escalating the threat.

Chapter 4

Swift had risen early and spent a couple of hours on the river. The water was murky and smelled of the season, with a hint of decay. There was a scent of smoke on the air and the trees along the river bank were turning shades of tawny yellow and orange. The horizon was misty and the still air soft and hushed. Contentment skirted his busy thoughts as he grasped the oars but edged away again as he remembered Mary and the conversation they needed to have.

He headed for home, needing hot food. He microwaved some of a risotto Cedric had given him the day before, his mouth watering as garlic and parmesan scented the kitchen. When he had eaten he brewed a strong coffee and phoned Teddy's Aunty Barbara in Dorchester.

'Hello, is that Barbara Stead?'

'Yes, unknown number. I'm not interested in changing my energy supplier or any other such rubbish so bugger off . . .'

'Hold on, hold on! This isn't a cold call. My name is Tyrone Swift. I'm a private investigator, hired by Rowan Bartlett.'

She laughed. 'Oh, sorry. Yes, Sheila did email me saying her father was back.'

'I hope you don't mind me ringing you. I just wanted to ask a few questions.'

'That's all right. Hold on a minute, I want to let the dog out.'

There were barks and sounds of doors banging. She returned quickly.

'Right, that's a relief. I can think now. He's a puppy and it's like having a toddler around. So Rowan's back in town. Feeling guilty and looking for answers about Teddy, is he? Pity he didn't want to at the time, when the poor boy was attacked. I hear Annabelle dumped him. That's justice, at least, some small satisfaction in the scheme of things. If only Tessa had lived to hear it. I mean, I know she was a difficult woman and hard going but isn't that what marriage is all about, navigating the good and bad times? I haven't seen any of the family since Tessa's funeral, by the way.'

Swift was pleased to hear that she seemed both garrulous and spiteful. Such informants usually offered rich pickings.

'I gather you don't much like your brother-in-law.'

She snorted. 'He's an utterly selfish bastard. He abandoned that family and left them to sink. My sister was never a strong woman and his leaving did her in. She never got over it. Annabelle was twelve years younger than her, you know. It was bad enough being replaced by a younger model, but your sister! I haven't spoken to that bitch since. I've never understood it. I mean, Rowan wasn't what you'd call a sexy man. I always thought he was a dry old stick but he clearly had some talents I didn't know about.'

'Did you see the family often after he left?'

She was a fast talker, rattling out her information. 'Once, twice a year. I couldn't make it any more often. I had a young family myself and a job. Life was busy. I was always encouraging Tessa to visit me here but she never did. She couldn't muster the energy to make any decisions, let alone get on a train. That's why I got Tim to visit here sometimes. At least he got some country air and a break from being smothered by his mum. I don't mean to sound horrible but Tessa did smother him, just like Sheila smothered Teddy. They were a rum bunch, I can tell you. To be honest, I worried about them but I was glad I lived at a distance because they got me down. Visiting was ever so depressing, with Tessa moping about, on pills or booze. I used to try to get her up and dressed, do her hair, you know — encourage her — but she usually didn't want to know. Then there would be Sheila looming around, looking surly. She always had a sort of negative aura clinging to her. Not an attractive girl and you couldn't get much conversation out of her. Seemed to spend a lot of time up in the loft. She said she kept stuff up there for charity shops although I can't imagine that family having anything worth giving away. She told lots of lies as well, did Sheila. If she said the sky was grey, I'd have popped outside to check.'

'Why did she lie?'

'No idea. It just seemed who she was and they were usually fibs told to big herself up, saying she was a school prefect when she wasn't, that kind of thing. I remember once she said she'd come top in all her school exams and then left her report lying around. I looked at it and it told a different story. Lots of comments of the *need to try harder* variety. When I challenged her she got angry with me and tore the report up. She didn't talk to me for ages after that.'

'What was Teddy like? Did he ever seem depressed?'

'Well, that's not an easy question. Quiet, basically, a bit of a shadow around the place. I used to call him the

Ghost Moth when I was talking to my husband about him. We're both amateur lepidopterists, you see. He always wore pale shirts or T-shirts and he would just give me a sweet smile in passing, then head for his room or the garden. He had such a light tread, you wouldn't hear him moving around. Sheila was never far from him. She used to cut his hair and buy his clothes, scold him for not eating enough vegetables.'

'It seems that she acted as his mother, and your sister was Tim's.'

'That's how the cards fell, yes. Probably just as well, as Tessa wasn't really fit for any kind of mothering once Rowan took off. Sheila's a funny one but when you think about it, it's good she stepped up or the household would have ground to a halt. It's hard to warm to the put-upon look though. I do feel bad for saying that. As for Teddy being depressed . . . He was such a vague presence, so . . . *muted*, I'm not sure that anyone would have noticed.'

'Do you have any thoughts on the odd note he left?'

'I never understood it. I do know that he was into mystical stuff about Druids and such, and teenagers can be so weird. My daughter went through a strange phase at fifteen, flirting with Scientology, but luckily she outgrew it when her hormones settled down. They're an alien race, adolescents. Of course, maybe his father's departure left him a lot unhappier than we realised. I know Tim struggled with it but he was always more vocal and emotional, which is probably better in the long run. He used to have terrible nightmares and he sleep-walked. He was still wetting the bed when he came here, I felt sorry for him because he was so ashamed. I do think coming here helped him and he had male company with my son Luke and my husband. I always think that's so important for boys.'

Swift didn't enlighten her about Tim's real feelings. She seemed a well-meaning woman.

'I believe the last time you saw Teddy was when you picked Tim up during that July.'

'That's right. I'd visited just after Christmas and he was his usual unobtrusive self. He was pleased at getting a book about Druids. I remember he showed it to me. It was called something like *Secrets of the Druid World*. Then when I fetched Tim in the summer, he waved from his bedroom window. Poor lost boy. Poor Teddy. They look after him well in that care place, but what kind of life is it?'

'Presumably you don't have any ideas about why someone would have attacked him?'

'Heavens, no. He was such an inoffensive boy. He didn't deserve what happened to him. Well, nobody would deserve that, would they?'

'Okay. Thanks for your help.'

'I probably haven't been much help to you. What do you think you can find out?'

'It's early days to make any prediction.'

He gave her his contact details and rang off. He looked through his notes so far. Quiet, mystical, unobtrusive Teddy. Poor Teddy. Even the diminutive of his name with its echoes of the nursery seemed to accentuate his passive presence in the family. Yet there was anger and resentment in his note that belied the picture of a studious homebody. Swift made more coffee and browsed the web for a while, reading articles about the Otherworld. He flagged one about Druid beliefs for further study:

> *Druids believed that the soul was immortal and that the dead were transported to the Otherworld by the God Belenus. Life then continued in this location. After the person died in the Otherworld, they were reincarnated to live again in another entity. This might be a plant or the*

body of a human or other animal. The soul rested in the Otherworld between each incarnation. After a person learned enough at each level, they moved to a higher realm, with its own Otherworld. This path continued until the individual reached the highest realm called the "Source."

Swift, who held no beliefs about supreme beings or life after death, thought it sounded a relentless and exhausting process. He could see that if you were a miserable teenager who viewed life through a bleak lens, believing that people were self-serving and exploitative, it would hold its attractions. You might well be enticed by the magical promise of better things to come and animals and birds helping you. He thought back to when he was fifteen and his mother died. He recalled the feelings of desolation and confusion that swamped him, emotions that no kind words could alleviate. He remembered also how secretive he had been as a teenager, needing to fly under the radar. His stepmother's blundering, well-intentioned interest in him had sent him scurrying to stay at his Aunt Lily's house, where he could operate unscrutinised and pour his anguish into the Thames as he rowed.

He returned to his laptop and looked up the significance of animals and birds for Druids. The hind indicated positive change and happiness to come. The raven was regarded as a messenger between this world and the next and was believed also to represent healing and protection. He read Teddy's note again. What was he a victim of or needing protection from and what secrets had troubled him? Had his bitterness and despondency stemmed purely from the loss of his father or had he been speaking of some other betrayal?

A web search brought up a contact number for a Druid group near Belsize Park. Swift rang the name given, Lochru Adamsbreath. The man who answered sounded cheerful and eager to help when Swift explained his role.

'Has your group been in existence for long?' he asked.

'Since 1921. I've been in the group for twenty-five years.'

'I wonder if you've ever heard of or been contacted by an Edward or Teddy Bartlett. We'd be talking about the 1990s and he was in his early teens.'

'Doesn't ring a bell. We're a small group, you see, and there's not much coming and going. I'd say we get a new member every couple of years and it would be unusual to be approached by someone so young. If you'd like to hold on, I can look in my record book. It's in the study, so I'll be a few minutes.'

Swift waited, hearing the chimes of a clock in the background. When Adamsbreath returned, he was panting.

'Study's at the top of the house. I've looked through enquiries and membership from 1990 to 2000 but there's no one of that name or age group. We only had five newcomers in that time and they were all women, which is usual these days.'

'Are there any other groups in that area of north London?'

'No, not to my knowledge. Although, of course, belief in the Druid way doesn't necessitate joining a group. That is what many people like about it. You can attend ceremonies or gatherings as you wish, or not at all. It can be a private, spiritual search. Would you like me to send you some information about our beliefs?'

'No, that's fine, thanks. I can look on the web. Can you tell me about the significance of blackthorn and whitethorn and why someone might carry both in their pockets?'

'Well, you know there can be different interpretations. Generally speaking, I would say that blackthorn would be used for strength against adversity. Whitethorn could be to protect from harm and help to communicate with the spirits of the Otherworld. Someone carrying both would probably be feeling the need for support in their life and in their spiritual quest.'

'I see. Thanks for that. I'm interested also in the significance of the yew tree for Druids, if you can tell me anything about that.'

Adamsbreath was clearly delighted at these enquiries. Swift thought he probably didn't get many phone calls like this, where he could air his particular knowledge.

'I can indeed. The yew tree has a reputation for long life. It has always been a symbol of death and rebirth, from the time of the ancients. It speaks of the new springing from the old. The yew grows in a particular, quite unique way. The branches grow down into the ground to form new stems. They then rise up around the old growth as separate but linked trunks. After a while, they become indistinguishable from the original tree.'

'That's very helpful. Thanks so much for your time.'

'We're having a mistletoe thanksgiving ceremony next month, if you would like to come. It's in my garden and you would be very welcome.'

'I'll think about it. Thanks again for your help.'

Swift rang off, not wishing to be sold any belief systems. It seemed that Teddy was planning to enact some kind of ritual in The Yew Grove that symbolised leaving his old life behind and moving to another way of living. He made a few notes about what he had learned and found the details Sheila had given him for Teddy's form teacher. He phoned Fairacres School and asked if Deaven Harrow still worked there. He was told by the icy-sounding receptionist that Mr Harrow was the head teacher. Swift explained the reason for his call and asked to make an appointment to see Mr Harrow. The receptionist said it seemed an irregular query and Mr Harrow was a very busy man. Swift advised that he would call the query unusual rather than irregular and added that he too was a busy man. The receptionist said she would consult Mr Harrow's diary but it could be weeks before an appointment might be available and perhaps Swift would prefer to send an email. Swift asked her for her name, then inserted a chip of ice into his own voice and told her that he wanted to see Mr Harrow in person. Presumably the head would wish to be as helpful as possible regarding what had been a tragic episode for one of their pupils and his family. There was a brief silence, then a request for him to hold. He walked around with the phone, bending and stretching. The afternoon was mild and the river beckoned. The receptionist returned, her tone slightly less arctic, and offered a half hour appointment at four on Friday afternoon. Swift accepted and thanked her for being so helpful. He rang off before she could respond to the sarcasm.

* * *

Mayfields was a single-storey, functional building run by a charity. Swift waited for Teddy Bartlett's key worker in a pleasant room furnished with magazines, pictures of wildflower meadows and a water dispenser. He could hear strange, high-pitched cries now and again and the rhythmic sound of tambourines.

'Mr Swift? I'm Peter Alfonso. How can I help a private detective, with regard to Teddy?'

Alfonso's handshake was firm. He was dressed in jeans and a white T-shirt with the slogan *don't tell me I can't*. He wore an earring and a stud in his left eyebrow. Swift had been expecting a nursing uniform of some kind and was pleasantly surprised.

'Teddy Bartlett's father has engaged me to try and find out who attacked his son back in 2000.'

Alfonso put his lips together in a soundless whistle. 'The police never charged anyone?'

'No.'

'I've worked with Teddy for two years so I know he was critically injured, but not any details.'

'I felt I should come and see him. He is the victim of a terrible crime and it seemed the right thing to do.'

'You know he can't communicate, or at least not in any way that anyone's able to understand?'

'Yes. Do you think he has any awareness of who or where he is?'

'It's hard to say. All I can tell you is that Teddy has lived here since 2001 and there's been no evidence of it.'

'Okay, I won't stay long. Would it be alright to tell him why I'm here and mention the attack?'

'I don't see why not. He won't respond, though. Have you met anyone with a severe brain injury and paralysis before, or been to this kind of centre?'

'No.'

'It's just that you might be shocked. We work with people who are profoundly in need. Some visitors can find it difficult to deal with.'

Swift nodded and Alfonso led the way to a large, airy room, saying that Teddy was having massage therapy. The room held a pool full of brightly coloured plastic balls. Scattered about were plastic percussion instruments and glowing lava lamps. Quiet choral music played. There were half a dozen people, a couple in wheelchairs and several in recliner chairs. In a corner, lying on his side on a large sheepskin, was a thin, shrunken man. A young woman was kneeling beside him, massaging his hands and speaking quietly to him. There was a scent of lavender in the air. Swift wasn't easily shocked but he was taken aback as he and Alfonso approached.

'Hello, Teddy. You have a visitor today. Mr Swift has come to see you.'

Teddy's face was shrunken and blank. The skin over the missing eye was dark pink and neatly folded, the other eye unseeing. He was wearing shorts and a sleeveless sweatshirt. His limbs were almost skeletal, his frame twisted, his mouth drooping. It was impossible to tell what age he might be. Swift would never have recognised him. The therapist smiled up at Swift.

'It's okay to talk to Teddy. You could crouch down and touch his hand as you speak.'

Swift knelt at the other side of the sheepskin and touched Teddy's hand lightly. It was warm and supple from the massage oil but he could feel the frail bones through the skin.

'Hello, Teddy, my name's Ty. We haven't met before. That hand massage looks good.'

There was no reaction. The therapist had moved to Teddy's right leg and was massaging the calf.

'This is your regular time with me, isn't it, Teddy? We always have a chat while we do this. I think you like this oil.'

A woman in a wheelchair let out a high shout. Teddy made a soft noise in his throat. The therapist carried on. Swift felt intrusive. He touched Teddy's hand again briefly.

'I've come here because your father contacted me. He's living back in London now. He's asked me to try and find the person who attacked you in Epping Forest.'

Teddy gave no sign that he had heard. The music changed to Vivaldi, a burst of bright violins. There seemed little reason to stay longer.

Swift stood. 'Take care, Teddy. It was good to meet you.'

He walked back to the waiting room with Alfonso and drank a cup of water. He was used to seeing victims of violence, yet he felt more distress than he had anticipated at the sight of the damaged young man. Perhaps it was the contrast between his broken body and the caring environment around him.

'What's Teddy's life expectancy?' he asked.

'Hard to say. He has low level antibiotics to ward off infection but with someone with such complicated needs, life can be tenuous. But he has good care so he might live a good many years.'

'Does he have visitors?'

'His father's been once. His sister Sheila comes a couple of times a year. There's a brother who never visits. Says he can't face it.'

'It seems strange that Sheila doesn't come more often. She and Teddy were very close when they lived at home.'

'It is difficult for families when someone can't respond to them. I know she's a nurse but that doesn't necessarily make it any easier when it's personal. And so many years on, it can be hard to maintain visits because life moves on and gets busy. We don't pressurise families, we make them welcome when they come.'

Swift was glad that he had seen Teddy, the visit had made him a real person. But he was deeply relieved to walk away from the confines of Mayfields into the busy hum of the city.

Chapter 5

Swift met Nora Morrow in The Parterre, a bar near Portobello Road. She had told him that she liked its eastern bazaar décor, with shabby leather chairs and ethnic throws, because it was a world away from the soulless offices she worked in. She was there, tapping on her laptop, when he arrived and she had a glass of merlot waiting for him. She was wearing one of her natty suits and string ties and trainers with purple laces and flashes. He felt a rush of pleasure at seeing her as she smiled at him.

'Hi there, Ty.' She stood and kissed his cheek. 'How're you doing?'

'I'm fine. Thanks for the wine.'

'Slainte!'

They clinked glasses and she took a long draught of her drink.

'I can smell that you've been on the river,' she said.

'I did have a shower, honest . . .'

She laughed. 'It's lingering in your hair. It's lovely, something wild and tangy.'

They talked for a while about work and ordered two more drinks. She woke her laptop with a tap.

'I had a look at the file on Edward Bartlett. It's pretty inconclusive. You've seen the strange note he left?'

'Yes. Despairing but ambiguous.'

'Hmm. The area in Epping Forest where he was found at eight in the morning was combed but nothing was retrieved except his leather rucksack. His wallet was gone but there were no fingerprints or DNA other than Teddy's, so whoever attacked him came prepared with gloves. It had poured with rain all night, so it's possible that evidence was washed away. He had no defence wounds, no scratches on his hands, nothing under his fingernails.'

'So the attack came as a complete surprise, no chance to put up a fight.'

'So it seems. We're looking at a sudden, frenzied assault. His house was searched. There were interviews with family, teachers and a couple of classmates. He appeared to have led an oddly quiet, unsocial life for a teenager. No leads to anything or anyone. The family seem to have been quite strange. There's a medical report on the mother, saying she was on big-hitting anti-depressants and appeared to be in a bit of a fog most of the time. The sister, Sheila, was hysterical in the early stages and took quite a bit of calming before she could be interviewed. She turned up in Epping Forest and caused a fuss, demanding to see the exact spot where Teddy had been found. She was in such a state the local police had to drive her back to London. The father was in Australia and flew back, but just temporarily. That's about it. Have you already got all that?'

'Pretty much. The father had run off with his wife's younger sister.'

'Ouch! I've heard of keeping it in the family . . .'

'Hmm, a touch biblical. Nothing significant was found in Teddy's bedroom? He was big on mysticism, Celts and Druids.'

Nora shook her head. 'There were a number of books and drawings he'd done but nothing that seemed important. No diaries. No links to any Druid activities or organisations were found. Have the family still got stuff of his?'

'According to Sheila, the sister, the mother burnt it all about a year later. Sheila told me that a DI Peterson was in charge of the investigation.'

'That's right. I checked him. He's retired now, living in Brighton. He wasn't highly thought of, I have to say. The consensus seems to have been that he was a corner-cutter, serving his time, waiting to retire. I have an email address for him, so I'll send it to you.' Nora shut her laptop. 'Well, I wish you good luck with it. Let me know how it goes. It would be a result if someone was nailed for it.' She sat back and finished her drink, saying it was good to be at this end of the day.

Swift smiled at her. 'I wondered . . . would you like to have dinner? There's a decent bistro up the road.'

As he spoke the door opened and Nora's eyes lit up. She beamed over his shoulder, waving her fingers. A compact, well-built man with cropped blond hair and carrying a briefcase came over and sat beside her. He nodded to Swift and touched Nora's arm in a way that indicated intimacy.

'Ty, this is Alistair,' she said. 'We're off to dinner now, in fact.'

'Hi there,' Alistair said, 'good to meet you. I hear you're a rower.'

'That's right. Do you row?'

'Only on the machine at the gym, but I think I'd better learn to keep Nora happy.' He took her hand and squeezed it, leaning in to her.

Nora laughed. 'Ah, a man whose mother has taught him the secret art of hanging on to a woman!'

Swift nodded and drank up, thanking Nora for the information and wishing them a good evening. He headed into the night, that tasted now of disappointment. He shook his head ruefully. He could only be grateful that Nora's new man had arrived when he did, before he had made a complete fool of himself.

* * *

Swift stood looking despairingly at his much-loved boat. It had cost him four thousand pounds and now it lay mangled at his feet. Thierry, the manager of the rowing club, had called him first thing, saying that he had discovered a break-in. Swift's boat was the only one damaged.

'Looks like someone's taken an axe to it,' Thierry said glumly.

'Yep. It's a thorough job.'

'I've called the police. You'll be covered by our insurance.'

'I'm sorry about this. Someone is harassing me and now it's spilled over on to you.'

'You've suffered the only damage. The door lock can be fixed easily. I've been suggesting an alarm system for a while. I think it's time to do something about it.'

'The police will no doubt suggest it.'

'You're welcome to borrow a boat until you get a replacement. I know it won't be the same but . . .'

'Thanks. I'll take you up on that.'

Swift crouched by the wrecked boat, touching a splintered segment. It had become a part of him, his companion on many river journeys, as familiar to him as his friends. He stood at the club door and looked out at the choppy, fast-flowing Thames, waiting for the police to arrive. Maybe this time they would get a fingerprint, but somehow he doubted it. He had planned to row for an hour before breakfast. He could almost taste his anger and frustration. *Who are you?* The river flowed on, unheeding.

His phone rang and he heard Sheila Bartlett's breathy voice.

'Hello, Mr Swift. I just wondered if you'd found anything out yet.'

'Nothing significant, no. Investigations do take some time, you know, especially when the incident occurred years ago.'

'Oh yes, of course. I understand. But you have started? You've been speaking to people?'

'I've talked to your brother, your aunt and the police.'

'Oh, that's good. I've just snatched a moment between meetings. The head of service is visiting us today so I've had to make sure everything is ship-shape. The buck stops with poor old me and if I don't check all the staff and equipment myself there are things that just don't get done or left in a mess and—'

Swift cut across her bragging. 'You didn't tell me you went to Epping Forest after your brother was found.'

'Oh, didn't I? I suppose I forgot. As you said, it was a long time ago and so much was happening, I was all over the place. I have to go now to chair a meeting with the top brass, no rest for the wicked! I'll keep in touch.'

It was PC Simons who arrived to take details about the break-in, part of trying to offer a seamless service, he said. Swift guessed he had been on a training course recently. He was a robust, fresh-faced man with a strong handshake. He stood, gazing at Swift's boat, shaking his head and stroking his neat beard.

'This is crap, isn't it?' he said cheerily. You still have no idea who might be targeting you?'

'No. I've given it plenty of thought. I take it you have no useful information for me?'

'Afraid not. I suppose whoever it is has moved away from your home, at least.'

'Oddly enough, I don't find that terribly comforting.'

'No. Sorry, sir. A bit crass of me.' He coloured up.

'That's okay but you do need to be more tactful with the public. I can't tell you anything about this incident, except it's my boat. Whoever's doing this is a careful planner and using their imagination to keep changing tactics.'

'We'll do what we can, as you know. I'll make sure you get a crime number today for your insurer.'

Swift spent twenty minutes with him, then left for home. He stocked up on wine, cheeses and bread on the way, reflecting on Sheila's call. She seemed selective about her memories in a way that snagged his interest. Her phoning him seemed another expression of her need to exercise control. Barbara Stead's comments about her lying were also worth further exploration. He couldn't help guessing that she was brewing the tea for the important meeting rather than chairing it.

* * *

Swift had an arrangement with Cedric. He borrowed his tenant's car occasionally, in return for takeaway meals, odd jobs or a bottle of wine. He had decided that, having met Teddy, he should visit Low Copsley and see the place where he had been attacked. Studying his map, he had seen that there was a village of the same name and decided that he would park the car there and walk to The Yew Grove, which was marked as a feature of the area. It was about two miles from the village but after a chill start the sun was warming the day and he looked forward to exploring a place he had never visited before. Browsing information about the area, he read that for centuries it had been a royal hunting ground and Elizabeth I had had a lodge there. Queen Victoria had declared it *The People's Forest* and Swift learned that if he wished, he could collect 'one faggot of dead or driftwood' when he visited. The woodland comprised of heaths, bogs and rivers, and the trees had not been cut since the nineteenth century. He was astonished that he had lived in London most of his life but had missed this particular jewel.

He drove the rarely used Mini Cooper along the busy North Circular and took the turning for Woodford. The road became less congested, the forest encroaching on either side. He slowed as he saw several deer grazing amongst the trees. One raised its head and stood absolutely still, gazing at him for several moments before moving away. He wondered what significance Teddy might have read into the encounter. He had noted that farmers were allowed to graze cattle in the forest in summer and that the occasional wild pony might be seen, having escaped from travellers. He drove on as the ancient trees grew ever thicker and more majestic, shading the road. Some had massive crowns with branches like trunks.

Low Copsley was a pretty, quiet village with a fourteenth century church, a pub called, aptly enough, the Forester and a modest supermarket which housed the post office. Swift parked the car by the small village green which had a covered well and two wooden benches. Mid-week and mid-morning, there seemed to be no one around. He checked that he had a bottle of water in his pocket and looked at a signpost, turning left out of the village for The Yew Grove. After about half a mile, he took a turning to the right, branching onto a forest track. The trees in this part of the woodland were mainly beech and hornbeam, their trunks abundant with moss and lichens. Autumn leaf fall added to the quiet hush around him and his own footfall was muffled. The thick canopy above filtered the sunlight into a greenish, watery haze. It was soothing, calming. Swift stopped and listened. London was close by, yet there was no sound but his own breathing.

He passed across open, bracken-covered ground by a pond. A small sign told him that it had been formed by a Second World War bomb. Here sunlight glanced in golden drifts off the water and the thick reeds growing by the edge. Another twenty minutes along a further path brought him to a branching, smaller track. As he walked along it, brambles tore at his legs and there was a strong scent of wild garlic.

The track opened suddenly into the grove. Twelve huge, ancient yew trees stood in a circle. They were massive and stunning. Swift felt their power and his own insignificance. He walked to them, placing a hand on reddish brown, scaly bark. It was cool and rough. He walked around the outside of the circle. The yew trunks had deep furrows and ridges. A couple had wide cavities near the base, showing internal roots. Their leaves were long and narrow, like lances, and there were red berries hanging, attractive but poisonous.

Swift walked into the circle and stood, looking up at the dense, almost closed canopy. Then he sat on the rough earth, which lack of sunlight left bare except for ivy and leaf mould. In the deep shade, all was still. The silence was intense. It seemed like a green wilderness. He thought how easy it would be to come here and sense enchantment, the spell of ancient things, the magic of tranquillity. He pictured Teddy, setting out that day in hope, eagerly seeking his Otherworld. He had travelled here because it was a spiritual place of safety but someone had come from behind one of these trees. They had anger in their heart and a rock in their hands. What they had done was a kind of sacrilege. Swift closed his eyes for a moment. The sudden call of a bird roused him and he shivered in the dim light. He wanted to be back in the sun and the open. He picked up a piece of wood, as was his right, and put it in his pocket as a memento.

Two horses and their riders passed him on the way back to the village, nodding greetings. He was glad of the sun's warmth on his back as he strode quickly and glad too that he had come here. It had helped him get a better picture of Teddy. In the Forester he ordered a ploughman's lunch and coffee. He was the only customer.

'It's a quiet place,' he said to the barman, an older man with a florid complexion.

'This is a dead time, mate. Commuter territory now, this village. We get busy at evenings and weekends when the city workers are back from town or Londoners come for some fresh air.'

'Have you always lived here?'

'Moved here from Walthamstow when I was six, so pretty much. What are you doing out this way? Exploring the forest?'

'Sort of. I'm a private detective. I'm looking into an attack that happened at The Yew Grove fifteen years ago. I wanted to have a look at the scene.'

The barman propped his forearms on the bar. 'I remember that. Young lad, wasn't it? We had reporters in here. Didn't they get anyone for it?'

'No. His father would like some answers.'

'Well, you can understand that. He still alive, that lad?'

'Yes, but very disabled.'

The barman straightened and wiped the spotless counter with his sleeve. 'Terrible, what happened. I've never liked that place. Those big old yews give me the willies. Too dark and cold. They remind me of graveyards. I always told my kids not to go there.'

'Do people hold ceremonies there?'

'Sometimes. Druids and the like. You know, solstice and that sort of stuff. New age, I believe they're called. Never any trouble from them, I have to say. They're very polite when they come in here.'

'I can't say I've ever heard of Druids rioting.'

The barman threw his head back and laughed. 'That's a good one, mate!'

Swift smiled. 'Did the police ask you if you'd seen anything suspicious at the time?'

'They were in here, yeah. I couldn't tell them anything. Tell you what, they were good for business, propping up the bar at all hours.'

Swift took his lunch to a table by an open fire. He was never hopeful regarding pub food; too often it consisted of stale bread, slimy coleslaw, limp lettuce leaves and ageing potato salad. This ploughman's was a delight, the bread was fresh, the cheese strong and tasty and the pickle home-made, with delicious chunks of gherkin and cauliflower. He savoured every mouthful, enjoying the warmth of the fire and the view of the village green outside. He glanced at the TV screen at the side of the bar, then turned away as pictures appeared of helpless refugees floundering in the Mediterranean. His appetite had vanished suddenly. He finished his coffee. As he left the pub he heard the barman chuckling to someone about rioting Druids.

* * *

At seven that evening Swift was sitting on his sofa with his laptop, drinking a glass of Shiraz and reading more about Druids and Celtic beliefs. He was particularly absorbed by an explanation that the Otherworld was not always used to refer to a place where the dead went. It could also be a place or state that was visited during earthly life and attained through meditation, trance or dreams. He was interrupted by a ring on his doorbell. He found Simone outside.

'Hi,' she said. 'I hope you don't mind me calling on the off-chance. I was in the area so I decided to stop by.'

He was surprised and a little wary; he hadn't been aware that she knew his address. He invited her in and led her through to the living room. She put her briefcase down and ran her hands through her hair so that her curls stood out like a burnished halo.

'This is lovely, so cosy and comfortable. I love the Art Nouveau style.' She ran a hand across a ladder-back chair. 'Is that William Morris wallpaper?'

'It is. Mary calls the look "shabby chic." I haven't changed the décor since my Aunt Lily died. I thought about it but decided I like it the way it is.'

'If it ain't broke don't fix it?'

'Something like that. Would you like a glass of wine? Red or white?'

'Whatever you're having.'

Swift fetched another glass from the kitchen and brought the bottle of wine through. Simone had settled herself in an armchair, her elegant legs crossed. Her pale blue dress and jacket looked businesslike.

'Sorry to interrupt you,' she said, gesturing at his laptop.

'That's okay.'

He handed her a glass of wine and sat opposite her, closing the laptop. He sipped his wine, leaving a silence as she glanced around, smoothed an ankle and settled her hair behind her shoulders.

'There was something I wanted to say to you. It's concerning what we talked about when you came to dinner, mine and Mary's wish to be parents. I don't know if you've thought about it, I hope you have.'

'I have thought about it.'

'Okay, good. Have you come to any conclusions?'

'Yes.'

She drank some wine. 'It's so important to us, you see, and as we said, we need to make a start as soon as we can. I find that I'm thinking about it all the time. I suppose wanting to be a mother can affect you like that. Now I know what women mean when they talk about feeling broody! We would love if you could see your way to helping us.' She looked at him.

'You and Mary explained that to me.'

'So, will you let me know what you're thinking?'

'No.'

'Pardon?' She made a little surprised movement with her head.

'I want to speak to Mary first.'

She looked annoyed, and bit her bottom lip. 'Ty, we are a couple, you know. I realise that you and Mary are close but this is about more than your friendship. I have to say, given how crucial this is for us, I'm finding your attitude difficult to understand.'

He felt anger rise and suppressed it. 'I didn't invite you here, Simone. I won't be pressurised. I understand how important this is to you. I can only repeat that I want to speak to Mary, then I'm happy to talk to you both.'

She looked down, clasped her hands together and took a breath, then a deep gulp of wine.

'Look, I came here because I wanted to say . . . if the clinical aspect of it all bothers you, you know, donating sperm — and I do understand it might seem a bit cold and impersonal, then . . .' She stopped, a bright flare of red blush appearing on her neck and travelling up to her cheeks, then rushed on, 'I would . . . we could, you know, actually have sex and see if I can get pregnant that way. We could be business-like about it, couldn't we? I'd be happy to get on with it now, if you like.'

Swift stared at her. He didn't know what he had been expecting, probably a lengthy lecture about child-rearing and blood ties. He put his wine glass down.

'Simone, you're gay. You don't want sex with men. With me.'

She rubbed at her neck. 'You're not "men," are you? This would be — it would be . . .'

'The means to an end.'

'Yes, if you like.'

'And if I agreed to this, how would that make Mary feel?'

'Would she need to know? I mean, we could still say we'd gone through with the donation and she'd believe it had happened that way. Other people come to this kind of agreement and if it achieves the desired result there's no harm done. Ty, I want a baby. We want a baby!' She started to cry quietly.

Swift rose and passed her a box of tissues, then closed the curtains while she composed herself. Had he ever had a stranger proposal? He could see what it had cost her to make it and he felt an exasperated compassion.

'I know you want a child and I understand that the hoops you have to jump through are hard and demanding. I do realise that this is an emotional time for you,' he told her. 'I think I understand what's made you come here and say this, make this offer to me, but I won't consider it and I think you'll regret making it. I'm amazed that you thought there was any chance I would agree. I want you to go home, Simone. Neither of us will ever mention this visit to Mary and we'll forget you came here.'

She leapt up and in one fluid movement, threw the remains of her wine at him and smashed the glass to the floor. He wiped flecks of the drink from his face as she ranted.

'Oh, it's all very well for you with your comfortable, well-ordered life! Don't tell me what I'll regret or what I will or won't say to my partner. You're so insufferably measured and composed about everything! Don't you ever get so emotional you could explode? I'm sure *your* life has never felt topsy-turvy. Bully for you! Where's your bathroom?'

He indicated the way. She crunched glass as she left the room. Swift fetched a cloth, dustpan and brush and swept up the broken glass. When she emerged from the bathroom he saw her out. She left without speaking and he too remained silent. He finished cleaning up, washed his face and changed his shirt. He sank back on to the sofa and stared up at the ceiling for a while, shaken and furious. Simone's assumptions about him were offensive. No doubt she would have liked it if he had told her all about Ruth and the torment he had endured when she left him. She belonged to that tribe who enjoy hearing about and dissecting the drama of other people's lives. He might enjoy reading pulp fiction but he had no intention of living it. He would prefer never to see her again but that wasn't possible. He finished the bottle of wine and emailed Mary, asking if he could meet her in the next day or two.

* * *

Fairacres School was a two-storey, sprawling building with a sign outside informing Swift that its fairly obvious purpose was *Learning for the Future* and it had been rated as *Good* in its recent Ofsted report. The school day had ended and the building was quiet, the air inside smelling of cheap sweets and something sharp and indefinable that Swift decided was probably adolescent hormones. He followed the sign to the head teacher's office, expecting to be snubbed by the icy receptionist but saw a tall man in a silver tracksuit standing in the doorway.

'Mr Swift? I'm Deaven Harrow. Do come in.' A massive hand grabbed Swift's and gave it a firm shake.

It was a small office and Harrow dominated it. He pulled out a chair for Swift and sat at his side of the desk, which was covered in yellow post-its, files, an open bag of Brazil nuts and another of dried fruits.

'Thanks for seeing me,' Swift said.

'My pleasure. Apologies for the informal garb but I'm playing in a charity rounders match at five, an ongoing inter-schools fixture that Fairacres is winning at the moment.' His voice was a smooth baritone with just a trace of Caribbean accent. He was a fine-looking man with round, luminous eyes and deep acne scars on his left cheek.

'I'll try to keep this brief, then. You know I've come about Teddy Bartlett?'

Harrow nodded. 'Yes, although not why.'

'I did give a brief explanation to your receptionist. I assumed she would have told you.'

Harrow rolled his eyes and shrugged. 'She is something of a martinet and a law unto herself as you probably gathered. I inherited her from my predecessor and as with many inheritances, there are unlooked for complexities.'

Swift smiled sympathetically. 'Mr Bartlett, Teddy's father, has returned recently from Australia and has asked me to try to establish what happened to Teddy and who perpetrated the crime.'

'I see. Well, I was Teddy's form teacher. I also taught him English. He was an avid reader.'

'You must have been shocked when you heard about him?'

'Yes, of course. Although I wasn't in London around that time. My father had died back in Jamaica and I'd gone to Kingston for the funeral. I had a month's compassionate leave so I was away until the end of September. A colleague rang to let me know about Teddy.'

'So presumably you'd last seen Teddy in that July?'

'That's right, when the school year ended. The father had left the family, I recall, another continent, another marriage. Would you like some of these? They're good for energy, you know.'

Harrow offered the bag of Brazil nuts to Swift, who said he would pass. He tipped some into his hand and ate them as Swift continued.

'You're correct about Mr Bartlett. He's retired now and back in the family home. I've spoken to him and his two other children and their aunt. I have a picture of an odd, disturbed family.'

Harrow put his hands behind his head, rested his right foot on his sturdy left knee and chewed thoughtfully. 'All three children attended this school. I didn't teach Sheila or Tim but I remember them because they all presented certain challenges in the classroom and were sometimes the subject of discussion at pastoral care meetings. Tim had outbursts of anger, Sheila was suspected of occasional theft and caused problems by telling lies about other girls. Teddy . . . he was the opposite kind of problem — withdrawn, difficult to engage with. Bright, though, wrote beautifully.'

'Did his writing reflect the Celtic mysticism he was interested in?'

'Sometimes, although I think he was more into drawing symbols. The triskele covered most of his exercise books. I remember when we were studying Macbeth he got caught up in whether or not the witch's cat, Graymalkin, was drawn from Celtic lore.'

'Did he talk to you about his home life?'

'No. Teddy didn't say much unless you asked him a direct question, and then he would speak so softly it was hard to hear him.'

'How did his classmates get on with him? Did they find him peculiar?'

'The boys tended to leave him be. Although he might have seemed a suitable soft target for bullying, he had a kind of self-possessed manner that kept them at bay. Teddy might have been diffident but he wasn't a pushover. There was a silly rumour that he knew ancient spells that he could use as curses. I've no idea how that started but it played its part in protecting him from the school bruisers. Some of the girls liked him, probably because as well as being intelligent, having a charming smile and waif-like appearance, he didn't tease or harass them. I wouldn't say that he had many friends as such.'

'That's what I've been told. It seems to have been true of the whole family.' Swift glanced at the clock and saw that half an hour had vanished. He focused on other information he needed. 'Sheila gave me the names of two girls Teddy knew: Imogen Thornley and Judith Saltby. I've confirmed that the police spoke to them at the time. I'm hoping to contact them.'

Harrow shifted in his chair. 'Sadly, Imogen was killed in a car accident when she was eighteen and Judith went to Ottawa for a while. I believe she married a Canadian. I still see one of her other friends occasionally and if you like, I could ask for Judith's current location.'

'Thanks. That would be a help.'

Harrow made a note on a post-it and stuck it to his phone. 'About that family being troubled. We referred them to an educational psychologist at one time because we were worried about the children's behaviour and the home situation but she got nowhere, as far as I can recall. The mother wouldn't cooperate and attempts at meetings failed. Then a round of cuts came and the services were "realigned," meaning they pretty much vanished . . .' Harrow sighed and checked his watch.

'Thanks for your time. I know you need to get to your match. That last summer before Teddy was attacked, you didn't have any particular worries about him?'

'No. He'd done very well in his GCSEs and was due to start in the lower sixth form, studying English, History and Spanish. He was his usual quiet presence.' Harrow tapped the desk, frowning slightly and sealed the packet of nuts.

Swift sensed that the head teacher was weighing something up. 'If there's anything you think might be helpful, I'd appreciate it. Fifteen years have elapsed and memories fade,' he prompted.

Harrow nodded and rubbed his chin. 'I used to wonder if Teddy might be gay. These were thoughts I kept to myself, you understand. Looking back and with the hindsight that comes with experience, I think it's a strong possibility. It would help explain why he kept a low profile. It's not easy to be a gay adolescent even now, but a lot has changed for the better in the years since he was injured. I would say that at times he acted as if he was guarding a secret.'

'If that's true, he had an awful lot happening in his life. His father married to his aunt, a mother who didn't function, troubled siblings and confusion about his sexual identity.'

'Yes, quite a brew. Struggling with all those complexities might have resulted in significant depression. How many times have you read about people who have done something out of character and their families say they had given no indication that they were feeling desperate?'

'Did you tell the investigating police at the time that you thought Teddy might be gay?'

'I wasn't interviewed by the police. As I said, I was away in Jamaica.' Harrow reached into a desk drawer. 'By the way, I found an old exercise book of Teddy's in my cupboard when I was looking up files about the family. It was one of his English books from 1999. It's just essays but I thought you might like to see it. I'm happy for you to borrow it but I would like it back. His father might like to see it too.'

He handed over a blue folder, glanced at his watch and asked Swift if he could see himself out as he needed warm-up time. As Swift left he was on the floor of his office, doing rapid press ups. Swift exited the school, thinking back to his own head teacher, a dry, finicky man with little empathy for others. He was annoyed that in 2000, the police had failed to speak to Harrow when he returned from Jamaica. He wondered if this important omission indicated other lapses in the investigation.

Chapter 6

Cedric knocked on Swift's door at eight a.m. as he was making his first coffee of the day. His tenant was looking dapper in a corduroy jacket and chinos and the checked trilby hat he wore as soon as autumn approached, but his face was grave.

'Ty, I assume you haven't you been out yet today?'

'No, just getting organised.'

'I think you'd better come out and take a look. I was on my way for my morning paper and breakfast but that can wait.'

Cedric led the way down the steps on to the pavement and gestured at the front of the house. The bricks, front door, basement door and window and the wall and gate had been sprayed liberally with red, purple and green paint, random daubs with the odd profanity thrown in. Cedric put a hand on his arm as he groaned.

'The "hoaxer," Ty?'

'Presumably. What a mess!'

'Must have been done after midnight because I got home from the pub around then and everything was fine.'

A neighbour from two doors up stopped on her way to work, staring at the graffiti. She said helpfully that someone seemed to have it in for him and that it made the neighbourhood feel unsafe, knowing that this kind of thing was happening. Swift didn't respond and she glared at him before walking on. He looked carefully around the area and the steps to the basement but could see no trace of the perpetrator.

'Is it worth asking the police to fingerprint?' Cedric asked.

Swift shook his head. 'Whoever did this will have worn gloves. I'll report it but I want it cleaned off today.'

'Anything I can do?'

'No. Thanks anyway, Cedric. You head on and get your paper.'

'Come and have breakfast in a while, maple syrup pancakes on me.'

Swift rang PC Simons. He explained the latest event, asking him to log it but adding that he didn't see any point in the police visiting. Simons confirmed that no useful evidence had been found at the boat club.

'We're no further forward, I'm afraid. We have previously advised CCTV for your home of course . . .'

'Yes, I know. I'm going to act on that now.'

'And you really can't think of anyone who might be behind this?'

'No. If I do, you'll be the first to hear about it.'

He rang several cleaning companies and found one that could visit with a pressure washer later that morning. The cost made him wince. He called at the nearest neighbours, explaining that the graffiti would be gone by the end of the day. Then he returned to his cold coffee and heated it in the microwave. He took it outside while he photographed the scrawls, forcing a smile as the postwoman commented that it wasn't exactly Banksy, was it?

He found a nearby CCTV company and decided to have cameras installed by the front and basement doors. He sighed and paid the deposit on the huge cost. He set off to meet Cedric, knowing that his friend hated CCTV. He had often talked about big brother and being snooped on everywhere in London. Swift could see no other option for now, hoping that the cameras would be a real deterrent.

* * *

Swift sat on the bus to Tufnell Park, listening to Amy Winehouse through his earphones. The previous evening, he had leafed through Teddy Bartlett's English exercise book. The front cover was decorated in black pen with various Celtic symbols: the triskele, crosses, sun wheels, a tree of life and many versions of an intricate circular pattern that he had googled and identified as a symbol for water. On the back cover was a circle with three dots and three lines fanning out from them. The marks Deaven Harrow had allocated in red pen throughout were never below 90/100 and the margins were dotted with comments such as *excellent interpretation* and *thoughtful, thorough study of the text*. There were essays on Sylvia Plath's poems, *Macbeth*, *To Kill a Mockingbird* and *Brighton Rock*.

Swift had turned back to the cover of the book and considered Teddy's illustrations of water signs. His own reading on the Internet had informed him that Celts and Druids revered water as a source of life and vitality, believing that it absorbed the healing power of the sun. He looked again at his notes about the Bartlett family. Teddy and Sheila had been 'conjoined' according to Tim, yet they were as unalike as siblings could be. The plodding, lacklustre, food-obsessed Sheila and slim, elfin Teddy and his keen intellect and imagination. He had decided to return to the Bartlett house without notice and at a time when Sheila was likely to be out at work.

He closed his eyes as the bus ground through Kentish Town and thought of the lunch he had shared with Mary. He had worried that Simone would have said something about her visit to him, maybe even blurted out her offer to have sex but, thankfully, she seemed to have thought better of it. Mary had been a little downcast when he explained that he couldn't agree to father a child, but she had accepted his decision without trying to persuade him further. He had offered to meet again with both of them but to his great relief, Mary had said that wasn't necessary and she would tell Simone. She added that she knew it had been a long shot; knowing him as she did, she couldn't see him embracing the idea. They had already visited a clinic to discuss the matter and they could initiate the procedure as soon as they wanted.

Then she had brightened, her eyes regaining their usual sparkle, saying she had important news. Simone had proposed to her the previous evening and she had accepted. She confessed that she'd been a bit bowled over as they had never discussed marriage. Simone felt that, as she hoped to be pregnant soon, they should marry for their own sake and for the sake of their child. The wedding was to be in December. The registrar was already booked. It would be a small, low-key celebration. Would he be best man? He had said of course, hugging her, expressing his delight. Afterwards, he had thought that it was all happening very quickly and wondered if Simone's proposal had anything to do with the outcome of her visit to his house. Then he chided himself for being churlish, reflecting that he mustn't let his antipathy for Simone get in the way of celebrating his cousin's happiness.

Rowan Bartlett answered the front door at just after nine fifteen, a slice of toast in his hand.

'Oh, was I expecting you? Sheila's gone to work. Have you got news of Teddy?'

'No, Mr Bartlett. I hope you don't mind me calling without an appointment. I was in the area and there was something I wanted to check.'

'Well, you'd better come in. As you can see, I'm breakfasting.'

He led the way through to a cluttered kitchen at the back of the house. There was a pot of tea on a pine table and the shells of two boiled eggs. Bartlett sat and indicated a chair opposite. The table was sticky with layers of grime.

'Would you like a cup of tea? I think there's one more in the pot.'

'No thanks. If possible, I wanted to look at the room that used to be Teddy's. I realise his things have gone but sometimes it can be useful.'

Bartlett looked puzzled. 'What are you looking for?'

Swift had no idea, inspiration, probably. 'It's hard to say. Even after fifteen years, it might help to look at his room as part of building a picture.'

'Well, it's empty as far as I know but take a look. Will you be long? I have an estate agent visiting at ten. I thought you were her at the door and she'd got the time wrong.'

'I won't be long. Are you thinking of selling?' Looking around, Swift thought he would have given the place a thorough clean if he was inviting a valuation.

Bartlett dropped his eyelids and looked shifty. 'I've asked the agent to do an appraisal. Look, I'd rather you didn't mention this to Sheila if you're talking to her.'

'If that's what you want, of course.'

'To be honest, Mr Swift, I would prefer a place of my own. I'm fond of Sheila and things worked out well to start with but I'm used to being master of my own house. She fusses over me and I find it increasingly difficult. Also, this place is far too big for two people and the bills are ridiculous. I would prefer to live somewhere more rural.' He sounded testy and hard done by.

'Presumably she might find it tough to leave here. It's been her home all her life.' Her empire, more like, from what Swift had established.

'Yes. I'm afraid when I raised the possibility with her she got very angry. I do own the house still, so it's my decision in the end. I thought that if I get a realistic idea of the market price, I can help her with a deposit on a flat. She'd only need one bedroom, after all. I'm sure she'll see the sense of it.'

'That's between you and Sheila. May I take a look upstairs? I understand Teddy's bedroom was at the front of the house.'

'Yes, first door on the right at the top of the stairs.'

Swift took the shallow steps two at a time. What a callous, self-absorbed man Bartlett was. He'd abandoned Sheila, returned to her life when it suited him and now he was going behind her back and planning to sell her home from under her. He opened the panelled door facing him at the top of the stairs and stepped into a good-sized, bright room. It was almost empty, containing one broken dining chair and a small chest of drawers. The walls were covered in a gold and cream striped wallpaper and bare. Swift opened the three drawers in the chest. They held only musty-smelling lining paper.

He stepped back on to the landing and listened. Bartlett was still in the kitchen with the radio playing. He opened the next door along and found a bathroom. Opposite the bathroom was another panelled door. On it hung a white plastic plaque with tiny rosebuds forming a garland around the name *Sheila*. He pushed the door and looked in. A clean, pressed nurse's uniform hung from the dado rail by the window but it was the only sign of order in the midst of chaos. The double bed was unmade, with magazines, clothing, underwear and books strewn across it. At least a dozen dirty mugs were scattered along window ledges and there were several plates smeared with food lying on the dun-coloured carpet. Chocolate bar wrappers were piled on the bedside table. A trap door was inset into the ceiling, presumably access to the loft. Swift left the door open behind him and looked at the magazines and books, which were of the celebrity watching/chick-lit variety. It was a teenager's grubby nest, not the space of a mature woman with a career.

He hadn't planned to search Sheila's room but now that he was in it, he decided it must have been at the back of his mind. What he knew of her bothered him and what bothered him made him curious. He looked in drawers and on shelves, moving rapidly. He didn't think she would notice if he moved anything out of place. Everything was a jumble. There was a good deal of cheap jewellery, scores of magazines about health and slimming and in the corner of the dressing table, a tin tea caddy with a fat roll of twenty pound notes secured with an elastic band. The drawer of the bedside table was crammed with diet aids: sachets of dried foods, boxes of fat-burning capsules and cartons of detoxifying drinks, promising to suppress or satisfy appetite. The chocolate wrappers lay above them and Swift wondered if Sheila saw the irony. He moved soundlessly across to a built-in wardrobe and looked at a rail holding jeans, jumpers and coats. There were four shoe boxes on a top shelf. He lifted them down, placed them on the end of the bed and looked inside. One held a pair of beige patent leather court shoes, the next a small pile of airmail envelopes from Australia, another a stack of photographs and the fourth just a small package in white tissue paper. Swift opened it carefully and saw a baby's jacket made from a fine yellow wool with tiny white bows as ties. It looked unused. The label inside said *Mothercare*.

The doorbell rang. He replaced the boxes, glanced around the room and headed downstairs as Bartlett greeted a suited woman who held a clipboard. Swift waved a goodbye, saying he'd be in touch and headed for Victoria, planning to spend the rest of the day in Brighton.

* * *

The day had started with heavy rain, which had now ceased, leaving a washed out silver sky. The fields looked sodden and the train carriage smelled of drying clothing and of the bacon sandwich the man in the next seat was eating. Swift was on his way to meet ex-DI Colin Peterson, who had sounded bright and breezy on the phone and eager to talk.

He bought a coffee at Brighton station and drank it as he walked to Peterson's house. It was a bungalow in a quiet residential area with a neatly pruned garden. Peterson waved to him from the front window.

'Have you heard my coffee's that bad?' he asked, gesturing at Swift's cup and laughing at his own joke. 'Come on into my humble abode.'

The living room was decorated in shades of oatmeal with fluffy rugs scattered on the carpet. Ceramic dogs and cats featured on the shelves on either side of the fireplace. There was a bored-looking budgie in a cage by the window. On the wall beside it hung a ceramic dish with the inscription; *my idea of a night out is sitting on the patio.* Peterson sat in his chair, a large black leather recliner and Swift took an armchair nearby.

'I won't offer a beverage just yet,' Peterson said. 'The ball and chain is out for the day so we can please ourselves.' He winked and rubbed the side of his nose.

Swift wondered what he had in mind. Perhaps when his wife was out he raided the drinks cupboard. He judged Peterson to be in his mid-sixties but he wasn't wearing well, with a flabby stomach propped up on a straining belt. He was tall, with thinning hair and puffy bags below his eyes. There were broken veins in his cheeks. He looked out of place in this suburban living room, as if he would be more at home propping up a bar. Swift imagined he might be finding retirement a challenge, hence his enthusiasm to discuss an old case.

'Thanks for seeing me,' Swift said. 'As I said on the phone, I'm looking into Teddy Bartlett's case, for his father.'

'No worries. I was looking forward to a chat about it. It was my last but one investigation. You used to be in the Met?'

'That's right, then Interpol.'

'Ah, a bright young spark; climbing up that greasy pole.'

Swift ignored the jibe. 'You remember Teddy?'

'I remember him. Nothing wrong with the old grey matter, luckily. The lungs haven't worn so well, which is why I'm sucking on these bloody things.' He picked up an e-cigarette and waved it about. 'Nothing like the real McCoy but the wife insists on it.'

He appeared and acted older than his age, with his outmoded idioms. Swift had met men like him, during his days in the Met. He thought of them as dinosaurs. They were the kind who liked practical jokes, were lazy thinkers, usually badmouthed female officers and headed for the pub at the end of every shift.

'Did you have any likely suspects for what happened to Teddy Bartlett? His sister told me the police thought it was random.'

'Nope, no suspects. A woman walking her dog found him. That sister of his, Sheila, she was a right weirdo. Mind you, they all were in that family. I didn't tell her it was random. She fixated on the fact his wallet had gone and went on about it being a robbery. I reckoned the wallet was probably taken to make it look that way. There was no DNA found at the scene, so it must have been a planned attack. Whoever bashed him with that rock was wearing protective clothing and gloves. None of that was found, of course. The rock had been chucked in the bushes and was covered in Teddy's blood and brain matter. He had bits of blackthorn and whitethorn in his jacket pockets. They seemed to be part of all that Druid hokum he liked. Is he still alive?'

'Yes. He lives in a care home.'

'I was amazed he survived. Whoever did it thought he was dead. There was real rage behind that attack, but I couldn't find anyone who might have felt like that about him. Everyone said he was a mild-mannered boy. The studious type. No evidence of drugs or any illegal activities, the kind of thing that might have got him on the wrong side of some low life.'

'Did anyone you interviewed indicate that Teddy might have been gay?'

Peterson grinned. 'Ah, a homophobic attack. Very PC. I can see you were a university entrant to the force.'

'It can be a motive for hate crime,' Swift said icily.

'No one told me he was a poofter, no.'

'Deaven Harrow was his form teacher at the time. He's the head teacher at the school now and he told me Teddy might have been gay.'

'Don't remember him.' Peterson pressed a lever and put his legs up as his chair extended, wriggling himself in more comfortably.

'He was in Jamaica that August, when the attack happened. He said the police didn't speak to him after he returned some time later.'

'No? Well, can't have seemed important. It was all looking pretty hopeless after a couple of weeks. You know what it's like if you don't establish something concrete pretty fast. I spoke to a couple of his friends — *girlfriends*, by the way, which means it's not likely he was . . . you know . . .' Peterson flopped a hand from side to side. 'They were big-eyed and tearful. They came out with the same stuff, Teddy was quiet, imaginative, and keen on Druids and all that new age mumbo jumbo. As I said, the whole family were nut jobs. They'd have kept a psychiatrist busy, if you ask me.'

'None of them were suspects?'

Peterson ticked them off on his fingers. 'We checked that the sister had been on her shift at the hospital at the time he died, the brother was in Dorset, the father in Oz and the mother . . . well, the mother was so out of it on prescription drugs she could barely lift a tea cup, let alone a rock. She hadn't left the house for years.'

'I understand that the spot where he was found in the forest, Low Copsley, is a sacred place for Druids?'

Peterson folded his hands over his stomach. 'I spoke to some Druid bloke who confirmed that they held the odd meeting or ceremony there at solstice. They regarded the trees as holding special powers. They had nothing planned there around that time and we couldn't establish that Teddy had been in any formal contact with Druids or the like.'

Swift watched the budgie rocking from side to side, staring through the window at freedom.

'It doesn't make sense, does it? Teddy had no apparent enemies. He left that ambiguous, heart-rending note, then headed to a place he believed was sacred where he met someone who came prepared to attack him.'

'That's true, nothing added up. That note. In the end I reckoned it was some flight of fancy of his. He was an airy-fairy kind of kid, head in the clouds, always drawing and writing about nature and stuff. Teenagers do attention-seeking things. Unless a stranger was roaming Epping Forest that day in protective clothing on the off-chance of finding a victim to attack, he'd got on the wrong side of someone all right. We couldn't establish why he'd gone to Low Copsley. The bizarre Bartletts didn't have the Internet or mobile phones so there was nothing to trace that way. We looked at the landline records but they hardly ever phoned anyone and the only numbers used were that aunt in Dorset and the GP.'

'There hadn't been any other random or unexplained attacks in the area?'

'No. Epping Forest has its share of murders, as you probably know. Nice big space on the outskirts of London with woodland and hidey-holes. We'd had a couple of bodies there over the years but one was a clear domestic and the others were crime-related. We got convictions for all of them. That crime didn't fit with anything else. Want a cuppa, or something stronger? I've a good single malt.'

'No, I'm fine, thanks.'

'Please yourself.' Peterson turned to the birdcage and pushed it gently from side to side, making cheeping noises.

Swift looked at him, knowing that his investigation had been sloppy. He recalled the barman at the Forester saying the police had been good for business. Peterson clearly hadn't had much respect for the family or the victim.

'What do you think happened, then?'

Peterson shrugged. He looked bored now. Swift suspected he had been hoping to meet an ex-policeman more in his own mould, someone he could brag to about the old days over a glass or two.

'I don't know why Teddy went to the forest that day. I reckon someone arranged to meet him but I don't know who or why. That someone bashed him over the head, with intent to kill. That's all I got from months of investigation. From what you say, maybe he was gay and got in with bad company, but from what I could gather he liked the ladies alright. Good luck to you if you think you can find a perp after all this time.'

Chapter 7

Swift left Peterson pouring his whisky. He walked down to the beach and sat outside a café in the late afternoon sun with a beer and a sandwich. The salty breeze cleared his head. He checked his emails and saw one from Deaven Harrow:

> *Judith Saltby moved back to the UK six months ago and lives in Cambridge now. I emailed her and she said it would be okay for you to contact her. See below.*

There was an email address and a phone number. He sent his thanks and signalled for the bill. As he waited he looked down to the beach and froze as he saw Ruth slowly pushing a man in a wheelchair along the tarmac walkway. She was bending forwards, chatting to him. It was the first time Swift had seen Emlyn Taylor. He had a red wool scarf knotted around his neck and wore a checked tweed flat cap. He held a shopping bag on his lap. They came to a stall selling second-hand books and stopped to look. Swift watched them for a few long moments, paid his bill and walked quickly away from the front.

On the train, he was unsurprised to receive a call from Sheila.

'I've just got back from a manic day at work to hear that you visited this morning.'

'That's right.'

'What did you want?'

He registered truculence. 'Have you spoken to your father?'

'Yes, of course.'

'Then he'll have told you what I wanted.'

'Well, I don't think you should turn up unannounced and start poking around.'

'Really? Your father didn't seem to mind and he's paying me to poke around.'

She snuffled. 'Dad's not a well man. You should give him notice of things.'

'Sheila, I think your father is well able to look after himself.'

'You don't know the half of it,' she told him.

He thought, *I think you're the one who doesn't know the half of it but it's not my place to tell you*. He said, 'I'm being paid to conduct an enquiry. That's what I'm doing. Are you worried that I might have found something?'

There was a pause, then she said, 'Of course not! I have to go, actually, someone's having a problem with a patient and I have to check on the situation.'

'Don't let me keep you from your work. I know how much you're in demand,' he said sweetly. The woman was clearly anxious about his involvement and what he might discover. The maddening question was why?

When he reached Victoria, he felt jaded and frustrated by his day and disturbed by the sighting of Ruth and her husband. He had managed not to think or dream about her since their parting and now he had the image of them both to remember. His melancholy mood led him to the

Evergreen. There was a scattering of people there in the early evening, having a drink after work. Krystyna was behind the bar and her bright smile cheered him a little. He ordered a glass of wine and some olives, read the evening paper, then watched as she sped around in her slim black trousers, snowy cotton shirt and squeaking plimsolls. The warm, low lights and the hum of conversation soothed him.

After a while the place emptied and Krystyna stood at the till, pressing buttons with fleet fingers.

'Cashing up,' she explained to him. 'My shift's nearly over.'

'Do you work here full time?'

'No. I used to but now I do a couple of days a week. I've started my own Internet business.'

'What kind of business?'

'Selling items related to the nineteen fifties. I'm mad about that decade. I love the clothes and the music, the style, everything. The website's called *Fifties Beat*. Take a look!'

He said he would, realising that he had never really looked at her properly before, Ruth had always been his focus. She wore her honey-coloured hair in a bob with a short fringe. Her wide face with high cheekbones and her accent suggested a Slavic background. Her expression was open, her eyes soft and a little dreamy.

He held out his hand. 'My name is Tyrone Swift. Can I buy you a drink when you've finished work?' He was hesitant. She was sure to have a partner although she wore no rings.

She shook his hand, looked at him and considered. 'The woman you used to meet here — Ruth — is definitely back with her husband for good?'

'Yes, for good. We don't meet any more.'

She nodded. 'Okay. But not here. And I need to eat, I'm famished.'

They ate in a small Lebanese café, drinking a bottle of Musar wine and sharing platters of kibbeh, tabbouleh and falafel with hummus. Fast, rhythmic flutes and drums played in the background, music that swirled and raced. Swift asked her about herself and she spoke readily. She had been born in Lodz, Poland, and emigrated to London eighteen months ago. She rented a tiny flat in Kennington.

'I was living at home with my parents in Lodz because I couldn't find a job, so I came west. A typical story. I shared a room in a house in Balham to start with, got a job at the Evergreen. Then my business started to take off so I managed to get my own place. It's tiny but I love it. My first name is impossible for most people here to spell and I get tired of repeating it, so I shorten it to Kris. Are you Irish? You look Irish, like people I saw in a documentary whose ancestors are said to have mingled with Spanish traders.'

'My mother was from Connemara so I suppose I might have Spanish ancestry.'

She told him that she hadn't made many friends in London as yet, because she had been too busy working and setting up her business. She went into more detail about it. She made fifties-style clothing and sourced and sold fifties artefacts. Her client list was growing as more people got to know about her. She gave him a business card with a black-and-white silhouette of a woman in a flared dress and hat.

'You have a talent not found in most men,' she told him. 'You pay close attention when I'm talking. Believe me, it's an attractive quality.'

'Thank you. It may be because my career has been about investigation of one sort or another and careful listening is crucial.'

It helped him that she knew about Ruth and that he didn't have to start explaining his recent emotional history, at least not immediately. They ordered coffee as he told her about Swift Investigations, and outlined his current case. Refreshingly, she didn't say she'd never met a private detective before. She smiled as the small cups arrived on a tray with a brass coffee pot, accompanied by tiny squares of baklava.

'No shortbread!'

'That's a relief.'

'You know, I feel as if I know you, even though I don't and I only heard your name tonight. I used to watch you with Ruth and wonder why you always looked sad, troubled. I thought maybe you were a couple heading for divorce and trying to rescue the marriage. I wondered if the baby was a relationship saver. I hope you don't mind me saying this? I've been told I'm too blunt sometimes. I wonder if it might be a cultural difference. The English have so many ways of not saying what they mean!'

He laughed but winced inside at this reflection of him and Ruth through her eyes. 'We tormented ourselves, certainly. I'm glad those days are over. I'm not going to say any more about that now. It will keep.' He liked her directness. 'Who told you you're too blunt?'

'Oh, a customer I had a while ago. She wanted a dress that wouldn't have suited her body. I know the customer is always right but I didn't see the point of her wasting her money and looking bad as well.'

He saw her on to her bus home, kissing her on the cheek. They agreed to meet again and he waved to her as she boarded and touched her travel card on the reader. The evening in her company had sped past, simple, untangled and not fraught with unspoken emotions. It was a long time since he had relaxed so thoroughly in a woman's company. A long time since he had allowed himself to.

* * *

He had been out on the river and was just pulling his borrowed boat up the slipway when Judith Saltby rang and said she could see him the following day. He would have to travel to Cambridge as she had just had a baby and she was currently inhabiting a different time and space continuum. She sounded tired but when he said they could discuss it over the phone, she replied that she would rather see him and that she was looking forward to talking to him about Teddy. Swift headed home to shower and have a late breakfast. He was tucking into a bowl of porridge laced with honey when he got a call from a Serena Clayhurst at Mayfields.

'I thought I should ring you, Mr Swift. Peter Alfonso informed me that you visited Teddy Bartlett and that his father has asked you to look into the attack on him.'

'That's correct.'

'I'm the manager here. I was on holiday when you visited. I took over here eighteen months ago. The administration of the facility had been sadly lacking and my predecessor was asked to leave. It took me a while to get things in order. I saw that Teddy Bartlett has an account with a substantial amount of money in, more than twenty thousand pounds, with the interest accrued. I assumed that this was money saved from benefits and family contributions or gifts. Such an arrangement isn't unusual and I was concerned that none of the money had been used on Teddy's behalf.'

'Did you tell the family?'

'I contacted his sister Sheila, last autumn. She said she knew nothing about this money. I was very worried so I looked through Teddy's file and I found a typed note. It's unsigned and undated. It states that there is a gift of twenty thousand pounds enclosed, to be used for Teddy Bartlett's care.'

'When was the account opened?'

'In April 2011, by the previous manager. At least he did that much and the money is safe. There is no envelope, just the note. We've had major changes in staff here and the handful who were here at that time know nothing about it.'

'So it sounds as if the gift was in cash.'

'That is confirmed by the financial record. Presumably no one would send that amount of money through the post.'

'I wouldn't have thought so. There's definitely no envelope?'

'I'm afraid not, I checked thoroughly. I don't know if this is of any significance but it seemed odd, so I wanted to inform you'

'Thank you. It could be significant. Can you scan the note and send it to me?'

'Of course.'

He put his cooling porridge on low in the microwave and watched it spin. It had to be guilt money. Rowan Bartlett undoubtedly harboured guilt but could hardly have delivered the cash from Sydney. An attack of conscience from the assailant?

The scanned note had arrived by the time he sat down again with his warmed bowl.

> *Twenty thousand pounds here for Teddy Bartlett. Use it if he needs extra things or for something special. Whatever makes his life easier.*

Such a large, anonymous gift had to be significant. He phoned Rowan Bartlett and asked him about the money. He said this was the first he'd heard of it. Swift updated him on progress and said he would be in touch again soon.

* * *

Later that night, Swift and Cedric returned from their local, the Silver Mermaid, where they had played dominoes. The talk had turned to Swift's work and Cedric mentioned that there was a woman who sometimes attended his reading group who was a Druid. She was

94

called Lucy Magee but her Druid name was Gwencalon, which meant shining heart.

'She told me she attends magical camps and various meetings in glades and forests and wears flowing robes. She always looks fairly formal and quietly dressed at the group so I was surprised when I found out. Good to have your stereotypes challenged now and again.'

'Are you expecting to see her soon? I'd like to speak to her. I'm not getting very far at the moment and she might tell me something useful.'

'We meet next week so hopefully she'll be there, although she does have to travel for work. I'll ask if you can contact her.'

They turned into their street. It was good to hear Cedric laughing. Since his son had departed for Spain, his spirits seemed lighter. He was explaining how Lucy Magee had divulged her Druid connections over fruit punch at a midsummer party when Swift touched his arm and stopped. He was sure he had seen a thin beam of light through his downstairs front window. The curtains were thinly lined and translucent. He looked again and saw a flicker.

'Can you wait here, Cedric? I think there's someone in my living room.'

'A burglar?' Cedric took a step forward but Swift shook his head.

'I don't know. Just stay here for now, please, while I take a look.'

Swift opened the front door and the inner one to his own flat, noiselessly. He pushed the door back a few inches and looked through. The living room had been turned upside down, with cushions, books and furniture thrown randomly about. A man dressed in black and wearing a mask and LED head torch had raised a can of spray paint and was about to decorate the wall over the fireplace. Swift stepped quickly towards him. The man turned, launching himself forwards and landing a hefty punch on the side of Swift's face. Swift tasted blood in his mouth and his ear was ringing. Swift shoved his calf between the other man's legs, trying to throw him off balance. He was much taller but the man was solidly built and felt like a small dynamo as they grappled and shoved. Swift ripped the LED light off his head, flinging it into a corner where it spun on the floor, casting dancing shadows. He landed a punch of his own in the man's diaphragm, winding him. Swift tripped over an upturned chair and fell, landing heavily on his right leg. As he struggled up he heard a *snick* and saw a blade glint. He dodged sideways as the intruder lunged towards him. The blade caught his upper left arm and he felt a hot, sharp pain. He grabbed the wrist holding the knife and with his other hand, rammed his fingers into the man's eyes. There was a satisfying howl as the knife flashed away through the air. Swift followed through with a knee to the groin. The man dropped to the floor, groaning loudly. Panting, Swift heaved him over to his front and shoved a knee on him, leaning his weight down and pinning his arms with one throbbing hand. With the other, he undid his belt and tied it around the man's wrists.

Light flooded the room as Cedric stepped through the door.

'Ty, are you all right? There was the most awful noise.'

'Kitchen drawer under the toaster. You'll find handcuffs, bring two pairs through.'

Cedric vanished, his mouth open. Swift panted, keeping his weight steady. Blood was trickling from his mouth. He let it run, glancing at his jacket arm, where the knife had penetrated. It burned but he didn't think the blade had gone too deep. The intruder tried to flex his back again but Swift slammed his knee into his spine and he groaned. Cedric was back with the handcuffs, holding them out.

'Want me to help?'

'Yes. Put a pair on his ankles. I'll hold him down.'

Once the ankles had been cuffed, Swift dragged the man to the only upright chair and slammed him into it, looping his arms over the back. He attached handcuffs to the powerful wrists and retrieved his belt. Then he pulled the mask off. Cedric had found a box of tissues and handed them to Swift, who wiped blood from his chin. He eased his jacket off and looked at his arm through his sliced shirt. There was a cut but it had already stopped bleeding. Cedric looked on.

'That might need stitches.'

'It can wait. There are plasters at the back of that same drawer in the kitchen.'

While Cedric fetched the first aid, Swift righted a couple of chairs and sat on one, facing his intruder. He was small, only about five feet five but he carried a muscular bulk that indicated regular workouts. He had the flattened nose of a boxer, short wiry hair and a crust of blood forming under one nostril. He blinked rapidly, clearing tears from his eyes where Swift's fingers had jabbed.

'I'd take a guess that you're the person behind the call-outs to the emergency services, the graffiti outside and the other stuff. What's your name?'

The man shrugged his shoulders, blinking again. Swift rose and stood behind him, taking care to pin an arm across his neck and reaching into the pockets of his jacket. He found a wallet with a driving licence inside.

'Okay, Francis Howell. Want to tell me why you're here?'

Cedric came back, dabbed antiseptic on his cut arm and applied a plaster, then handed Swift a glass of water. He drank deeply, tasting the metallic blood washing from his mouth.

'Who is this vermin?' Cedric asked.

Swift handed him the driving licence and looked back at Howell.

'You need to tell me something. Start with who's paying you.'

Howell shrugged again and pulled his mouth down. He shifted in the chair, wincing and taking a sharp breath. Swift was glad he'd made a good connection with Howell's genitals. His head, leg and arm were throbbing and he could feel his lip swelling. He finished the glass of water, then turned to Cedric.

'I think heavy rain is forecast tonight, isn't it?'

'That's right.' Cedric looked startled at this introduction of the weather.

'Good. Okay, Howell, you'd better speak to me or things might get very difficult before I call the police.'

Howell ran his tongue across his lips and looked at the floor. Swift turned to Cedric.

'You get off to bed now, it's late. Thanks for the help.'

'Good heavens, dear boy! I'm not leaving you here with this specimen of primitive man.'

Swift looked at Cedric meaningfully. 'Poor Howell. Whoever is paying him hasn't told him about my previous careers. I know you've lived a sheltered life and what's going to happen here might not be pretty, if you know what I mean. I don't want to give you nightmares, my friend.'

Cedric nodded. 'Ah, I see. Well then, I'll be off upstairs but I won't be asleep.'

Swift sat back in his chair and look at Howell's bloodshot eyes.

'I intend to establish why you've been doing these things, Howell. You can talk to me or not, it's your call. I'm not going to spend time trying to talk you into it, especially as my mouth hurts. If you don't start telling me in the next ten minutes, I'm going to gag you, drag you out to the garden and lock you to a rain barrel. You'll get a good cold drenching overnight. Maybe in the morning you'll feel like talking — if you haven't got pneumonia. I can leave you out there as long as I like, come to think of it, with a nice robust gag. It's in a spot where the neighbours can't see you. Nobody would blame me. I've got a knife you brought with you and the cut where it went in, not to mention a witness. I'm going to make myself a coffee, so have a think.'

Swift picked up the knife in some tissues and took it to the kitchen, where he placed it in a polythene bag and sealed it. He brewed coffee and took a couple of aspirin for his aching jaw and limbs. He rubbed his leg, wincing. It would have to be the right one, where he had been stabbed in the thigh. Moving his tongue around, he discovered a chipped back molar. He took his coffee back to the living room and sat, sipping cautiously. Howell was looking a little anxious now.

'Two minutes left,' Swift said conversationally. 'The rain's started. I've unlocked the back door.'

He left a silence as the forecast downpour began to lash the windows. After a couple more sips of coffee, he rose and started to pull Howell's chair with his good arm, dragging him backwards across the floor and through the kitchen. He had got as far as the back door, throwing it open, when Howell spoke.

'Okay, okay! Cut it out. I'll tell you. I might as well, right? I've had the payment anyway.'

Swift let go of the chair so that Howell rocked back and forth.

'Pay-off before it's done? Very nice arrangement. Tell me more when I've fetched my coffee.'

He sat with his hot drink by the table, leaving Howell in front of the open door where the cold air and rain whipped at him.

'Go on.'

'This barrister bloke rang me a couple of months back. He was in court once, years back, when I was on a charge. He was just a solicitor then, right? He remembered me when he wanted this job done. Anyway, he said there was a bloke who'd crossed him and he wanted to teach a lesson to. Gave me your details, right?' His voice became whiny. 'Here, can't you close the door? It's bloody freezing and I'm telling you everything.'

Swift ignored him, masking the dismay he had felt at the mention of a barrister.

'What's this barrister's name?'

'A poncy name: Emlyn Taylor. He said to cause you a bit of misery, like. Told me the kind of stuff to do and said to use my imagination. First time anyone's paid me to do that, I can tell you. Money for old rope really.'

'How much did he pay you?'

'Three hundred a go. Listen, I'd checked you was out tonight, right? I wasn't going to hurt you, just trash the place.'

'Strange, carrying a knife when you don't intend any harm.'

Howell shivered. 'It's for protection, right? You've got to look out for yourself in my line of work. I only used it cos you came at me. It wasn't nothing personal, mate, and I wouldn't have touched the old geezer, like, I wouldn't do—'

'Oh shut up,' Swift snapped. 'What were you going to do next?'

'I dunno. I'd have to put me thinking cap on. Taylor rings me after each time, the next day. He likes to hear the details. He had a good laugh when I told him about the animal gizzards through the door, and smashing up your boat tickled him — he suggested that. I don't contact him, that's the deal. I expect I'd have put dog shit through the letterbox, smashed windows, stuff like that. Maybe damage your mate's car. I'd have had to be more careful, mind, now you've put the CCTV up.'

All in a day's work, his manner said. He had grown confident as he described his activities, clearly pleased with his accomplishments. Swift finished his coffee and poured another.

'I suppose all the arrangements were by phone and the money paid into your account?'

'Yeah. I haven't met Taylor, if that's what you mean. That's it, the lot. He don't like you, does he? Got it in for you, that's for sure. You must have caused him some grief to make him come after you, right?' Howell smiled slyly, his tone a little bolder. He had sensed that he had touched a nerve. 'Shag his missus or his girlfriend, did you? Blokes like him don't like that, they're used to calling the shots, owning their territory. It can turn them nasty.'

Swift rubbed his aching chin, thinking, trying to ignore the tiredness nagging at his bones. He reflected that he was now between a rock and a hard place and that in many ways this difficult position was his own fault. Above all, he needed to protect Ruth.

'Like I said, it ain't nothing personal. Taylor's behind it all. I suppose you're going to call the cops now,' Howell said in a hard-done-by voice.

Swift stood abruptly. Howell flinched.

'No. I'm going to let you go. If you come anywhere near me again, I'll make sure you suffer and not just through the courts. Your knife will be kept safe. You won't be receiving any more business from Mr Taylor.'

Howell looked surprised but evidently knew when to shut up. Swift unlocked the ankle cuffs and told him to get up. He groaned as he stood, pressing his knees together. Swift pushed him roughly to the front door. Howell stood on the doorstep, holding his cuffed wrists out behind him.

'Don't forget these.'

'That's okay. You can have those on me. A little keepsake.'

Howell turned. 'What? How am I going to get them off, you bastard?'

Swift shrugged. 'Not my problem. I'm sure you have friends who can help.'

He shoved Howell out into the deluge, slammed the door and locked it. He leaned against the wall for a moment and sighed. Cedric appeared on the landing, in his dressing gown and slippers.

'Are you all right? You've let him go?'

'I'm okay. Yes, he's gone.'

Cedric started down the stairs. 'But surely you're calling the police?'

'No. I know why Howell's been targeting me and I can deal with it. It's best that way. You get some sleep. Thanks for your help, Cedric. Howell won't be back. I'll see you in the morning.'

Cedric went to speak, looked carefully at Swift's determined face, then nodded and returned to his flat. Swift looked at the mess in the living room and decided it could wait. He locked the back door, made himself another strong coffee and sat at the kitchen table with his phone. He looked up Emlyn Taylor and found a landline number. He made a note of it, then sat drinking and considering the conversation he needed to have with Ruth's husband. Hopefully, Taylor would now feel honours were even.

Chapter 8

Swift had borrowed Cedric's car again for the journey to Cambridge. By seven a.m. he was heading out of London, fuelled by strong coffee and painkillers. He had slept fitfully, waking in a sweat several times, thinking of the previous stabbing when his thigh had been sliced open. He had checked the cut on his arm. It wasn't too open and didn't seem deep. He drenched it with antiseptic and put a fresh plaster on. It would have to do for now. His top lip was puffy and livid where Howell had landed the punch. He used a strong mouthwash, wincing as it stung. By the time he'd finished he smelled like a pharmacy.

Once he was on the M11 he stopped at a service station. It was eight fifteen and he gauged that Ruth would have left for work. It was a mild, sunny day so he got out of the car and sat on the bonnet as he dialled Taylor's number. It rang for a while and he was about to give up when it was answered. The voice was deep, musical.

'Emlyn Taylor.'

'This is Tyrone Swift.'

There was a pause. 'Yes?'

'I'm calling you about Mr Howell.'

'Who?'

'Let's not play games. Francis Howell broke into my house last night. I persuaded him to tell me who had asked him to carry out various damaging acts against me. He told me. Three hundred a go, he said. Reasonable rate.'

Taylor coughed. 'I don't know what you're talking about. I have no wish to speak to you.'

'We can either do this now, by phone, or I can come to your house. I'd rather Ruth knew nothing about it but that's up to you.' Swift had no intention of going anywhere near their home.

'How gentlemanly of you to consider Ruth's feelings.'

Swift took a breath. He needed to keep this calm and straightforward.

'Francis Howell attacked me with a knife and injured me. I have the knife and a witness. Pretty open-and-shut case. I don't want to involve the police. I let him go and told him he won't be hearing from you again. I won't contact you further if you guarantee you'll back off. If you don't I'll go to the police today. They have a log of all the previous incidents. It wouldn't do your career or your reputation much good.'

'I see. Have you suffered at the hands of that idiot? I do hope so. It was certainly my intention. He may not be sharp-witted but he has a certain way of crafting his work that is quite admirable.'

Swift swallowed an angry response and kicked a tyre, sending needles of pain up his bruised leg. A car drew up beside him. He walked to a line of trees where there was a picnic area and stood beneath one, a hand on the rough bark.

'I've been inconvenienced, angered, worried, put out of pocket and the knife wound hurts. Also my jaw, where I was punched. Does that satisfy you?'

'It does. It gives me enormous satisfaction. I enjoyed listening to all the details. I could almost hear the boat splintering. I found out from Ruth's text messages that she

104

was seeing you. I thought something was going on while she was in London so I checked her phone. So obvious and so stupid of her not to cover her tracks, but she probably thought my brain was deteriorating along with my body. She was different when she came home. It's hard to conceal deception, even when you think you are.'

She managed to deceive me efficiently about you, when she was seeing you, Swift thought but stayed silent.

'I enjoyed my revenge on you,' Taylor continued, 'even though it was risky. Thing is, when you've become a cripple in a wheelchair and your wife is cheating on you, you don't feel as if you have much to lose.'

'I can see that.'

'I was going to pay Ruth back by telling her to pack her bags. I might have told her about Howell too, just to make sure she understood cause and effect. Then she told me a couple of days ago that she's pregnant again. I'm delighted. I want to be a father. I'd decided to call off Howell anyway, now that life is going to take a new direction.'

'I see. Well, congratulations about the baby. Ruth and I finished seeing each other a while back, if it's any consolation.'

'Not particularly. I don't trust her now and I probably don't even love her any more. But in my position and with a child expected, I have to compromise. Howell has given me the consolation I wanted. Stay away from us and I'll stay away from you.'

'Fine. Agreed.'

Swift shoved his phone in his pocket, cursed and ran his hands through his hair. He bought a coffee and croissant and sat in the car with the door open. He felt grubby after the conversation with Taylor and sorry for Ruth, wondering what kind of future she would have. A man with a progressive disease was always going to occupy the moral high ground. He recalled that Ruth had said her husband was beginning to be subject to mood swings. He wondered if Taylor's judgement was being warped by the illness. He winced as he forgot to chew the croissant on the undamaged side of his mouth. He phoned his dentist and secured an appointment for the following afternoon, then drove on to Cambridge.

* * *

Judith Saltby opened the door. A tiny baby was strapped to her chest. It was to stay there, sleeping, for the duration of his visit. She looked startled when she saw him.

'Have you had an accident?'

'Sort of. Probably looks worse than it is.'

She led him through the hallway of her small terraced house, past a folded pushchair into a bright kitchen, painted white, which was very warm and full of baby paraphernalia. Wet wipes, creams, bright plastic toys, nappies, small suits and bibs lay all around.

'You'll have to forgive the mess,' she said, moving a box of nappies from a chair for him. 'Samuel is just three weeks old and I've discovered that a tiny human can overrun a house. My husband says it's like having a benign version of Attila the Hun move in.'

She was a petite woman with neat features, her hair coming loose from a hastily arranged bun. Despite her wrinkled T-shirt and jeans, there was an elegance to her movements. He watched as she put the kettle on, finished loading the dishwasher and tipped coffee into a cafetiere, asking if decaff was okay. She had the wild-eyed look of someone sleep-deprived but she smiled constantly. It was a smile of sheer joy. Swift regarded Samuel's pale, sleeping face. Babies seemed to be everywhere at the moment — born, expected, longed for. He suddenly remembered the tiny yellow cardigan he had found in Sheila's chaotic room, carefully hidden away. He thought it might be important, but had no idea why.

They sat at the kitchen table with coffee. Swift refused a ginger biscuit, pointing at his mouth. He explained about Rowan Bartlett contacting him and his enquiries.

'How is Teddy?' Judith asked. 'I must visit him one day.'

'When did you last see him?'

'Eleven years ago, just before I went to Canada.'

'I've seen him recently. He has to have special care.'

'He's never regained any speech?'

'He can't communicate.'

'So no one knows if he remembers what happened that day but just can't tell anyone?'

'No one can tell, but I think it's unlikely that Teddy has any recall, after the injuries he sustained.'

'It's so unfair. Teddy had so much promise.'

'I understand that he had few friends and you were one of them. I've established that the family were complex and troubled. Were you ever in their house?'

'Gosh, no. Teddy didn't want to take people home. He called his house misfit central, I remember. He used to come back to mine after school sometimes. He'd have to lie to his sister Sheila, and say he was attending a club. She was a strange girl, always keeping tabs on him and wanting to know where he was. Things improved for him after she started her nursing training. He could move around more freely. I only met her once when she was waiting for him at the school gate. She was spooky, I thought.' She looked down, then up at him. 'I need to explain that Teddy and I probably bonded because we both had odd, restrictive families. I was brought up in a strict religious household. We belonged to The Select Flock. Have you heard of them?'

'Vaguely.'

'It's a narrow, inward-looking faith with many rules. A kind of prison. I escaped the flock when I left school. It's one of the reasons I went so far away, and headed to Canada. When I told my parents I couldn't stay in the church they disowned me. That's what happens if you're not a believer. My father literally threw me out. He told me I was dead to them and said he wished I'd never been born. So I don't have any contact with my family. They don't know I'm married, or about Samuel.'

'I'm sorry.'

'Thanks. It's okay now. I've worked through it all. It took me a long time and I miss my mother sometimes. She was always kind to me, as far as her faith permitted. She preferred my brother to me, I knew that, but in the end she's the only mother I had. I'd like to be able to tell her about Samuel but she can't speak to me and I wouldn't put her in that position. Women in The Select Flock are very much governed by the males in the household. I've accepted that it's best just not to try to communicate and open up old wounds.'

'The Select Flock sounds almost like a cult.'

She nodded. 'It's on that spectrum, yes. At home, we weren't allowed music or television or fizzy drinks or other ungodly things, all the things that might make life pleasurable. We only got a landline phone two years before I left home. I have one brother, Joshua. He's three years older than me and he was almost more devout than my parents. I used to think that Sheila and my brother had a lot in common. They both liked to call the shots, tell other people what to do. Me and Teddy used to arrange to meet up on evenings when Josh was at bible class and my parents were still at work.'

'You didn't have to go to bible class?'

'Yes, but at different times to Josh. Boys and girls weren't allowed to mix. Heaven knows what might have happened.'

'Lust and fornication and such like?'

She smiled. 'Exactly. There were a couple of hours on Tuesdays after school when I had the house to myself and the coast was clear. Teddy would bring his music round and I'd buy cake, cola and crisps on the way home. We used to refer to those times as covert operations. Teddy took all the evidence away with him when he left. We'd listen to music in my room. It was ironic. To me my home felt like a jail, but Teddy said he could breathe at my place. We had a narrow escape one evening when my mum came home early from work with flu. Luckily, she'd forgotten her key and had to ring the bell so we had warning. We waited until she was lying down and then Teddy slipped out.'

'The Select Flock allowed women to work then?'

'Yes, but the job had to be approved by the pastor and they weren't allowed to work in shops or with any kind of merchandise. Clerical duties in offices were okay. My mother worked for a local solicitor.'

'Deaven Harrow said Teddy was also friendly with Imogen Thornley. Did she come to your house?'

'No. Imogen wasn't really my close friend. She and Teddy used to hang out together at art club after school and her mother gave him a lift home afterwards. Mrs Thornley liked Teddy, she approved of his good manners. She didn't approve of my family. She was a school governor and she'd had a run-in with my father when he complained about sex education lessons. She didn't want Imogen having anything to do with The Select Flock, and I can't say I blame her. Imogen was killed when she was eighteen, a drunk driver.' Samuel mewled and she kissed the top of his head, patting his back lightly.

'Tell me about Teddy, what he was like.'

Judith dipped a biscuit in her coffee and nibbled it.

'He was so sweet, and such good company when he wasn't melancholy. We just got on really well. People said we looked like brother and sister.'

'I can see that. I've seen photos of Teddy.'

'I didn't get on with my own brother and Teddy was easy to be with. A lot of the boys at school were objectionable. You know, testosterone-fuelled adolescents, unsure of themselves and making up for lack of confidence by pretending they were God's gift to girls. Sorry, you were a boy once!' She smiled and licked biscuit crumbs from her fingers.

'That's okay. Hopefully I wasn't that bad, but maybe the girls I was at school with would say different . . .'

'I'd guess you were a decent sort, judging by what I see now. I was friends with Teddy for five years so I got to know him well. He was like a restless spirit who was in a trap and trying to escape it. When he got into Druidry, life seemed to get better for him. I didn't always understand what he was talking about but it seemed to inspire him. He was such a gentle, kind boy and funny too. He used to call Sheila the Generalissima — we'd been studying the Spanish Civil War. Sometimes he'd salute or click his heels when he mentioned her.'

'Is that what you meant when you said she was spooky?'

'I suppose. She scowled when I met her, sort of stared at me. I felt she was jealous of Teddy having a friend.'

'Was he frightened of her?'

Judith took another biscuit and stroked the baby's head.

'I'm not sure. He used to joke about her, but he was wary too. He didn't want to get on the wrong side of her. His mother seemed a pathetic woman so Sheila ruled the roost. He rarely spoke about his father, except to say he was a waste of space. To be honest, he didn't talk about home much. I think he liked to forget about it when he was with me. He'd dance and we'd sing. You know, pretending to be pop stars, the way teenagers do. We packed an awful lot of fun into a couple of hours, letting our hair down. Also . . .' she paused, looking at him. 'There's something I'd rather you kept to yourself, something about Teddy. He trusted me with it and even now I wouldn't want you repeating it to anyone. It's why I wanted to speak to you in person — well, one of the reasons.'

Swift felt a tingle of interest. 'Okay, I can agree to that.'

'Sometimes, Teddy liked to put on one of my dresses or skirts and tops. He preferred a dress. He just liked to sit in it while we talked. It started as a joke when we were miming to Madonna, but I could see it meant something to him. Then, as time went on, it was the first thing he did when we got to my house. He'd say he was my sister, Edwina. I didn't know what to make of it back then. With hindsight, I'm sure it meant he was interested in transvestism or maybe confused about his sexuality. I was reading an article recently about people who describe themselves as "gender neutral," and what they were saying rang bells about Teddy. I'd let him go through my wardrobe and choose something. There wasn't that much to choose from and it was drab stuff, all dark colours and plain styles. The Select Flock didn't allow vanities. But Teddy looked really good in my dowdy dresses. He was so slim and fine boned, they were a nice fit.' She laughed warmly at the memory.

Swift regarded this kindly, thoughtful woman. He could see why Teddy had trusted her. She was the first person who had talked about him laughing and having fun. The shadowy, diffident character had a different, more substantial aspect now.

'It was good that he had you in his life, I think. You provided a safety valve for him.'

'Well . . . I hope so. He certainly helped me survive my upbringing. He was a good person. I missed him after he was injured. Life seemed very dull.'

'From what you've told me, I'm presuming that back in 2000 you didn't tell the police about Teddy's liking for dressing in your clothes.'

'No. I did wonder at the time if I should, but the detective who spoke to me was arrogant and patronising, a real macho man — heavy aftershave and big ego. He eyed me up and down in that way some men have, as if they're picturing you naked. I disliked him and I thought he would make fun of Teddy so I kept quiet. That was why I kept quiet about the other thing I knew as well.'

'Go on.'

She gathered biscuit crumbs from the table and tipped them on to a plate.

'Teddy's family was like ours in that they had no computers or mobile phones. Teddy used to go to an Internet Café in Fitzrovia a couple of times a week, when Sheila was on a shift at the hospital. I think it was one of the first in London. He swore me to secrecy about it. He told me he wanted to look up information about people who felt like him, men who wanted to put women's clothes on. He said once that he was talking to some people on the web about it. He was thrilled to find boys his age he could discuss it with. I knew nothing about the Internet back then. I didn't understand how he could do that.'

Swift let out a breath. 'That could be very important information, Judith. It may be that he got involved with someone who was pretending to be like him but who wanted to harm him.'

She looked sober, nodding. 'I realise that now. Back then, I had no idea and I wanted to protect Teddy from that detective. I imagined people talking about him, the boys at school ridiculing him, as he was lying in intensive care, more dead than alive. Do you think if I'd said it at the time, the police might have caught the person who attacked Teddy?'

'It's hard to say. If he did come to harm through Internet chat, the police might have looked at the computers in that café. Although fifteen years ago I'm not sure they'd have had that kind of handle on the technology or been able to trace anyone.' He thought of Peterson and it seemed unlikely.

'Hindsight is painful sometimes.'

'I wouldn't lose any sleep over it. It's helpful that you've told me now. When did he start going to the Internet café?'

'I'm not sure. I think it was sometime in 1999. Teddy had seen a newspaper article about it. Will you have to tell people now, about Teddy's interests?'

'Not necessarily. I'll only do that if I have to in order to identify his attacker, and I'll inform you.'

She looked relieved. 'Okay.'

'Did Teddy seem depressed to you that summer or say anything that indicated he was considering running away or harming himself?'

'No. As I said, he was often a bit melancholy. I think he was a bit quieter than usual around that time. He did say that Sheila was really getting him down, but then he often made that kind of comment about her. I thought everything had got too much for him at home. Since Mr Harrow contacted me, I've been thinking about Teddy a lot.'

They sat in silence for a moment. Swift touched the soft foot of some baby leggings on the table.

'Do you know if there were any births in Teddy's family? Did he mention new cousins, anything like that?'

'Not that I can recall. Why?'

'I just wondered. Why would someone keep a brand new baby cardigan tucked away?'

Judith tapped the table, beating out a soft rhythm.

'A gift never given? The person it was intended for had a miscarriage or stillbirth? It was forgotten about?' She smiled. 'A friend of mine crocheted a blanket but it's huge and a bit heavy. Samuel can have it when he's a toddler. I've put it in a drawer and I can imagine I might forget about it — although knowing my friend, she'll remind me!'

Swift left as Samuel started to wake, nuzzling at his mother's neck. He parked near the Quayside by Magdalene Bridge and walked along the river towards Midsummer Common. He passed a row of houseboats. A few of the owners were cleaning windows, seeing to plants, carrying out routine maintenance. He turned over this new information about Teddy, not sure what he could do with it. Checking Google, he saw that the Internet café used by Teddy had been called Cyberia and no longer existed. Teddy had been a confused adolescent exploring his sexual identity. His vulnerability was almost tangible, even across this time and distance.

Swift rang Tim Christie and asked if he could remember any births in the family or amongst people they knew. Christie sounded puzzled and said he couldn't recall any babies being born or being brought to the house. He sounded half asleep, as if the call had woken him up, although it was midday.

'By the way,' he mumbled, 'tell Sheila to leave me alone when you see her.'

'What do you mean?'

'She's been emailing, wanting to know if you'd been in touch and what you asked me. I ignored it, so she sent another message. I don't want anything to do with her or my father, so tell her.'

'I don't want to carry messages around your family, Tim. You'll have to reply and tell her yourself.'

Christie became excitable, stuttering his words in a rush. 'I wish you'd never got in touch about this. I'd got her out of my life and now she's back in and that bastard with her. I've been having bad dreams. Last night I found myself in the street in the early hours. I must have been walking in my sleep. I haven't done that for years. I have this dream that something's squeezing me and I can't breathe. My face is covered. I wake in a panic. Oh God! After all this time.'

'Tim, take a breath. Have you ever had any counselling about your childhood?'

'What, you mean a shrink or something?'

'A therapist, someone to talk it through with.'

'Nah. What's the point?'

114

'It might help you. I think you use drugs to ease the pain and if you talked to someone, a professional counsellor, you might not need to.'

Christie started screaming. 'Fuck off and mind your own business! I don't want to hear from you ever again. Fuck right out of my life and take those fucking bastards with you, ok?'

He rang off. Swift walked on for another fifteen minutes, raising his face to the late autumn sun, reflecting on the pain in Christie's voice, trying to ignore the pain in his mouth.

* * *

Swift called in to the health centre and was told that he was lucky, the practice nurse had had a cancellation. She looked at the knife cut, told him off for not going to A & E immediately and advised him that he had just got away with not needing stitches. She put a dressing on his arm, asking how it had happened and he explained it had been an accident. She nodded, clearly not believing him. She told him to come back if there was any sign of infection and gave him instructions on keeping the wound clean.

He stocked up with painkillers and some more dressings at a chemist, then made for home. He was opening the front door when a car pulled up and Sheila got out, waving. She was wearing her nursing uniform and a dark blue raincoat.

'Hi! I just thought I'd call by, see if you'd made any progress. That's a nasty looking lip.'

She came up to him, too close, wheezing in his face. Her breath smelled of eucalyptus. He didn't want to invite her into his home, so he indicated the basement.

'I had an accident. Come down to my office.'

She thumped down after him as he unlocked the door. He invited her to sit.

'This is nice,' she said. 'Handy for you, too.'

'Yes.' He sat behind his desk. 'If you wanted to know about progress, you could have rung. Hammersmith is quite a journey for you.'

'I was at a conference in Fulham today so I thought I'd call by on the off-chance.'

He thought she was lying. Her eyes were shifty. Looking at her, he knew he wouldn't want her touching his skin, cleaning a wound. There were epaulettes on the shoulders of her coat and he thought of *the Generalissima* and Tim referring to her as Stalin.

'I have nothing particular to report. If I had, I would have called your father. Does he know you're here?'

She pulled her coat around her. 'No. I'll tell him when I get home. So, who have you talked to?'

'The police, Teddy's head teacher, your aunt, your brother and a friend of Teddy's.'

'Is that all?'

'That's all. You know, given that you didn't think it was a good idea for your father to instigate this enquiry, you seem very keen to know about it.'

She picked at a nail. 'I just think I need to look out for him. Who's the friend you talked to?'

'Judith Saltby.'

Her brow furrowed. 'I don't see that she could tell you much.'

'No? Of course, you've already asked your brother what I talked to him about. He's pretty upset about you emailing him. I think you should back off.'

She bridled. 'I don't see why I can't contact my own brother if I want to. It's not for you to say.'

'No, but it is for him to say. I told him to let you know himself, but I think you must be aware that he wants to avoid contact with you and his father.'

'He's just troubled. He was always highly strung. I said to Dad that opening up this can of worms would do no good but he wouldn't listen.'

'Well, that's between you and your father. By the way, you forgot to tell me about the twenty thousand pounds someone donated to Mayfields for Teddy.'

She looked genuinely blank. 'Oh, that. I didn't think of that. It seemed peculiar.'

'It is, and it could also be important. Let me know if you remember anything else I should know. I do need to get on so if you'll excuse me . . .'

He got up, forcing her to rise too and opened the office door. She stopped halfway through.

'So what did Judith Saltby have to say?'

'Not a great deal.'

'You don't seem to be getting very far.'

'These things take time.'

He gestured for her to go ahead. She moved reluctantly and he waited until she was walking to her car.

'Oh, Ms Bartlett, just one question. Were there ever any births in your extended family or in friends' families when you were young? Did any babies visit your house?'

She stopped and turned slowly. Colour drained from her face, then rushed back in a fiery blush.

'Babies? No. What an odd question. Why are you asking me that?'

He wasn't sure what he could see in her eyes. Anger and confusion, certainly, but maybe fear as well.

'Oh, just something that was said. Detectives come up with all kinds of random questions you know.' He stepped towards her. 'Sheila, why do I get the impression that you're hiding something?'

'I don't know what you mean. What would I have to hide?'

He shrugged. 'I have an idea that you're concerned that my investigation might throw light on something else, something you wouldn't want revealed.'

She tightened the belt on her coat. 'Don't be so ridiculous. I can't waste any more time on this nonsense.'

He stood watching as she walked slowly to her car. She sat inside, her head down. Then she reached into her bag and took out a large pastry, which she rapidly consumed, stuffing it into her mouth. After she had driven away Swift tidied the mess Howell had made in the living room, amazed that nothing was too damaged, just one wonky chair leg. Sheila was worried about his questions, that much was clear, and the mention of babies had thrown her.

When he had finished clearing up, he sat with his notes, sifting through the information. There were dots but so far, none of them joined up.

* * *

Kris's flat in Kennington was at the top of a three-storey house. It was small with a living room, kitchen, one bedroom and a shower room but dormer windows made it bright and airy. Swift visited her after his dental appointment. The dentist had applied a temporary cover to his chipped tooth and said it would need a crown. The poking and prodding had been painful because of the bruising to his jaw. He had told Kris that he'd had a burglar and that he had an interesting bruise on his face. He was glad that she didn't make a fuss when he arrived.

She watched expectantly as he looked at the vibrant fifties décor. There was a free-standing cupboard filling the wall between the windows of the living room, painted in sections of pale green, yellow and sky blue. The wallpaper was green with geometric designs, lamps with shades in the same design lit the room and there was a sofa and chair in red fabric with yellow cushions. Pictures of cityscapes and a sunburst clock hung on the walls. A long white table with a laminated apple print occupied one wall. It held a sewing machine, an angled lamp and a length of orange fabric, patterned with triangles and squares.

'I haven't started on the kitchen yet. I have to earn some more money first,' she told him.

'You know, I think I like it. It's a bit of a shock but it works.' He turned around slowly. He admired the detail and the care she had taken. Also the fact that she knew what she liked and wasn't afraid to express her taste. She was wearing a black and white polka-dot dress with a full skirt, the kind he'd seen in films and on her website.

'Did you make the dress too?'

'Finished it yesterday. Look at the dents in my fingertips from my hard work!'

'Amazing. You have real talent.'

They ate macaroni cheese with salad at her narrow kitchen table, the kind with an extra flap that could open out. He appreciated that she'd made food he could eat easily. He forked the meal carefully into the side of his mouth, telling her his background with Ruth and the truth about Francis Howell and the reason for his attack.

She looked at him, food suspended on her fork.

'You're not going to go to the police?'

'I can't, Kris. I want to close the whole situation down, have done with it. Otherwise Emlyn and Ruth are still in my life, and they've been there long enough.'

She nodded. 'I can see that. I'm glad, actually.'

She had made a Polish fruit dessert called Kisiel, thick with apricots, cherries, oranges and red wine and wonderfully rich. He admired the vibrant colours, though its sweetness made him blink.

Over coffee they talked more about her business. She told him that she had an order for two halterneck dresses, a pair of pedal pushers and a circle skirt. Several more customers had contacted her and asked her to visit them to take fittings, and orders on her website were growing. She showed him the cupboards in the hallway and her bedroom. They were full of neatly packaged and labelled fifties-style hats, gloves, shoes and sandals, boleros, wraps and pieces of jewellery. Some of these she had made but most she had sourced on the Internet or through visiting second-hand shops and house clearances. She thought she'd soon be able to give up her shifts at the Evergreen. She had a delightful habit, he noted, of blowing her fringe back from her forehead when she became animated.

'Tell me,' he said, 'did you ever feel like running away from home when you were a teenager?'

She laughed. 'Loads of times! Is there a teenager who doesn't? All those things your parents forbid or don't approve of. I must have planned it a couple of times. You know — that'll show them, they'll be sorry for being so unreasonable!'

'What stopped you?'

'I couldn't think of where to go and of course in the end, home was in fact a pretty good place. How about you?'

'No, I never did. My parents must have been exceptionally tolerant and long-suffering.'

* * *

Later, lying in her not very comfortable bed, she whispered in his ear.

'You know, I was attracted to you when I first saw you in the restaurant. Thought it was just my luck that you were married.'

He held her close, stroking her hair. Her bedroom was so narrow he had already cracked his shin twice on the furniture but he didn't mind. He lay awake for a while after she fell asleep. This uncomplicated relationship was such a novelty. His heart was already lighter. He could see the outline of a tacked gingham skirt hanging on the sewing mannequin that stood in the corner. His thoughts drifted to a boy who liked to wear his friend's dresses.

Chapter 9

Swift was feeling irritable. He wasn't able to row for a few days because of his arm wound and he keenly missed his therapy. He knew that Sheila was hiding something but he couldn't tell if it was connected to Teddy. He rang Barbara Stead and asked her if she knew why any of the Bartlett family might have bought baby clothes. She laughed, her dog barking madly, and said she had no idea and none of that lot should ever have been left in charge of a baby. An idea was scratching away in a corner of his mind. He emailed Nora Morrow.

> *Hi Nora,*
> *Hope you're good. Could you do me a favour and run a check on Sheila Bartlett to see if she comes up in connection with any other incidents? There's something about her that doesn't add up. In return, I can borrow a boat for you and Alistair from my club if you want to go on the river.*

All best, Ty.

He walked to the Silver Mermaid just after nine o'clock. Cedric had told him to come along then, as the book club would be finishing. The members met in a room above the bar. The landlady was an avid reader so they got the place for free. Lucy Magee, auctioneer and Druid, was attending and had agreed to have a drink afterwards. Cedric was sitting in an alcove with her. Swift bought another round of gin and tonics and sat opposite them. The pub was noisy but she had a robust voice. She was a rounded, cheerful woman in jeans and a cotton jacket. Her long chestnut hair rippled down her back. Swift gave a quick outline of Teddy. He showed her the email with the copy of the note Teddy had left and the exercise book Deaven Harrow had loaned him.

'His beliefs were important to him,' he explained. 'I think that those beliefs might have played some part in him being attacked. He was a troubled young man, trying to understand his sexuality and gender identification. I've read up about Druidry, but any ideas you can come up with would be welcome.'

Lucy examined the email carefully, then scrutinised the exercise book. She looked up at Swift.

'It's a searing note, full of desperation and despair. But there's hope in it too, with the mention of the journey and Otherworld.'

'I've read that the Otherworld can be a state of mind as well as the next world after death, and I think that's what Teddy meant.'

She nodded. 'I suspect that Teddy was drawn to Druidry because it's free of dogma. There are no set beliefs and its tolerance would have been liberating to a young man who must have felt confined and confused. His goal of reaching the Otherworld would mean attaining wisdom, creativity and love.' She traced her fingers over the drawings on the exercise book. 'There are different kinds of Druid beliefs. Teddy's drawings and words indicate that he was drawn to animism or pantheism, the belief that the deity is present all around us, within ourselves and in nature.'

'He gave his brother a painting of a white hart in a forest. That would also fit with what you've said.'

'You've done your homework.'

'I've tried but it's a complicated subject, as are all belief systems. I haven't been able to work out the drawing on the back of the book, the circle with three dots and three lines.'

Lucy pointed to it. 'It's called Awen and symbolises the search for the spirit of Druidry.'

She sat back and looked through the exercise book. 'He was a very intelligent young man, judging by these grades.' She shook her head. 'Your difficulty is that Druidry is such a non-regimented way of living and believing. It's open to many different interpretations. Teddy was looking for meaning and structure, a sense of belonging and acceptance. By going to a place of trees, associated with sacred things, he may have believed he was starting his journey to Awen.'

'Do you know anything about Low Copsley, where he was found?'

'I know something of it, although I haven't been there. It's a sacred grove of yew trees. To Druids, the yew is the most potent tree for protection against evil. From ancient times, it has been a means of connecting to ancestors and a conduit to dreams and to Otherworld journeys. Yews are thought to have a powerful connection to the oldest magic.'

'So it could be that Teddy went there to make a positive, fresh start in life. I visited there and that's how it seemed to me.'

'That's how I would read his note and his actions. I think as a start of some kind of healing, too. Sadly, that wasn't to happen,' she said.

'No. His life effectively stopped that day.'

Swift left just before closing time, while Cedric and Lucy were still chatting over their drinks. He walked to the Thames to breathe the fresh night air, reflecting that the open-ended Druid beliefs and the strict ideology of The Select Flock couldn't be more dissimilar.

At home his thoughts turned again to Teddy and the likelihood that he had been targeted. He sat in his dressing gown, mulling over all the information he had gathered so far and writing down his thoughts:

> *Bartlett family; all damaged & in pain & locked in a strange dependency.*
>
> *Teddy's note; something caused Teddy great distress — someone in the family with a secret? Seems likely. A gentle, confused boy but with a strong belief and spirit. He was questioning his sexuality. He was using Internet to explore this. He responded to people he trusted. He had planned to get away from his family.*
>
> *Sheila was like an obsessed gaoler & she's hiding something. She's a liar. She was unwell that summer. Teddy told Judith that she was really getting him down.*
> *Teddy went to Low Copsley because it held sacred significance. Possibly arranged to meet someone there & that person arrived ready to kill him. Teddy believed same person was going to be part of his new start/helping*

him with it. Someone he met online or
in Internet café?

He considered Teddy's small social circle and his own options for trying to progress the case. The Internet café was long gone and there seemed to be nothing else he could glean from the Bartlett family, the school or Judith. She had mentioned that Imogen Thornley's mother knew and liked Teddy. He emailed Deaven Harrow, asking for a contact number.

* * *

Mary and Simone had sent out their wedding invitations. The marriage was to take place at a small hotel near Kew where Simone's brother was head chef. The request at the bottom of the card said, *please keep your dress informal!* Swift wasn't sure what this meant. He showed the card to Kris over lunch.

'I suppose it means you don't have to wear a suit.'

'Ah. I am the best man, though.'

'Better check with your cousin, then. What does it mean in the UK, being best man?'

'As far as I know, making sure there are rings and giving a speech at the reception. Some grooms ask the best man to organise a stag do but given that there isn't a groom, I'm relieved of that responsibility.'

'In Poland the best man has no responsibilities, other than to turn up.'

'That sounds ideal.'

Kris smiled, declaring that she was going to have a pudding and holding the menu close to her face. Swift had discovered that she was short sighted but didn't like wearing glasses in public. She had tried but failed to get on with contact lenses and admitted the world was often slightly blurred. She was wearing one of her home-made outfits: dark grey cigarette pants, a striped grey and blue shirt and a blue beret. Swift was becoming familiar with the names of fifties styles and could confidently distinguish between cigarette pants, pedal pushers, Capri pants and a poodle and a pencil skirt. He had discovered that she had been an enthusiastic gymnast as a child, which explained her balance and poise. She could still do handsprings with somersaults and something called an Arabian double front which she had demonstrated in his living room after pushing all the furniture against the wall.

'I'm going to have butterscotch and toffee sponge with cream,' she declared.

'I'll share it with you. There's something reassuring about a woman who likes puddings.'

'My mother makes wonderful desserts. Whenever anyone compliments her she's embarrassed and she says, "a beautiful plate won't feed anyone." She makes the best cheesecake I've ever eaten.'

Swift smiled at her. He knew she was getting under his skin and it felt good. He was being cautious, though, taking things slowly. He pictured her with him at the wedding and decided to ask.

'Would you like to come to the wedding with me?'

She looked delighted. 'Am I invited?'

'I've just invited you.'

'Yes, please! It will be my first English wedding. You'll have to draw me a diagram of your family so that I can be polite.'

'That won't take long. My stepmother will be thrilled to meet you.'

Joyce will be astonished and overwhelming, he thought. He would have to warn Kris. However, there was a determination to the tilt of her chin that persuaded him she would be more than a match for his stepmother. While they ate pudding, Kris sketched an outline of the dress she would make to wear at the wedding. It would probably be in heavy satin, she said, dark blue with a light aquamarine trim on the bodice, a full skirt and three-quarter-length sleeves, as it was a winter ceremony. She would match it with an ivory feather clip hat decorated with small beads that she had in her store. He watched the light, confident pencil strokes she made in her notebook. He took her free hand in his and she wriggled her cool fingers against his palm, glancing up at him, smiling.

* * *

Mrs Thornley lived in a one bedroom flat near Fairacres School. Swift was glad that he hadn't eaten more than a couple of spoons of Kris's pudding as Mrs Thornley had provided an old-fashioned tea, with scones, Madeira cake and meringues. She must have had Imogen later in life, he thought, looking at the deep lines under her eyes. Her blue jeans and jaunty floral quilted jacket belied her years. The small sitting room had too much furniture, with deep armchairs that dwarfed the space. Mrs Thornley explained that she had sold her house and downsized after her husband died.

'I should have been more ruthless in disposing of things but I think it's a process', she told him, gesturing at the room and buttering a scone. 'Imogen was our only child. There didn't seem to be any point, living in a three-bedroomed house. I'm not going to have grandchildren.'

'I understand that Imogen was killed in a car accident. I'm sorry.'

'Yes. She was just about to go to university to study architecture. The car driver was four times over the limit. He got seven years for taking her life.' She had a precise, slightly sharp tone but her eyes were kindly.

Swift took a slice of cake, deciding he didn't want to manage the cream oozing from the meringues.

'As I explained, I'm investigating what happened to Teddy Bartlett and I've been speaking to as many people as I can who knew him.'

'That was so awful, what became of him. Imogen was distraught at the time. The whole school felt the shock of it.'

'I spoke to Judith Saltby and she told me that Imogen and Teddy were friends, attending art club together. What can you tell me about Judith's family?'

Mrs Thornley chewed carefully and took a sip of tea. 'The Saltbys were . . . are . . . members of an exclusive church called The Select Flock. I believe that Judith managed to break free of them?'

'That's correct. She doesn't have any contact with her family.'

'I do believe that's a good thing, even though I put great faith in family life. I'm wary of people who think they are special and who judge others for the way they live. I know of the family because I was a school governor at Fairacres for eight years. Mrs Saltby only attended one school event during that time and that was when her husband was ill. She seemed a faded, downtrodden woman, meek. She wore a dark brown cotton dress and headscarf. All married women in The Select Flock wore a brown headscarf. The son, Joshua, was with her and she deferred to him. He was a handsome young man, tall and blond, but he had a severe, withdrawn manner. I don't think there would have been many laughs in that household.'

'Judith told me that one of the reasons she was fond of Teddy was that they laughed together.'

'They were ports in a storm for one another, those two. Imogen told me that Judith used to smuggle Teddy into her house when the coast was clear. I did worry about what might happen if her parents ever found out. Teddy's family were odd but I found the Saltbys sinister.'

'And Mr Saltby?'

'Hmm. Mr Saltby was dogmatic to the core. He was deputy to the pastor at their church. Mr Saltby knew best about everything. He barged into a governor's meeting where we were discussing the syllabus, including sexual health and education. He was shouting and denouncing us. I remember him saying we were *promoters and harbourers of promiscuity and debauchery.* I laughed, I'm afraid. I couldn't help it. He was so ridiculous but also terrifying. He was a big man, bulky, and he threw a chair over while he was ranting. The head had to threaten to call the police before he would leave.'

'Do they still live locally?'

'They're at the same address. Mr Saltby had a terrible accident about five years ago. He and his son run a plumbing business and he was injured in a house they were working on. I believe it left him in a wheelchair. I only know because it was in the local paper. I don't have anything to do with the family. Do have some more cake or another cup of tea.'

Swift was about to decline the cake when she placed another slice on his plate. He accepted more tea.

'What about Teddy? Did you know him fairly well?'

'Only in passing. I saw him about half a dozen times, when he accepted a lift home from the art club. He seemed a quiet, introspective boy. He loved drawing. Imogen told me a bit about his home life, which seemed rather inward and closed off. When I was packing to move, I found a few of his pictures amongst Imogen's things. I had no idea she had them and I left them in the folders. I thought you might like to see them.'

She fetched a plastic zip folder from a shelf and took out several pieces of A4 paper, handing them to him. She went to add hot water to the teapot while he looked. He fanned the three pages out on the floor. They were signed in the bottom right hand corner, *Teddy B.* Two were paintings with the kinds of interwoven Celtic designs that had featured in Teddy's English exercise book. The third was a charcoal sketch of a circle of trees with two shapes in the centre. Swift lifted and scrutinised it. The shapes were human figures in pale robes, holding hands. Underneath them Teddy had written;

The gift of the Druids

Two searching souls in the forest
Twin seekers at the sacred place
We need to be lost to find ourselves
Life will spring refreshed

When Mrs Thornley returned, Swift asked if she had any idea when the drawing of the trees had been done.

'I'm afraid not. As I said, I didn't even know Imogen had those. She had hundreds of pieces of art work. She probably picked some of Teddy's up after art club by accident.'

'Can I hold on to this drawing?'

'Of course. Is it important?'

'Yes, I think it is.'

It was a fine day with a mellow breeze. Swift decided to walk off the cake and headed along Dartmouth Park to Parliament Hill Fields. Teddy had intended to meet someone at Low Copsley, someone he thought of as a twin soul. A twin soul in terms of Druidry or sexual identity or both? He had probably intended to go away with this person to make his new start. At Parliament Hill, Swift sat on a bench dedicated to the memory of a Maggie Murphy. He gazed at the horizon. The anonymous money had been donated to Teddy four years ago and Mr Saltby had been injured a short time before. Serena Clayhurst had referred to compensation. Perhaps the payment had been compensation, but not for the reason she thought. He googled *Saltby* and found a newspaper article and a church reference. He read the newspaper first. It was dated May 12, 2010:

> *Local plumber Mr Steven Saltby, 59, was badly injured last Friday. Mr Saltby was involved in a house renovation in Palmerston Crescent when heavy scaffolding fell on him as he exited the property. He was taken*

> *to hospital and has had surgery. Top Tower, the scaffolding company, have been unavailable for comment.*

The second item was a website for The Select Flock. It was a no frills site with a home page that informed him:

> *We believe that Jesus Christ came into this world to save a **particular** people, who alone shall share this blessing.*

There followed a verse:

> *Free from the law, O happy condition,*
> *Jesus hath bled and there is remission,*
> *Cursed by the Law, and bruised by the fall,*
> *Grace hath redeemed us, once for all.*

There were links to local chapels. Swift followed the link to their London churches and found Hope Chapel in Tufnell Park. There was a short paragraph of information and a small photograph of the pastor.

> *Mr Joshua Saltby is the pastor of Hope Chapel.*
> *Our pastor leads The Select Flock Sunday service at 10.30 a.m.*
> *Bible classes are held on Sundays at 11.45 a.m. and Wednesdays at 4.30 p.m.*
> *When the righteous increase, people rejoice.*

Joshua had risen up the religious rankings since his sister left home. The photo was a head shot of a long-faced man with a constrained smile.

It was a while since Swift had been to church. He thought he would take a look at the righteous on Sunday.

Chapter 10

The following morning, a Saturday, produced two interesting contacts concerning the Bartletts. Nora Morrow emailed him:

> *Hi there, Ty. A sweep on Sheila Bartlett brought up something in 2002. She was interviewed because she had attended a party at a house in Islington. It was a birthday do for a nurse she was working with, an Amelia Olewo. There were over forty guests. Amelia had a baby, a girl who was asleep in an upstairs bedroom. The child was found dead in its crib when the mother went to check on her late evening. The final verdict was probable suffocation due to a loose blanket in the bedding.*
> *Take care, N.*

A baby again. There was something troubling in this. He rang the Bartlett house, deciding to visit and speak to Sheila. Rowan Bartlett answered, sounding exhausted.

'I believe I'm making some progress regarding Teddy, Mr Bartlett. I would like to speak to Sheila. Is she around today?'

'She's at work this morning, back at lunchtime. Actually, Mr Swift, this isn't the best time . . . things are difficult here.'

'Oh, I'm sorry to hear that.'

'Yes. On Thursday, Annabelle arrived here unexpectedly from Sydney. There has been a lot of arguing and difficulty with Sheila. Oh dear, I'm afraid it's all become too much . . . I can barely explain . . .'

Swift's interest grew. 'Perhaps it would be best if I called in. I'll keep it brief.'

'Very well, if you must.'

Swift arrived there just after noon. Bartlett opened the door, looking more faded than ever in a loose-fitting beige cardigan. He showed Swift into the living room. A woman with glossy blonde shoulder-length hair, wearing designer jeans, a silk shirt and sporting a ripe black eye was sitting on the sofa. The eye didn't prevent her from radiating a confident glamour.

'Annabelle, this is Tyrone Swift.'

She stayed seated, waving at him in a regal fashion while openly examining him.

'That's a nasty bruise,' Swift said, gesturing at his own jaw. 'We've both been in the wars.'

'You could say that. Mine's courtesy of my lovely niece. It's always nice to receive a warm welcome.'

'Now, Annabelle, there's no need to start telling Mr Swift. It's all very unfortunate . . .'

'Unfortunate!' Anabelle laughed, a tinny sound. 'I don't call a fist unfortunate. She's lucky I didn't call the cops.'

'Sheila hit you?' Swift asked.

Annabelle twitched her shirt collar and settled her hair. 'She certainly did. She landed a good one. I'd only been off the plane a couple of hours and *wham!* She's lucky I was still jet-lagged or I'd have been tempted to land one back.'

Bartlett was fidgeting around with the fire, poking logs and causing sparks.

'Oh do sit down, Rownie,' Annabelle said. 'You're making me nervous.'

Swift didn't think that Annabelle would frighten easily. She had sat forward and was looking him up and down, head to one side. He recognised a woman who responded to a new male presence with keen interest. Bartlett sat next to her on the sofa.

'Why did Sheila hit you?' Swift asked. 'If you don't mind me asking.'

'Oh, I don't mind at all. Let's see . . . to quote the lady herself, "*if you think you can just waltz in here and make yourself at home, you can think again.*"' She touched the eye gingerly. 'Do I look as if I've done ten rounds with a heavyweight?'

'I've seen worse.'

Bartlett made a throat-clearing noise. 'Sheila found out earlier this week that I'd had the house valued. She was already very angry about that, then Annabelle arrived without warning.'

'And the shit really hit the fan,' Annabelle said. 'Aunty wasn't welcome.' She pulled her mouth down. 'Poor me.'

Hardly surprising, Swift thought. Bartlett had put a tentative arm along the back of the sofa, behind his wife. She was aware of it but didn't sit back. Swift wondered why she had come all the way from Sydney. He didn't think she was lovelorn. Did she have a whiff of money, with the house being sold?

'So, have you come for a holiday?' he asked.

She smiled and patted Bartlett's knee. He looked like a puppy who's been thrown a treat.

'I just wanted to see my family,' she said.

The front door slammed and Annabelle pretended to be scared.

'Stand by your beds, it's Mike Tyson!' she hissed.

Sheila stomped in, eating a chocolate bar. She stood with her back to the fire, chewing.

'What are you doing here?' she asked Swift. 'Have you found something out about Teddy?'

'I'm making progress.' He smiled at her, making his voice gentle. 'I was sorry to discover that your friend's baby had died, a couple of years after Teddy's terrible accident. That must have been hard for you. And having to talk to the police about it. It must have brought back bad memories.'

She stared at him, chewing the end of the bar. She turned and threw the wrapper in the fire. Two red spots flared high in her cheeks.

'How do you know about that?'

'When you're a detective you come across random information while you're investigating. That was very bad luck for your friend. Emily, was it?'

'Amelia,' she corrected. 'Yeah, it was rotten.'

'What was the baby's name?'

Sheila ran a finger along the mantelpiece, then moved to stand by the window, sticking her thumbs in her uniform belt.

'She was called Clara.' She stammered a little over the name, reminding him of her brother Tim.

Swift knew he had hit a nerve. He pressed on. 'That's a pretty name. I expect you were fond of her, bought baby things for her.'

'Well you're wrong. I hardly knew her.'

'I never knew about this, Sheila,' her father said. 'How sad. I don't think you mentioned it in a letter. I'd have remembered something like that.'

'I didn't think you'd be interested.' She spoke stiffly, looking at Swift. 'I still don't understand why you'd want to come here, talking about it. It's nothing to do with Teddy.'

'I just felt for you,' Swift lied. 'How terrible to attend a birthday party that ends in tragedy like that.'

'The baby died at a party?' Annabelle asked.

'Amelia's birthday party,' Swift told her. 'Amelia found her daughter dead at the end of the evening. It was a cot death.'

'That's awful. The poor woman! You haven't had much luck, Sheila, have you? All these dreadful events happening to people around you. There must have been times when you felt like a jinx.' Annabelle took her husband's hand and patted it, leaving the barb in the air.

There was a silence, filled with Sheila's breathing. Then she erupted, seizing a china vase from the mantelpiece and throwing it at Annabelle, who ducked so that it bounced off her shoulder and smashed on the floor.

'Shut up, you fucking bitch! You're the jinx, ruining my parents' marriage and all our lives! I know why you're here and it's not because you miss Dad. It's because you think you're going to benefit from the sale of this house. Over my dead body you will!'

'Careful what you wish for,' Annabelle said calmly.

'Oh please, let's not start all this again. I can't bear the shouting. Mr Swift doesn't want to get involved in this.' Bartlett held up his hands pleadingly.

Sheila laughed, wheezing. 'Oh, I don't think Mr Swift minds our dirty laundry. He likes poking about in the bins. If you want a quiet life, Dad, it's not a good idea to go around behind my back planning to put the house on the market. This is my home. It always has been and it always will be. I'll go to court and do whatever it takes to stop you. You're not getting me out of here. My *memories* are here, my whole *life*!' She was screaming and trembling, punching her right fist into the palm of her left hand. 'As for you,' she yelled at Annabelle, 'you can fuck off back to Sydney, because you're not getting a penny from this this place. You're a whore and a bitch and nobody in this family wants you around!'

Annabelle went to speak, then thought better of it, glancing at Swift. Sheila ran to her bag and produced a large package which she brandished in front of her father's face, making him recoil.

'This is a padlock and two bolts and they're going on my bedroom door this afternoon. I can lock myself in and when I'm out you can't get in there or let any nosy Estate Agents and their grubby buyers in. I'm getting a microwave and kettle and I'll have my meals in my room until that fucking bitch leaves this house and there's no more talk of selling. D'you hear me, Dad? Loud and clear?' She leaned into his face, yelling and spitting. There were bubbles of foam at the corners of her mouth.

Bartlett shrank back and Annabelle moved into the corner of the sofa. She's becoming her mother, setting up a bedsit, Swift realised. He stayed sitting and spoke quietly.

'I'm sorry you're so upset, Sheila. Maybe it would be best if you get on with your locks now. Things are getting a bit heated.'

She turned to him, her face draining of colour. 'Has anyone ever tried to sell your home from under you?'

'No.'

'No. Well, it will get even more heated before it's finished.' She pointed at her father. 'He betrayed me once before and now he's planning to do it again. He's scum. I loved him all those years and asked him to come back here, made a home for him and he's scum. Tim's right about him. Maybe I'll change *my* name to Christie too!'

She ran from the room and thudded up the stairs. There were dragging noises and then the whine of a drill as she started to fortify her room.

'She's completely bonkers,' Annabelle said. Then, in a pronounced Australian twang, she added, 'Or as we say in Oz, "she's got kangaroos in the top paddock."'

Bartlett put his head in his hands. 'What am I going to do?' he asked.

Annabelle stroked his shoulder. 'Well, we're not going to be bullied, that's for sure. Let's make a cuppa and a plan while she builds Fort Knox. I'm relieved she's locking herself in. I might do the same! Want a cup of something, Mr Swift?'

'No thanks. I'll be going.'

She nodded. 'I can imagine you've had enough of this soap opera. The Tufnell Park version of Neighbours! Tune in soon for the next instalment!'

Swift wasn't sure if she was really taking the situation so lightly. He judged that she was a woman used to having pole position, especially with her husband and she seemed unheeding of the dynamics she had wandered into. He knew that Sheila was near the end of her tether and volatile.

'I'd tread carefully with Sheila. She's hurting.'

Bartlett didn't look up. Annabelle pointed to her eye and then the broken vase, saying smartly that she thought she was the injured one.

Swift left them to it. The drill was still boring through wood as he closed the front door. He was convinced that Sheila had had something to do with the death of that baby. She was clearly capable of anything if roused, capable, strong and terrifying. Could she have attacked Teddy? If he had crossed or disappointed her in some way, it was possible. The stifling bond that Sheila had woven might have been threatened and she clearly reacted viscerally if anything jeopardised her home. Peterson had said she had been at work when he died, but Swift's doubts about the thoroughness of that investigation were growing. It would be impossible to check her alibi, fifteen years later.

* * *

When Swift returned from a row in his borrowed boat he saw Cedric outside the front door, bowing to the CCTV camera.

'It's okay, Cedric. I've turned them off. I might as well leave them in place as a deterrent now they're there.'

'Ah, jolly good. I was feeling that I had to be on my best behaviour all the time. You've had no more trouble from Mr Howell, then?'

'No, that's all resolved.' He thought Cedric seemed a little despondent, his eyes strained. 'Are you okay?'

'Oh, yes, dear boy, just didn't sleep too well. I heard from Oliver yesterday. He'll be back at Christmas. He wants to spend it with me.'

'I see. Well, I'll be around so maybe we can get together.'

Cedric patted his arm. 'Kind of you to say that but you mustn't feel obliged. I'd best get going.'

'Where are you off to?'

'I need to buy a new shirt to wear to Mary's wedding. Milo is meeting me at Bond Street, then we're going to the cinema in the afternoon followed by a quiz in The Mermaid.'

Milo was one of Cedric's closest friends and his sartorial adviser. Milo's taste verged on the eccentric, so Swift was looking forward to seeing the purchase. He watched the tall, erect figure, imagining the conflict of emotions he must be experiencing, dreading his only child spending Christmas with him.

He showered, removing the dressing from his arm wound. It was healing well and the bruising on his lip was fading. Shaving was still a delicate process but it had to be done. Swift hated stubble on his skin and Kris voted it a turn-off. He rang her number. She had said she would phone him during the day to arrange where to meet for dinner, but he hadn't heard from her. He knew that sometimes she got delayed when she visited customers' homes for measurements and fittings. Her phone instructed him to leave a message. He said he would head for home and wait for her call. She had sent him a photo of the dress she was making for the wedding. Sitting on the train, he looked at it. It was pinned together on her sewing mannequin and looked like a gown from a glossy Hollywood film. She was going to look stunning. He had better get his own act together and consult Mary about suitable attire.

* * *

Hope Chapel was an anonymous-looking, squat brick building at the end of a row of shops. A plain board attached by the open door made a bald statement:

> *Hope Chapel of The Select Flock*
> *The LORD shall judge the people:*
> *judge me, O LORD, according to my*
> *righteousness, and according to mine*
> *integrity that is in me.*

Swift had decided to smarten up for his visit, donning grey chinos and a rarely worn khaki-coloured trench coat his father had given him years ago. He stepped through the door into a small, austere room with rows of wooden chairs and a table at the front with two white pillar candles and a large bible set between them. The bare windows were metal-framed. They were high and narrow, admitting a dim light. The air was chilly and looking around, he could see only one small wall heater. There were about thirty people seated in silence, men on the left and women and children on the right. A man with a weathered face and a bald patch on the crown of his head like a tonsure stepped forward. He was dressed in a dark grey suit and nodded to Swift.

'Good morning. You are a new visitor to our service.' He offered a tight smile.

'That's right. I'm interested in The Select Flock. Is it all right if I attend today?'

'Of course. We always welcome seekers of the true path. The service will start in a few minutes.'

He turned and lifted a hymnal and a pamphlet from a ledge beside the door. Handing them to Swift, he showed him to a chair at the end of a row. It had the kind of hard, shallow seat a tall man cannot get comfortable in. Swift wriggled against it, assuming that mortification of the flesh was part of the package and hoping the service wouldn't last too long. He looked around. All the men and boys were dressed in dark suits. Most of the women wore sombre dresses and dark brown headscarves, which were tied with a knot at the base of the skull. Younger girls were bare-headed but wearing plain coats, their hair scraped back into pony tails. Swift imagined Judith sitting there on Sundays, thinking about the music she would listen to with Teddy. Everyone was sitting with clasped hands, looking downwards. On the end of the front row of men's seats was a thickset man in a wheelchair, Steven Saltby, presumably.

A door to the side of the front table opened and a tall, blond man walked out and stood behind the table. He lit both the candles with long matches and opened the bible. He was better-looking than his photograph, slim and attractive, with high cheekbones in a long, narrow face. A Plantagenet face, Swift thought, one you might see in a brass rubbing. His black suit fitted beautifully and his white shirt gleamed. His pale-lashed eyes looked at the congregation and Swift knew he had been noted. He raised his hands and the congregation stood. He started to sing and they joined in the first hymn. Swift recognised it and mouthed the words: *O God our help in ages past, our hope in years to come* . . . There was no accompaniment, just the voices in the shadowy room.

Some prayers and another hymn, one that Swift didn't know, followed. The congregation stood for these, then sat as the pastor moved to the front of the table, joining his hands in front of him.

He had a thin but clear voice and confident stance. He spoke slowly and without notes for a good twenty minutes, stating that his sermon today was based on Isiah: '*and I will bring the blind by a way that they knew not; I will lead them in paths that they have not known: I will make darkness light before them, and crooked things straight. These things will I do unto them, and not forsake them.*'

Swift felt the chair boring into his back and thighs but kept still. The chill air was barely warmed by the bodies gathered and he could feel the muscles of his injured leg tightening. The rest of the congregation, even the young children, sat rigid and upright as they listened to the sermon. There was a good deal about sin and retribution, delivered clinically, without warmth or passion and ending with a warning.

'God will only forgive any of us if his strict justice has been satisfied. That is why Jesus had to die; he died to satisfy the justice of God, his father. Many people find that difficult to understand. How could a father demand this? We must understand that God is saying he will make straight what is crooked and warped. As soon as you accept this in the gospel you will come to a blessed place. If people will not believe in Christ and understand this there is only one place that they can go to. And that is a terrible place, a place of eternal punishment, hellfire, damnation and banishment from the love and presence of God forever. I do not tell you this to make you fearful but to make sure you know the way you must follow.'

Swift thought the chapel had been misnamed. The sermon didn't offer much hope. There a quiet communal 'Amen,' another hymn and the pastor extinguished the candles and exited through the door. Everyone stood and started to file out, without speaking. Swift stood at the back of the chapel and let them leave in front of him. A middle-aged woman in a headscarf moved to Steven Saltby and pushed him out. One of the wheels caught on a chair as she neared the door and Swift heard Saltby hiss, '*stupid!*' The woman flinched. The man with the bald patch moved quickly beside her and wordlessly helped to manoeuvre the wheelchair. Swift walked to the door at the front of the chapel and knocked. The pastor opened it, straightening his narrow black tie.

'Joshua Saltby?'

'That's correct. I haven't seen you here before. Can I help you, Mr . . . ?'

'My name is Tyrone Swift. I would like to have a word with you.'

'Of course. We're always glad to welcome new friends.' He gestured for Swift to pass into the tiny inner room which was narrow and even dimmer than the main chapel. It held a dozen chairs, and shelves with candles and stacks of bibles.

'Please, take a seat.'

'I won't, if you don't mind. I'm aching from sitting in the chapel.'

Saltby looked put out and straightened a row of bibles. 'Well, do you know much about our church or would you like me to give you some information? We have a special induction programme for those who wish to join us.'

'I'm not here as a believer or potential recruit. I'm a private detective and I'm investigating an attack that happened fifteen years ago to a young man called Teddy Bartlett. No one was ever convicted of the crime. I spoke to your sister Judith and to a Mrs Thornley. What they told me brought me here.'

Saltby stood absolutely still and folded his arms. He cleared his throat before speaking.

'We don't talk of my sister. She is lost to us, sadly. She has chosen a different path and one that can only lead to despair and damnation.'

'I see. Did you know Teddy Bartlett?'

'No.'

'Judith knew him. He was a good friend of hers at Fairacres. You didn't know him at school? '

Saltby shrugged. 'As I said, I didn't know him. I attended a different school from my sister.'

Swift took the school photo of Teddy from his pocket. 'This is Teddy. It might jog your memory.' He held it towards Saltby who glanced at the photo but didn't touch it.

'No, I don't recognise him.'

'Teddy used to visit your house after school when you were out. He and Judith used to hang out in her room, play music and such. Did you know about that?'

'No.'

'Do you think your parents knew?'

'No. If we had known, it would have been stopped immediately. Music is not allowed in the home and we do not socialise with people who are not of our congregation.'

'Did you know any of the Bartlett family?'

'No. As I said, we don't mingle outside of our church.' Saltby pressed his tie between his fingers. They were long and delicate with well cared-for nails. His hands didn't look like a plumber's.

Swift rested one foot on the rungs of a chair. 'Judith was very upset when Teddy was attacked. Surely she must have talked about it at home?'

'Not that I recall.'

'Someone anonymously contributed a significant amount of money for Teddy's welfare. It was four years ago. Do you know anything about that?'

'No, of course I don't.' He opened the door. 'I can't help you with your investigation. I don't appreciate you coming to our service under false pretences.'

'I was interested to observe your service and listen to your beliefs. I would like to speak to your parents. That was your father in the wheelchair?'

Saltby beckoned irritably. 'No, my parents would not want to talk to you. We know nothing about that young man. My parents don't discuss my sister. She is dead to us and I don't want you bothering them. My father isn't well. Now, I have a class to take. I'll see you out.'

He followed Swift to the door and banged it shut after him. There was the sound of a key turning. The congregation had vanished. Swift stood on the pavement, thinking. Saltby had maintained careful control but he had lied about Teddy visiting the house.

There was a small supermarket just across the road. A man came out and held the door open for Mr and Mrs Saltby. She backed the wheelchair out, then pushed it along the road and waited to cross. She was a tall woman but thin and somewhat stooped and the wheelchair was burdensome. She struggled on the kerb with it. Swift darted across and took one of the handles.

'I'll give you a hand if you like.'

She glanced at him, then quickly shied away, pale and alarmed. Saltby senior turned his head towards Swift. He had a broad, heavily lined face and bushy eyebrows. His thick skin reminded Swift of an animal's hide. His expression was impassive.

'That won't be necessary. We can manage.'

His wife pushed against the chair and moved quickly forward, her sensible lace-up shoes pattering across the road.

* * *

Simone was pregnant after a successful visit to a clinic. She and Mary beamed across the restaurant table, holding hands. Cedric, Swift and Kris had met them for dinner to discuss the wedding. They toasted the baby with champagne while Simone stuck to apple juice.

'Would you like a boy or a girl?' Kris asked. She was still out of breath, having rushed in late.

'We don't mind,' Mary answered. 'We'll take whatever is on offer!'

It was the first time Swift had seen Simone since the night she had visited him. They had kissed cheeks, both successfully concealing any discomfort. It felt like a mountain climbed. Simone started a long diatribe about wanting a home birth and the difficulties of having one because of the reluctance of doctors to take risks with women in their thirties. Swift tuned out and looked at Kris, who was nodding intently. He took her hand under the table and squeezed it. She returned the pressure, not taking her gaze from Simone.

Simone's mother was widowed and apart from her brother, who as head chef would be busy managing the wedding breakfast, she lacked family members to help out on the day. Cedric had been appointed as a general master of ceremonies for the occasion. There were lengthy discussions about table settings, wines, music, speeches and the disco. Mary stressed that she wanted people to have a good time as informally as possible. Swift asked if he could request a special favour as best man, not to be seated at the same table as Joyce.

'Fond as I am of her, I feel I am entitled to time off for good behaviour and I promise to have one dance with her.'

Cedric laughed. 'I think we might allow him that,' he said to Mary and Simone.

When Kris went to the Ladies, Mary leaned in to Swift and stroked his arm.

'You look well, Ty, lit up. Best I've seen you in ages. I think Kris must have something to with it. She seems lovely.'

'She is. I enjoy her company. She's talented too, a gymnast and seamstress.'

'Where did you meet?'

'In the bar where she works part time. And you? You're content?'

'Very. I have everything I want.' She turned to Simone and took her hand.

'Ah, young love. I remember it well!' Cedric said.

'Approaching middle-aged love,' Simone replied, resting a hand on her stomach.

'Simone is an interesting woman,' Kris said afterwards, when they were stretched out on the sofa in his flat.

'People are usually being tactful when they say someone is "interesting."'

Kris laughed. 'Hmm. It's an English word I've learned to apply. It's very useful.'

'She's certainly forceful. I have to confess I can't warm to her. Mary loves her, that's the important thing.'

'True, that's all that matters. I thought maybe Simone needed to claim so much attention because she came from a big family, so I was surprised to find that she only has a brother.' She stroked his face. 'Sorry I was late, by the way. I know you hate it. I'm a terrible time-keeper, always have been. I get caught up in something, lost in it really and lose track of things. I was dealing with a particularly tricky silk fabric and interfacing.'

It did annoy him because he liked punctuality. But he would just have to get used to it and he was beginning to appreciate the complexities of creating garments. He told her about his visit to Hope Chapel and his encounter with Joshua Saltby.

'I'm sure he knows something about Teddy Bartlett. I need to find a way in to that family but they're sealed off.'

'From what you've said and from what Judith told you, I would try the mother. She must be missing her daughter, whatever her religion and those men dictate. She will dream about her and think of her and wonder what is happening in her life. Her heart will be full of hidden sorrow. She will be the weak link, I'd guarantee it. Also, surely she should know she has a grandson? How can people be so cruel, rejecting their own flesh and blood? I am so lucky. My mother emails me every week telling me she loves me.'

He held her close, breathing in the biscuit scent of her hair. She was lucky, having a mother around to tell her she was loved. He appreciated that she had the wisdom to understand her good fortune.

Chapter 11

Swift recalled that Judith Saltby had said her mother worked at a solicitor's. He didn't want to ring her for more information and resurrect old ghosts, or at least not until he had good reason to. He reckoned that the women of The Select Flock wouldn't be allowed to travel far from home. He googled solicitors around the area and struck lucky on the website of the fifth, Pond and Reynolds. He clicked the *Our Team* button and saw that Dorcas Saltby was in charge of office administration. He assumed she must have a lunch break. He was in no doubt that she wouldn't be allowed to enter the flesh-pots of local cafes but would eat home-made sandwiches in the office. He hoped she would step out for some air or shopping, so the following morning he headed to the premises in Cedric's car. He parked in a side street, feeding a meter with an alarming number of coins. At eleven forty-five he walked past the large office. It had one of those plate-glass windows that allows a good view of the staff inside. Swift spotted Dorcas behind a desk, her scarf in place. There was a post office across the road. He stood in the doorway, out of the sharp wind.

Dorcas came out of the office at twelve fifteen, wearing a shapeless chocolate-coloured raincoat and carrying a hessian shopping bag. She started to walk slowly along the pavement towards a parade of small shops, her head down. Swift crossed the road and fell into step beside her.

'Mrs Saltby? Please don't be alarmed. I visited Hope Chapel last Sunday. You may remember me.'

She stopped and looked at him. There was a thin line of salt and pepper hair visible beneath her scarf. She had a sallow face with a large mole on her top lip. When she spoke her breath carried a sour scent.

'Yes, I saw you. You offered to help with the wheelchair.'

'My name is Tyrone Swift. I wondered if I could speak to you. Just a few minutes of your time.'

She touched her chin with a gloved finger. Her voice was just above a whisper. 'You speak to the pastor if you want to attend chapel.'

'It's not about the chapel.'

She glanced around and moved away, shaking her head. 'I can't speak to you. I'm busy now.'

He moved beside her. 'It would really help if I could talk to you.'

She walked on, head down. He could barely hear her. 'Speak to Joshua Saltby, the pastor.'

'I have spoken to him. Mrs Saltby, I saw Judith recently. She has a baby.'

She stopped, head still down. Her fingers gripped the shopping bag in front of her. Her hands shook.

'I've come here, not to your home because I know this is difficult. Please speak to me.'

She looked around again, blinking. This is what it must be like to worry about surveillance by the secret police, Swift thought, recalling the motto of the KGB: *Loyalty to the party. Loyalty to the motherland.*

'Judith?' she whispered.

'Yes. My car's just up here. We could sit in it for five minutes. That would be safe for you, no one would see us. Five minutes is all I ask.'

She stood, swaying slightly, then nodded. He led the way to the car and she sat beside him, still gripping the bag tightly on her lap with one hand, the other on the door handle. She looked around again, slumping down in the seat. He could feel tension radiating from her and hoped he could find words that wouldn't make her bolt.

'I met Judith. She is married and has a baby called Samuel. They're both well.'

She kept her head lowered. 'Is she in London?'

'No. I don't want to say where she is just now. I met her because I wanted to talk to her about Teddy Bartlett, a boy she was friends with at school. He was attacked fifteen years ago. His father has asked me to find the person who carried out the attack. This is Teddy.' He placed the photograph on her lap. 'Did you know him?'

She shook her head. Her fingers trembled on the door handle.

'Teddy doesn't look like that nowadays. He's blind and severely disabled, living in a care home. Judith told me she used to bring Teddy home after school sometimes, when you and your husband and Joshua were out. I asked Joshua about Teddy. He said he didn't know him. Do you think your husband knew him?'

He saw her mouth working. She glanced at him sideways. He wasn't sure what he could see in her eyes, maybe despair, but also a furtive look.

'We don't know him. Please, leave us alone.'

'I'm not sure I believe that, Mrs Saltby. I know that your family would have been very angry if Teddy's visits had been discovered. I think someone in the family might have wanted to stop Teddy because he was leading your daughter astray, away from the righteous path. The irony is that she left you anyway.'

She looked at him fully then, running her tongue over dry lips. 'You are a cruel man.'

'I don't think so. I think whoever put Teddy in a care home is cruel.'

'I have to go.' She depressed the door handle.

'Okay, you go. Judith misses you. Here's my card. You might want to contact me.'

He put it into her hand. She didn't reject it. He watched in the mirror as she scurried away. She was a mouse-like creature, with her drab browns and timid movements, but her eyes held knowledge from a world beyond the confines of her controlled life. He sat, thinking about her. She held down a job, so she must have some abilities. She wasn't just Dorcas Saltby, downtrodden wife and mother. In a solicitor's office, she would hear about all kinds of disputes and unpleasantness. She would know that other lives were messy and unpredictable. Were the mother and son involved together in the attack on Teddy?

* * *

In the afternoon Swift was out on the river at Putney. He was still adjusting to his borrowed craft. His insurance claim was in progress but he was going to have to wait a couple of weeks for his new boat. The sun was shining through a light mist but there was a distinct wind chill and he was glad he had brought an extra fleece. He could see the majestic mirrored buildings of the City, beyond Putney Bridge. Buses in the distance looked tiny. Birds were busy, swooping and diving across the water, filling the air with their calls. He had passed the stone which marks the start of the Oxford and Cambridge University boat race and sculled steadily. His purpose was to exercise his wounded arm and put it to the test while allowing his mind to ponder the information he had on Teddy Bartlett. His arm was behaving, it was his thigh that started to play up, his old scar tissue tightening. He steered in by the river bank and massaged it, watching a pair of swans grooming themselves. His thoughts went back to the Saltbys, and Teddy's visits to the Internet café. The possibility of a connection niggled at him. As one of the swans extended its wings and shook them vigorously, a potential line of enquiry occurred to him. He found his phone and rang Mark Gill, a friend and ex-colleague who still worked in the Met, in digital investigations. He and Mark shared an interest in pulp fiction and they briefly discussed their latest reading. They exchanged some other news and Swift explained he was interested in an Internet café called Cyberia.

'Do you remember that guy we worked with on the Villiers case about twelve years ago? He was a computer specialist when the role was still being developed. He was annoyingly geeky but had amazing recall, never forgot a face or name. He used to get irritated when we didn't understand his tech-speak. I remember talking to him once and he said he got into computers really young and he was delighted when Internet cafes opened in London. Ian . . . ?'

'Ian Wareham. He wore a tie with a keyboard design on it. He works in fraud now. I can find you his number if you want to speak to him.'

'Please.'

Mark gave him the number. They agreed to meet for a drink soon. Swift phoned Ian Wareham who answered immediately.

'Yep?'

Swift recalled Ian had always been succinct. 'Ian, hi. It's Tyrone Swift here. I used to be in the Met. Mark Gill gave me your number. We worked together once, on the Villiers case.'

'Yep, I remember.'

'I'm a private investigator now.'

'Cool, yep.'

'I've got some information concerning a case I'm working on. It's about an Internet Café in Fitzrovia called Cyberia. I wondered if you knew it.' He could hear that

Wareham was typing fast as they spoke, fingers rattling a keyboard.

'It's closed now.'

'Did you use it?'

'Yep. I kind of almost lived there. It was the first Internet café in London. Terrific place. Rock stars used to go there, Bowie, Jagger. Quite a buzz.'

'What years would we be talking?'

'I found it in 1995, a year after it opened and used it till around 2004. From 1997 I used to run courses for Internet virgins.'

'Do the names Teddy Bartlett and Joshua Saltby ring any bells? Teddy definitely went to Cyberia and Joshua might have.'

'Don't think so but you know, it was a busy place, people came and went. Names weren't important.'

'Could you take a look at their photos for me? I can scan you one of Teddy. If you look at a website for a church called The Select Flock, then follow a link to Hope Chapel in Tufnell Park, there's a photo of Joshua Saltby.'

'The Select Flock?'

'Yes, it's a church. Saltby is the pastor.'

'Okay. Yep, can do.'

'Terrific. I'll email you.'

It was wonderful dealing with someone who didn't waste words. He turned the boat and headed back to Hammersmith, feeling energised. Within ten minutes of scanning Teddy's photo, Swift received an email from Wareham:

> *I remember Saltby. Can't say from when. I helped him with password access one day. He badly needed the help but seemed to resent it. Don't recall Bartlett.*
> *Cheers, IW.*

Swift sat back in his chair. He had something tangible at last. Saltby had been a devout young man, according to his sister, so devout he had been promoted to church pastor. Yet he had strayed far from the strictures of home and church. His presence at Cyberia was astonishing and had to be connected to Teddy. Time for another visit to chapel.

* * *

Hope Chapel was even chillier that Wednesday evening. Late autumn was growing colder and overnight frost had been forecast. Swift walked up and down for a while, then braved one of the hard chairs in the back row, waiting for bible class to finish. The man in the dark grey suit who had given him a hymnal on his previous visit was watching him warily. He had approached Swift when he arrived.

'Does the pastor take bible class at this time?' Swift had asked.

'That's right. Class is held in the study room.' He gestured to the small room at the front of the chapel. 'You're late, I'm afraid, and the pastor doesn't like interruptions.' He had a scrawny build yet his suit was a little tight for him, straining on the shoulders.

'That's okay, I don't want to attend class. I want to speak to Mr Saltby. I'll wait here.'

'I see. Can I help you? Is it concerning the church?'

'Well, Mr . . . I don't know your name. Mine is Tyrone Swift. I'm a private detective, here on business.'

There was a pause, a quick purse of the lips. 'My name is Graham Manchester. You have business with Mr Saltby?'

'That's right. It's about someone his family used to know, someone who was attacked some time ago.'

'Oh, I see.' Interest flickered behind his eyes.

'Are you his deputy?'

He straightened, asserting himself. 'I am the assistant pastor, yes.'

'I suppose you know the Saltby family well.'

'Oh yes, I've known them a long time. Who is this person you referred to who was attacked?'

'His name is Teddy Bartlett. Judith Saltby knew him well. They were good friends.'

'Judith Saltby has been gone from us for many years. I've never heard of this person. I must get on with my tasks now. Class will finish in fifteen minutes.'

Swift read his newspaper while Manchester busied himself with tidying. He could feel the man's eyes on him. After a while a group of young boys exited the class and filed in silence down the chapel, eyes to the floor. They held their bibles against their chests in both hands. Swift rose and walked to the front as the last boy left the study room. Saltby was standing just inside the door, buttoning his suit jacket. He frowned when he saw Swift, stepped forward and glanced down the chapel. Manchester was observing them. He retreated through the door.

'I have nothing more to say to you. Please leave this chapel.'

'I think you do have things to tell me. I know you do.'

'I don't know what you mean. I'm going to see you off the premises.'

Swift took a step towards him. 'Cyberia,' he said softly, 'and I don't mean the place in Russia. A café called Cyberia.'

Saltby blinked and touched his throat. A lovely tell, signalling discomfort.

'I don't know what you're talking about. I'll show you out.'

Swift shook his head. 'Mr Manchester is more welcoming. He said he's known your family a long time. Shall we ask him to join us? Maybe he knows you used to go to Cyberia and that you met Teddy Bartlett there.'

Saltby stared at him, panic flitting across his face. He was weighing up fight or flight. Swift put his hands out, palms raised, a gesture of appeasement.

'Mr Saltby, I have a witness who met you in Cyberia and remembers you from your photograph. He happens to work for the Met police now.'

Saltby froze for a moment, then stepped back, allowing Swift into the study. He called out to Manchester, telling him he could go now, he'd lock up. He kept his voice under control but a tinny note had crept into it. Then he closed the door and stood for a moment with his back to Swift, holding on to the handle.

'I think I'll sit this time,' Swift said, hooking a chair with his foot.

There was a scent of sweat and of hot wax in the airless room. A white candle was still smoking. Saltby pinched the wick firmly. Swift could see he was trying to marshal his thoughts. He sat, pressing his knees together.

'You lied to me last time I came here. You lied about Teddy, even when I showed you his photo. Isn't that a sin?'

Saltby's eyes flashed. 'I don't need lessons about sin from you. And just because I went to Cyberia doesn't mean I knew Teddy Bartlett.'

'Oh, please. Judith told me that Teddy went there several times a week. My witness puts you there in the same time period. Of course you knew Teddy. Let's find a way in. Tell me about how you ended up at Cyberia,' Swift suggested.

'I didn't attack Teddy Bartlett.' Saltby's long face was drained of blood. He looked more than ever like an effigy on a tomb.

'If that's the truth, then you needn't worry about telling me why you were at Cyberia. It might help you to be honest about it after all these years.'

Saltby swallowed. 'This is very difficult.'

Swift said nothing. He could sense Saltby's struggle and the need for confession and relief that was building in him. He watched the candle vapour curling to the ceiling and vanishing.

'Very well, I'll tell you why I went there.' He made an effort, pulled himself up straight. 'I came home early one evening and overheard my sister and Teddy. That was when I found out she was bringing him to the house. They were playing music, they didn't know I was there. I stood outside her room. She'd left the door slightly open. I was about to go in and put a stop to it but then I saw Teddy. He was wearing one of her dresses and dancing around. It was the first time I'd seen him. He was . . . beautiful, entrancing. He looked so alive and full of energy.' He looked down, then continued, almost whispering. 'I wanted to see him again. I came home several more times after that to watch them, to watch him. One evening, I heard him tell my sister about an Internet café called Cyberia. He said he was able to chat online to other boys who wanted to wear women's clothes.' He stopped, wincing.

'You wanted to do that too?'

A long pause. 'I knew I liked boys, not girls, in *that* way and yes, I sometimes dreamed about wearing female clothes.'

'That must have been hard for you, given your beliefs.'

'Yes. I despised myself. I am full of disgust at myself now for those weaknesses but I have overcome my base self through prayer and commitment.'

'So you went to Cyberia to see more of Teddy and to chat online? Teddy didn't know who you were, of course.'

Saltby stood and fetched a bottle of water from a cupboard. He took a long draught. 'Yes, I gave in to temptation. I went there and sat next to Teddy, got talking to him. He had no idea who I was. I introduced myself as Luke, my middle name. We had coffee and he showed me

159

online conversations he was having. I knew nothing about the Internet and I couldn't get the hang of it at first but once I did, I saw that there were lots of men who felt like me, like Teddy. There were photos to look at, men who dressed up.'

'Did you fall in love with Teddy?' Swift asked softly.

Saltby blushed. 'I suppose you could say that. I liked him very much. Too much. We got on really well. He was a sinner and lost in so many ways and also a pagan. But he was the only man I've ever really grown fond of. I should never have allowed it.'

'How many times did you go to Cyberia?'

'Half a dozen or so. I was in torment. It was a terrible place, full of deviants and misfits. A godless place. I tried to stop going there, I tried to pray but of course the devil was distracting me, whispering in my ear.'

'Did you see Teddy at other times?'

He shook his head. 'No, only in Cyberia. I thank God that I was saved and came back to the straight path of righteousness.'

Swift pulled his jacket around him to ward off the creeping chill.

'What saved you?'

Saltby reached for a bible. 'This, and my mother.' He placed the bible on his lap and crossed his hands over it. 'My mother found me one day, trying on a dress. I'd gone to a charity shop and bought a couple. They were pretty, colourful. I was lured by the temptation. I hid them at the back of my wardrobe and put them on sometimes when I had the house to myself. I was so ashamed that she had found me out in my wickedness. I told her all of it, about watching Teddy and my sister and about the visits to Cyberia. We wept over my sin. We knelt and prayed together and I swore on the holy book that I would never do such a thing again. And I didn't, I never returned to that place. I returned to goodness and the true path.'

'It must have been quite a shock for your mother, discovering that both her children were transgressing. What did she do about Judith?'

'She told me to say nothing to my sister. She was going to deal with her.'

'How long after this did Teddy's attack take place?'

'A couple of weeks later. I only knew because my sister came home and spoke about it. Of course, she couldn't explain the truth of why she was so upset. That is how lies and evil corrupt the innocent.'

Swift looked at him with pity and dislike. 'Can you not say your sister's name?'

'She has chosen the wilderness. I was led there too through her sin but by God's mercy, I was brought back to the fold. I was recalled to the words I should not have forgotten: *"do you not know that wrongdoers will not inherit the kingdom of God? Neither the sexually immoral nor idolaters nor adulterers nor men who have sex with men nor thieves nor the greedy nor drunkards nor slanderers nor swindlers will inherit the kingdom of God."* My mother made me repeat that verse from Corinthians, over and over.' He held the bible up and kissed it fervently.

'I suppose there must be verses about not attacking and blinding someone too. Or is that permitted if they are found unworthy?'

Saltby shuddered and looked up. 'I didn't touch Teddy Bartlett. I kept away from Cyberia and from him and anyone like him. I have forged my soul anew with God's forgiveness and his grace.'

Swift stood and switched the light on, stamped his feet to encourage circulation. He couldn't see Saltby having the fire and fever to almost kill someone. He was a zealot but an oddly dispassionate one.

'Did your mother tell your father about your activities?'

'No. She said that she had failed as the mother of her children, not keeping them from sin and wickedness. In

161

our church, women set the moral compass for the family. She had to repent for her failure and put things right. She promised me she wouldn't tell my father once I had given her my vow that I would never harbour those deviant thoughts again.'

Swift wanted to ask if thoughts were so easily banished but he didn't want to encourage any further biblical quotations. He assumed that Mrs Saltby would also have been frightened of telling her husband of her terrible failure.

'How did you find Teddy, during those visits to Cyberia? Was he depressed? Sad at all?'

Saltby looked uncomfortable, crossing and recrossing his legs. 'You're asking me so many questions. It's in the past. I've tried hard to forget about it and now you're dragging it all up.'

Swift had no time for this man's self-pity. His voice turned icy. 'You might be experiencing a bit of temporary discomfort, but Teddy is inhabiting a permanent twilight world. His family are still suffering. You spent time in his company at a crucial period. I believe that what happened to him has some link to Cyberia. The least you can do is try to remember how he was, the things he said. Come on, Saltby, do the right thing!'

Saltby looked angry but he made an effort. 'He did have mood swings, I think. He would be very lively when he was chatting online. Sometimes he seemed tense. One afternoon he said that his sister was doing his head in. He hinted at some major problem that he was having to help her with.'

'Anything specific?'

'No. He was vague but he said that secrets were a burden. That's truly all I can tell you. When we talked, it was mainly about websites. I didn't want to discuss my life or my home, for obvious reasons.'

'Have you any idea why Teddy went to Epping Forest? Had he said anything to you about it?'

Saltby rubbed his brow. 'Not Epping, no. Sometimes he talked about Druids and the magic of woodland places. He was very wrapped up in it all.' He stood and straightened the chairs. 'I have to go. My mother will have dinner ready.'

'I haven't quite finished. Do you recall any other people Teddy was friendly with at Cyberia, or any of the men he was talking to online?'

Saltby leaned heavily on a chair. 'No. There was a constant stream of people in and out of there, engaging in nonsense and wickedness. It was a long time ago, Mr Swift, and I have put those days when I was lost in the wilderness out of my mind. I have prayed for Teddy over the years.' He blinked and tapped the chair with his fingers. 'I hope you can keep this conversation confidential.'

Swift opened the door. 'I'm not interested in making difficulties for you, or your church. I am interested in finding out who left Teddy for dead. I won't divulge what you've told me unless it's crucial to finding the perpetrator.'

Saltby let him out of the chapel and locked the door. Rain had swept in on a strong breeze and Saltby raised a huge black umbrella.

'Do you pray for Judith?' Swift asked him as he zipped his leather jacket and turned the collar up.

'I include my sister in my prayers. I pray that she will be saved one day.'

Swift watched him move away, stiff and straight. The man was repressing so much. He must feel always as if he was walking on eggshells. Swift walked fast through the stinging rain to an Italian café where he bought a large coffee and warmed his hands at it, then dipped the numb end of his nose into the steam. He drank thirstily, thinking. Dorcas Saltby had lied about not knowing Teddy. Judith hadn't mentioned that her mother ever indicated that she knew about Teddy, or had spoken to her daughter about him. He rang Judith's number, knowing that he needed to be careful about what he told her. Despite her apparent security in her new life, she would still carry the deep trauma of her family's rejection. He didn't want to alarm or hurt her.

'Hi, it's Tyrone Swift. I hope I'm not interrupting your evening meal?'

She laughed and yawned. 'I wish! My husband is just attempting to get Samuel to sleep and I'm going to fetch something from the freezer.'

'I just have a few quick queries. Did your mother ever talk to you about Teddy or indicate that she knew he had been in your house?'

'No, never.' Her voice tightened and dropped. 'Have you spoken to my mother?'

'I have, recently, near her work. I needed to ask her a few questions. She said she didn't know Teddy.'

'Well, that's right.'

'Okay. You did tell your family what had happened to him?'

'Briefly. It was difficult not to talk about him because I was so upset. I referred to him as a school friend, that's all. Have you found something out about him?'

'Nothing definite but the information you gave me has been helpful.'

He heard her take a breath. 'Did you tell my mother you'd seen me?'

'Yes. She asked if you were in this country. I confirmed that you are and that you have a baby.'

'What did she say?'

'She didn't say much. She looked affected. I would say she misses you.' Judith wouldn't know about her father's accident or that he was in a wheelchair. He decided not to tell her. Her own parents had chosen not to. That was between her and her family, if there was ever any future contact.

'I'm not sure you're right about her missing me. As I implied before, I always felt that I was trying to attract her attention. Joshua absorbed her time and energy. He was the one she had ambitions for.'

'I see. I suppose she might have regrets. I can't say.'

'Well, thank you.'

'Just one other thing. Did you know Graham Manchester?'

'Of course, yes, I knew him throughout my childhood. He was one of the church wardens. He's my mother's cousin. They were always very close. They were very fond of each other because he had been brought up by her parents after his own died. More like siblings, really. He came to us for Christmas and Easter and was often with us at weekends. I used to think my father was a bit jealous of him sometimes because he was so fond of my mother. Why are you asking about him?'

'I've met him a couple of times. I just wondered.'

She cleared her throat. 'I rang Mayfields to ask after Teddy. I said I'd visit him before Christmas.'

'That's good. Well, thanks again. Take care.'

He sat, deciding that he was hungry and couldn't be bothered to cook. Delicious aromas were snaking from the kitchen. He ordered mushroom and ham cannelloni and a large glass of house red. The café was muggy and he had warmed through. He shrugged his jacket off and used a couple of paper napkins to dry his hair. His thick curls absorbed and trapped water like blotting paper. The waiter came over with his order and grinned, pointing to his own bald pate.

'Wish I had your problem, mate. Pity I can't borrow some!'

'You'd be welcome, if it was possible.'

'I enquired about a transplant but it's too expensive. I've got a bathroom chock full of stuff I've bought on the net — you know, it will make your hair grow if you rub it in daily. Complete rubbish. I haven't grown a single strand, just a bit of bumfluff on my head. Anyway, *buon appetito!*'

The cannelloni was herby and delicious, the wine fruity. The waiter's description of a bathroom full of hair products made Swift think of Sheila's crammed bedroom. Teddy had spoken to Saltby of his sister having a secret. Something else teased at his memory, something someone had said, but he couldn't retrieve it. He was going to have to see Dorcas Saltby again. In the meantime, he rang Bartlett to give him an update but there was no answer. Swift left a message and sat back, savouring the last of his wine.

Chapter 12

Swift had finally capitulated. Cedric and Kris had persuaded him to let them go shopping with him for best man clothes. Swift liked natural fibres and well-made jeans and jackets but he hated shopping of any kind, which was why his wardrobe contained so many slightly fraying garments. His dislike of social functions meant that this rarely mattered. His favourite items of clothing were his leather jacket, his rowing leggings and gilets. He had only agreed to the outing because he had no idea what to buy and didn't want to let Mary down on her big day. *Make sure you scrub up nicely*, she had warned him. Also, he trusted Kris's judgement. Given more time, she said that she could have made him a jacket and trousers but on this occasion, manufactured would have to do. Cedric alone wouldn't have been reliable, with his penchant for bold patterns. The shirt he had bought for the wedding was yellow with pink stripes. Mary had seen it and said it was a brave statement.

Kris had decided that given his aversion to shops and shopping, they should go on a Monday, when there were fewer people about. She had got an idea of his budget, taken his measurements and researched the market. She told Swift and Cedric to meet her at Baker Street. She was only ten minutes late and led them through back streets in Marylebone to an airy, brightly lit shop. Before he could blink, Kris had provided him with an outfit to try on: tapering dark grey cotton trousers, a cotton shirt in the same colour with a mandarin collar and a slim-fitting burgundy velvet jacket with a matching waistcoat. She informed him that the jacket had shawl lapels and its single button opening suited his long, lean frame.

'Burgundy, hmm,' he said, examining the rich colour. He thought he liked the combination. It was certainly smart while keeping a casual feel, which was what Mary wanted. 'What do you think, Cedric?'

Cedric put down a bright blue paisley shirt he had been looking at longingly. 'I love it, Ty, fits you like a glove. You look younger.' He ran a hand down the soft jacket sleeve. 'Colour's good on you too. Goes with your eyes.'

'The deep red is good,' Kris reassured him. 'It adds warmth to the grey and Cedric's right, it compliments and softens your smoky eyes. You don't want to look so serious. It's a celebration! Also, the shirt collar means no need for a tie. I know you hate that.'

'You know things about me I don't recall telling you. How does that work?' he asked her.

She tapped the side of her nose. 'It's a woman thing. Don't worry about it.'

Burgundy. Maybe . . . He looked in the mirror again. He thought he would do and on the plus side, the whole experience had taken only half an hour and he hadn't even developed a headache.

They had lunch to celebrate his purchase, in a small French bistro. Cedric had bought two of the paisley shirts, the blue one for himself and a rose-hued one for Milo.

'I love your outfits, their style and simplicity,' he told Kris. 'What's this coat called? It has such a soft shape.'

She was wearing a bright yellow needlecord coat with matching beret. 'It's called a swing back, because of the pleat at the back. I didn't make this one, I got it on eBay. Couldn't resist.'

Cedric nodded. 'Seeing you, I can picture myself strolling around London in 1958 or watching Audrey Hepburn in *Gigi*.' He went on to tell her about a couple of Polish colleagues he had worked with during the early fifties.

Swift watched them, taking pleasure in their liking for each other. He wished he could warm to Simone the way Cedric had to Kris. He recalled that in his early days in the Met, he had confided to Mary that he disliked a colleague he had to work with closely and found this difficult. She had shrugged and said, *just pretend*. Not bad advice. He made a mental note to himself to be extra friendly to Simone next time he saw her. His phone rang. He saw that the call was from Rowan Bartlett and excused himself. He stood by the door of the small restaurant, holding his wine.

'Mr Swift, I got your message. I've been rather tied up, at the airport with Annabelle.'

'She's gone away?'

'Back to Sydney. Sheila had the most awful row with her and attempted to push her down the stairs. She managed to save herself by clinging to the banister but she has a nasty bruise to the chest. She decided to leave. I'm relieved, to be honest. The situation here was worsening by the hour. Sheila stayed in her room for a couple of days after the incident and wouldn't respond or come out. She's gone to work this morning, thank goodness. She hasn't spoken to me since it happened. She must still be upset because she forgot to lock her door. I glanced in her room. It's in the most terrible mess, as if a storm's blown through.'

At that moment, Swift recalled the remark that had been eluding him. Sheila's aunt had said that she spent a lot of time in the loft. There had been a dead baby in

Islington, a secret that troubled Teddy and a baby's knitted jacket in a wardrobe. He knew he needed to revisit Sheila's room and go up into the loft.

'I wanted to update you about Teddy. Will Sheila be out all day?'

'Presumably. She usually finishes work between five and six.'

Swift glanced at his watch. 'I'm coming over. I'll be there in half an hour.'

He asked Cedric to take his outfit home and gave Kris money for the bill. He thanked her again, kissed her cheek and hurried away. She and Cedric were happily perusing the dessert menu, debating the merits of strawberry pastries with crème patissiere and tarte citron.

* * *

The Bartlett house smelled stale. The living room was much grubbier than on his first visit and littered with papers and used cups. Bartlett had referred to a storm in Sheila's room and he looked as if he had been in one himself. His thinning hair was dishevelled, one leg of his jeans had a trailing hem and his shirt collar was stained.

'What did Sheila and Annabelle argue about?' Swift asked.

Bartlett made a hopeless gesture. 'Annabelle was fed up with Sheila. She banged on her bedroom door and told Sheila she'd have to come out when the house was sold and cleared. Said if she wasn't careful, she'd end up being chucked in the removals van.'

'Pretty unpleasant, given that this is Sheila's home.'

'I know, I know. I have to say though, it's been very difficult living with a . . . a . . . brooding *presence* in the house. Sheila came rushing out of her room and went for Annabelle. It could have been much nastier if Annabelle had fallen down the stairs.'

'What happened afterwards?'

'I took Annabelle to A & E. Sheila went straight back into her room. She didn't even bother to check how Annabelle was. I hardly recognise my daughter these days . . . Did you say you had news about Teddy?'

'Would you mind if I look in Sheila's room first? I'd like to check on something.'

'Oh . . . very well.' He sounded tetchy, near the end of his tether. 'I must make a hot drink and toast. I feel empty, haven't been able to eat with all this upset. I'd like to be on a desert island somewhere right now, or perhaps in a monastery. Somewhere with no women and no arguments.'

Swift ran up the stairs and entered Sheila's room. It was littered and rank smelling, reminding him of the stench of animals at the zoo. What was it Christie had said about his mother's room? It had been a stale and fuggy burrow. Sheila was certainly following in her footsteps. He looked around in the mess for a pole to open the loft trapdoor, treading carefully on the clothes and rubbish on the floor. Finally he saw one hanging on a hook by the window. He pulled down the metal ladder, checked it was stable and climbed the ten steps. There was plenty of light up there, from a window in the slope of the roof, overlooking the back of the house. The loft was fully boarded so he stepped up and stood, avoiding a low central beam. He was glad of the dry, sweeter-smelling air. He had expected the room to be stuffed with items but it was surprisingly empty and tidy. The inner wall had been papered with a design of huge red tulips. There were several large cardboard boxes, a couple of suitcases, an oak gate-legged dining table propped against a wall and four stacked dining chairs.

He moved to the boxes and opened the flaps, going through the contents before replacing them. There were faded, musty curtains, bedspreads and linen, five duvets, towels and some women's clothes and raincoats. He sneezed as dust rose and drifted through the air. One suitcase was empty, the other contained well-worn shoes and sandals. With their cracked leather and bent soles, they were hardly worth keeping. He stood and looked around, turning full circle. He went to the table and moved it away from the wall. Behind the table, low down, was a small rectangular door with a knob. He knelt down, pulling at the knob. The door opened easily and he peered in to a narrow dark space. He took his LED torch from his jacket pocket and shone it in. To the side, pushed up against the brick of the outer wall, was a thick cardboard box, about twice the size of a shoe box and a little deeper. He shuffled in on his knees and caught the edge of it, pulling it towards him and backing out with it. It was light and fairly new looking.

He placed the box on the floor and opened the lid. There was another box inside, not quite so new and fitting snugly. Swift took a breath and lifted the lid. A dark blue crocheted blanket was folded along the top. He peeled it back slowly. Beneath it was a tiny skeleton of an infant, carefully arranged on a matching strip of blanket with dried flowers of lavender surrounding it. The lavender was still faintly aromatic. Swift judged it had been placed there in recent months. Sheila's secret. He looked down at the frail, miniature bones. He couldn't gauge how old they were. He knew that corpses kept above ground deteriorated fast but this baby must have died many years ago. He knew now why Sheila had contacted him so frequently, averse to the past being raked over, desperate to know what he had been told. She had been unwell and piling on weight the summer when Teddy was attacked. He knew as well why Teddy had to help her with a major problem and why his note had said that the innocent suffered. Her visits to the loft had been to tend this dead child, perhaps to hold it. In her bedroom was a brand new baby jacket that had never been needed. His heart felt heavy.

He stood, brushing dust from his legs, went to the trapdoor and called Bartlett. The man appeared after a few minutes, standing at the door to Sheila's room. He was wiping his mouth with a tissue.

'I've found something disturbing up here. You need to look. Can you get up this ladder with your arthritic hips?'

'Yes, but I'd prefer not to. What is it?'

'Please come up first. I don't want to move it any further as the police need to be informed and they'll want to investigate.'

Bartlett stared at him, about to protest, then saw the seriousness of his expression. He climbed the ladder slowly, wincing once and pausing before he took each step. Swift helped him up the last rung and held on to him until he gained his balance.

'Here.' Swift took one of the stacked dining chairs and placed it near the box. 'You'd better sit down.'

He guided Bartlett to the chair. He sat slowly, then saw the box and its contents. Swift turned it so that it was facing him.

'What on earth?' He leaned forward. 'That's a human skeleton.'

'Yes, a baby. I found it in the cupboard behind the dining table.'

Bartlett gazed at him in bewilderment, then back at the box. 'But I don't understand. How did that get here?'

'Mr Bartlett, I believe that this is the skeleton of Sheila's baby, your grandchild.'

He shook his head, as if to clear his thoughts. 'But Sheila didn't have any children. I would have known. No, that's not possible.'

Swift knelt down again by the baby. 'Only a DNA test will prove whose baby this was but I have reasons for being fairly sure that Sheila did give birth.' He told Bartlett about Sheila's apparent ill health and weight gain in the summer of 2000, the carefully wrapped baby's jacket, and the references to her spending time in the loft subsequently. He wasn't sure how much the man was taking in as he rubbed at his forehead.

There was a long silence. The only sound was Bartlett's rapid breathing.

'But someone would have known,' he said finally. 'If this is true, surely someone must have helped Sheila.'

'I think Teddy did. That is why the note he left talks about things being hidden and the innocent and suffering. I've also spoken to someone who heard Teddy refer to Sheila having a secret he was helping her with. Sheila must have told Teddy she was pregnant. They were close, and if she chose anyone to confide in, it would have been him. She must have given birth at home and he probably assisted. I would guess that the child was born some time that August. Certainly it had died and been concealed by the time Teddy was attacked.' He waited to see if Bartlett was going to ask the obvious question.

Bartlett leaned down and touched the edge of the box. Swift was relieved to see that he had steadied his nerves. He had after all spent years as a surgeon, dealing with flesh and its complexities.

'The body would have decomposed quite quickly, above ground and in a warm, dry environment. There would have been an amount of liquid and odours from decomposition, although with such a tiny child it would have been easy to deal with. Its container would have needed replacing regularly for a while. Probably it was originally wrapped in plastic.' He spoke dispassionately, then looked at Swift and back at the bones. 'But how did this child die?' His voice held a sudden note of fear.

'That we don't know. Perhaps it was a stillbirth or something went wrong, with no medical help. Only Sheila can say. Teddy probably knew.' Swift suspected there might be a darker explanation, thinking of Teddy's note and the dead baby at the party. If Sheila had killed her baby and Teddy knew, there would be a strong motive for her to want rid of him too.

'My God. What was happening in this house?' Bartlett sat back, shoulders slumping. 'How could Sheila have been pregnant without her mother knowing? How could Tessa not have noticed a baby being born in her own home? What kind of mother was she?'

Swift noted Bartlett's usual willingness to shift blame on to anyone but himself. He didn't respond but listened as Bartlett carried on, listing again the reasons he had left his wife and her failings as a mother, complaining at length that she had allowed the family to fall to pieces.

Sheila was at the top of the ladder before they realised she had come home. She was still in her belted raincoat and sturdy shoes. She stepped in to the loft and stood in silence, staring at the opened box.

Her father looked at her. 'Sheila, what has been going on here? Can you explain this? Mr Swift thinks this is the skeleton of your baby.'

She said nothing. Her chest was rising and falling rapidly. Her hair was lank and her skin shiny with grease. A crop of tiny spots had sprouted on her chin. She took her inhaler from a pocket and drew in medication. Swift stood, watching her. He wondered how long she had been at the ladder, listening.

'This is your baby, isn't it, Sheila?'

'Yes. My baby. My business. *My* baby was resting nice and peacefully. Now look. People gawping.'

Bartlett put his hands out. 'Sheila, you must have known that this child would be found sometime.'

'I kept him so safe from everyone for so long. Safe and warm and cosy, all tucked away.'

Swift said quietly, 'I'm going to go downstairs and call the police. You might want to talk to your father. Please don't touch the skeleton, either of you.'

She said, as if to herself, 'They'll take my baby away.'

'They will have to, to start with. But they will return him or her to you for a funeral.'

'Him. His name was Ambrose.'

'My father's name,' Bartlett whispered.

Sheila waited until Swift had crossed to the loft opening, then stepped quickly behind her father. She slipped a small screwdriver from her pocket and held it to the front of his throat, clamping her other hand hard on the top of his head as he tried to get up.

'I'll stick this in you, I will. Tim's right. You're a joke of a father.'

Swift stood still. Bartlett turned his eyes towards him, blinking rapidly.

'Don't you move,' Sheila told her father. 'I'd love to stick this in you. Bringing that slut back here, lying to me, slagging off our mother.' She looked at Swift. 'You want to know what was happening in this house, do you? You're Mr Know-it-all, how come you can't tell him?'

Swift kept his voice neutral. 'If you were listening to us, you'll know that I did make some observations to your father. You must have gone through a terrible time. Hurting your father won't solve anything.'

'Oh, it might. It might make me feel better.'

'I don't think so, Sheila, not in the long run. Surely your family has had enough sadness.'

'All caused by him.' She angled the screwdriver, prodding it against her father's throat, and he gasped.

'Your father had nothing to do with your baby being born or dying. Did Ambrose die soon after he was born?' He thought it was best to distract her, get her talking about herself.

'A couple of days. I was all on my own.' She fixed her gaze on the box.

'Teddy was with you though. Teddy helped you.'

'Oh yes, Teddy helped me. Teddy knew all about it. We read what to do in one of my textbooks. But then when Ambrose died he said we ought to tell someone.'

'And you didn't want that.'

'No.' She shook her head violently. 'I wanted to keep my boy. People would have been all over us, asking questions. They'd have taken my baby. I wanted to keep him safe by me. And I did.'

'Yes you did, Sheila. You kept him and looked after him, giving him new flowers and blankets. You kept him close by you and safe. You did everything you could.' Swift took a step nearer as he talked.

She noticed. 'Don't move. If you come any nearer, I'll stick this in his throat. I know where to aim.'

'Sheila . . .' Bartlett whispered.

'Okay, Sheila, okay, I won't move. Did you argue with Teddy?'

'A bit. Then he went quiet, wouldn't talk about it. I came home that day and he'd taken off. Even he left me. In the end, they all left me.' She tugged her father's hair. 'You started it, all the rot.'

'I'm sorry,' he said. He had turned a waxy colour.

'And you brought that bastard detective here,' she continued. 'I told you not to. All he's done is cause trouble. I'd like to stick this screwdriver in him when I've finished with you.' She rolled her tongue and spat at Swift. 'You had no right going into my room, you fucking bastard, no right coming up here. You've been a thorn in my side since the first day you came here, with your poking and prying. And what's it all been for? I bet you still don't know who bashed Teddy's head in!'

'I'm sorry if I've upset you. I know you've been having a hard time. If you put the screwdriver down, we can talk. I'm sure we can help you.'

She looked around and smiled. 'Help! No one has helped me for a long time. The police will question me, won't they? There'll be hours of questions, raking it all up and pretending they care.' She clenched her free hand into a fist and wheezed, banging the fist against her chest.

'The police will ask you questions, yes. Sheila, you might find it helps to talk about it. Police have special training now. They'll be sympathetic and careful when they discuss it with you.' She seemed to be listening. He decided to try playing to her self-importance. 'The police will understand that they're dealing with a fellow professional who has a good reputation. They'll know that you have a very responsible job, with colleagues and patients depending on you. They'll know how valued you are at work.'

'It's true. I do have a good reputation. Workhorse, that's me. Good old Sheila, she'll stay late and do the weekend shifts, she's got no other life going on! Pathetic, fat old Sheila, no husband or boyfriend! I see the glances when they're chatting about parties and family events. Sad old Sheila, that's who I am. Now I'll be mad old Sheila with the dead baby.'

She smiled at Swift, a deranged grin, and suddenly shoved her father to one side. As he tumbled from the chair, she stabbed the screwdriver into her own stomach and fell to the floor with a scream. Blood spurted. Bartlett shouted her name and scrambled up. Then he was beside her, fumbling with her belt and tearing open her coat and uniform. Swift dialled 999 and requested an ambulance, describing the wound. Bartlett was pressing down on the area around the screwdriver's hilt. Sheila groaned softly.

'Has she cut an artery?' Swift asked. The blood wasn't pumping.

'No. But the blade's in deep and her pulse is weak. She's conscious, which is good. This is all I can do for now. Can you get something to keep her warm?' He seemed calm, in control.

Swift opened the nearest box and took out a bedspread, tucking it gently over Sheila's legs.

'I'll go down and let the paramedics in. They're going to struggle getting up and down from here.'

Bartlett nodded. He spoke gently to his daughter, repeating the words reassuringly. 'Sheila, it's all right, we've got help coming. Everything will be all right. I know you can hear me. You're going to be okay.'

Swift called the police as he opened the front door, and waited. The ambulance crew had Sheila strapped to a stretcher and lowered down in record time. One of the crew kept her hand on the screwdriver, ensuring it didn't move. Bartlett insisted on going with her in the ambulance and climbed in, his hands and shirt blood-soaked. Someone draped a blanket around him. Swift told him he would speak to the police and explain what had happened. He nodded, distracted, and asked a paramedic to check Sheila's blood pressure again.

Swift closed the door and went through to the kitchen. Dirty crockery was piled in the sink and cluttering the work surfaces. He rinsed a glass and filled it with water, then drank another. He didn't want to return to the loft. He would leave that to the police. He looked around but there was no dishwasher. He thought he might as well make himself useful until they arrived and took the dishes from the sink, stacking them on the drainer. He filled the sink with hot water and started scrubbing plates and saucepans. It was a useful process, imposing some order on the chaos and he felt his own heart rate quieten. The sky outside was turning a bruised violet as dusk approached. He had always found it a melancholy time of day. He pulled the window blind down and concentrated on his repetitive task.

It was almost eight by the time the police had finished examining the loft and questioning him. A DI Archie Lorrimer listened to his explanation of his involvement with the family, over a cup of tea in the kitchen. Lorrimer knew of Nora Morrow and gave her a quick ring to check Swift out.

'I have wondered if Sheila attacked Teddy and if she was responsible for the death of that other baby,' Swift

179

told him. 'Up in the loft, she said nothing that indicated she did harm Teddy, although she acknowledged that she argued with him about Ambrose.'

'What kind of woman is she? As chaotic as her bedroom indicates?'

'Self-important, angry, damaged, food-obsessed, jealous, frightened, a liar, sad and lost. The keeper of a dead baby. She has a nasty temper. I think she'll need psychiatric help.'

Lorrimer finished his tea. He was a small, sharp-eyed man, watchful but pleasant. Swift had heard him instruct a constable to tuck the covering blanket over the skeleton before the box was taken away.

'She might have killed Ambrose,' he said, rinsing his cup in the sink. 'I don't know if a pathologist will be able to determine that. Hopefully she'll survive and we can talk to her.'

'Can I head off soon? I'd like to ring the hospital, see how she is.'

'Yeah. I'll need you to come and make a statement in the next few days. We'll secure the house before we leave.'

* * *

Back home, Swift opened a bottle of wine. The hospital had told him that Sheila had been operated on and was expected to recover. He ran pictures of that summer of 2000 in his head: Sheila carrying her growing secret, Teddy knowing about the pregnancy, their mother hiding away, Tim unaware. He poured a second glass. His phone rang. It was Tim Christie.

'What's going on? My father just rang me from a hospital to say Sheila had stabbed herself. Bastard. I cut him off.' His speech was slow and slurred. Swift assumed he was on something.

'That's right. Sheila stabbed herself in the stomach. She's okay, as far as I know.'

'What's going on? Why'd she do that?'

180

'Look, Tim, you'd better speak to your father tomorrow. A lot has happened in your family recently and he'll need to talk to you about it.'

'Oh yeah? Well, I don't want to talk to him. You tell me.'

Swift felt weary. The last thing he wanted was to start explaining a dead baby to a drugged-up sibling.

'I can't do that. It's not for me to discuss. Either talk to your father or don't. Or maybe just go and see Sheila and when she's able to, she can tell you.'

'You know how I feel about those two, they do my head in. I can't face them and I can talk to you, you treat me like—'

Swift interrupted. 'Tim, I'm not your parent. I have to go now, I've had a long day. Sheila's okay. Go to bed and sleep off whatever you've taken.'

He stepped out into the garden and breathed in the cold air, trying to clear his head of other people's secrets and torments. His next task was to confront Dorcas Saltby with her lies.

Chapter 13

She came out of her office at the same time, head down, scarf tied tightly. There was a strong wind and she swayed slightly, buffeted. Swift had decided not to bring the car and offer her a secure environment. Let her feel the pressure. He crossed the busy road and fell into step beside her.

'Mrs Saltby, you lied to me about Teddy Bartlett,' he said conversationally. 'Your son told me you knew all about him.'

She stopped, looked around, peered at him. There was shock in her eyes and a cold hostility. An angry-looking cold sore had appeared on her lip, cracked and peeling.

'You've spoken to my son?'

'Twice now. Didn't he mention it?'

'No.' She moved in to the side of the pavement, up against the window of a launderette.

'Joshua lied to me the first time. When I saw him again he told me the truth, all about finding Teddy in your house with Judith and about the dressing up and the Internet café.'

She leaned against the window. She flicked her tongue on the cold sore and winced.

'I can't talk to you,' she said hopelessly.

'You have to. Otherwise I'll come to your home. I am going to find out what happened to Teddy.'

'I can't tell you anything about what happened to him.'

'Can't as in won't?'

She was silent, fiddling with the handles of her shopping bag.

'You know something. I will come to your home if you won't talk to me. I don't think your husband would like that. There's a café along here. It's cold in the wind. Let's sit down.'

She glanced around again. 'I can't stay long.'

She walked on with him, shrinking into herself. In the café she insisted they sit right at the back, away from the window, and found a table tucked into an alcove. He ordered coffee for himself and still water at her request. She poured it into the glass, spilling it and dabbing the puddle fussily with a paper napkin. He saw that she bit her nails, the skin rough and torn around the cuticles.

'So stupid of me,' she said. 'Look at this mess.'

He suspected she was often told that she was stupid, but he thought otherwise. It seemed to him that she had hidden reserves to draw on. 'It's only water, Mrs Saltby. Let me take you back to the summer of 2000. You came home and found Joshua dressed in women's clothes and he confessed to you.'

'Yes.'

'Was that the first you knew of Teddy's visits to your home?'

'Yes.' She drank and patted at her lips.

'So how did you feel when you found this out?'

She pressed her lips together. 'I felt ashamed and frightened.'

'Angry, too?'

'I suppose. It was all Judith's fault. She encouraged wickedness into our home. She showed Joshua her sin and he was tempted.'

'Did you tell your husband about Joshua and Teddy?'

'No.'

He stirred his coffee. 'Why not?'

She pulled her chair in, crouching over the table. Oddly, she seemed happier to talk about Steven Saltby. He was clearly in some ways a safer subject.

'My husband didn't need to be burdened with such unnatural behaviour. There would have been dreadful trouble in our home. Also, he had important church responsibilities at the time. He needed to concentrate on those. It was my duty to deal with it.' She linked her fingers and intoned: "*Older women are to be reverent in behaviour, to teach what is good, to be self-controlled, pure, and submissive to their own husbands, that the word of God may not be reviled.*" It was my error that our children had strayed and mine to put right.'

'You told Joshua that you would speak to Judith but she says you didn't. She still has no idea that you knew about Teddy. Why didn't you deal with Judith? She was breaking all your rules as well.'

She took another drink. She was all sepia tones, her clothing and scarf, her skin, her hair. Her voice was muted, her movements sluggish. Everything about her spoke of a subservient, downtrodden woman. Yet he sensed an adversary in her. Now and again antagonism flashed across her face. She gripped her glass so tightly he thought it might break.

'I was going to. My daughter was always more questioning than Joshua and harder to talk to. She was wilful. I had to build up my resolve through prayer. Then she came home and said that the boy had been attacked.'

'A handy solution to all your problems.'

'I prayed for the boy. His sin had found him out but I prayed that God would guide him.' She nibbled at a ragged thumb nail.

'Did you tell anyone else about this, at any time?'

'Never. I spoke only to the Lord. He answered my prayers by raising Joshua to pastor some years later.' Her voice had grown stronger, her son's status evidently gave her satisfaction. 'You've spoken again to my daughter?'

'Yes. I told her that you know she's back in the UK and has a baby.'

She blinked and shook her head. 'I tried to steer her on the right path but she chose the road to damnation. I don't want you troubling my son again. He has fought his demons. He has won the battle with my help and redeemed himself in the Lord's eyes. Leave us alone now. There's nothing more we can tell you.' She looked at him and her eyes were suddenly lit up with animosity. 'He was wearing a pink lacy dress with bows. My son, *my* son. That sight was an outrage. I burned those dresses, all four of them. They were like something a fallen woman of the streets might wear. Thankfully the Lord called Joshua back.' She lifted her bag. 'I have to go back to work. I hope you too can find the Lord, Mr Swift.'

'How do you know I haven't?'

She made no reply but walked away, checking the street from the café door before slipping out to the pavement.

He felt frustrated at the blank wall she had presented to him. He was convinced she knew more, he could sense it. Back in 2000, she must have felt desperate. She had believed that she had failed in her responsibilities as a mother. She had let down her children and had to make amends, restore her family. If they had been exposed, Joshua's and Judith's exploits would have brought terrible shame within the closed world of The Select Flock. Steven Saltby's position in the church would have been undermined and he would have turned his anger on her.

She had favoured her son, loved him the most, and invested the most in him. Had she resorted to violence to shield him? Had she attacked Teddy to protect her family? He turned over the theory. She was a tall woman, she could have, especially armed with anger and an element of surprise. Then maybe she had paid twenty thousand in guilty-conscience money from her husband's compensation. But how did she get Teddy to Epping Forest or know that he would be there? Teddy would hardly have agreed to meet Dorcas. He thought he was going to join someone who shared his beliefs. Swift tapped his spoon on the table in annoyance, trying to think of another lever to use on her. He wrapped his scarf around his neck. As he stood, he saw Graham Manchester outside, seated on an old-fashioned bike. He was wearing the same dark grey suit, with a quilted body warmer and bicycle clips. He was turning to look at the traffic before he pedalled away. It was hard to tell if he had been out there, observing the meeting inside. Perhaps it was just coincidence that Dorcas's cousin had materialised, but Swift didn't believe in coincidence.

* * *

Rowan Bartlett phoned Swift later in the day. He was on his way with Cedric to Saffron House, the wedding venue in Kew, for a run-through. Cedric was driving in the erratic fashion of a motorist who rarely takes to the road. He seemed to have forgotten that he should give way to the right at roundabouts. Swift was gripping the edge of his seat with his left hand.

'The police have spoken to Sheila,' Bartlett told him. 'She's recovering now. A psychiatrist saw her and said the police could conduct a brief interview. They allowed me to sit in.' He sounded exhausted.

'I'm glad she's going to be all right.'

'Depends on what "all right" means. I'm going to talk to her about booking into a private clinic for further psychiatric help when she has recovered physically. I'll be happy to pay. I hope you don't mind me phoning you about this. I know it isn't strictly to do with Teddy but I have no one else to talk to. Annabelle's not answering my calls.'

Swift thought that Bartlett would be happy to palm off the problem of his daughter elsewhere. He would probably sell the house while she was out of the way. He put a hand on Cedric's arm to stop him pulling out in front of a bus at a junction.

'That's okay,' he said. 'At this stage, all information from Sheila might be relevant to what happened to Teddy.'

'About the baby . . .' Bartlett coughed drily. 'He was born on August eighth. Initial results indicate that he died from sepsis. If he had been taken to hospital and treated with antibiotics, he might have survived. It's hard to say.'

Swift felt deeply relieved that Sheila hadn't killed the child. 'That's very sad. What did Sheila tell the police?'

'Ahm, let me see . . . well, the main topic was the baby of course. They told her about the sepsis. She said that he died at two days old. She found him dead in her bed. She had noticed nothing untoward. He had been snuffling but not in a way to worry her. Sepsis can be very sudden and rapid, of course.'

'Did she say who the father was?'

'No. She wouldn't speak about that and they didn't press her. She's very tearful and of course in pain from the wound, although that's quite well controlled. She said that she told Teddy as soon as she knew she was pregnant and they agreed to keep it a secret. By the time she realised what was wrong with her, it was too late to have an abortion. She worried that she would be expelled from her nursing training. She managed to hide the pregnancy by talking about the weight she kept gaining, and luckily she was healthy throughout. Some larger women are able to conceal the fact that they're expecting. She took the last weeks before the birth off work, saying she was anaemic.

Teddy helped her with the birth. She had spent some time on a maternity ward and instructed him.'

'But what was she planning to do with the baby? She could hardly keep him a secret for long once he was born.'

Bartlett heaved a heavy sigh. 'She was going to leave him at a hospital during that first week, somewhere he would be found quickly. When he died, Teddy said they had to tell someone but Sheila refused. I think that Sheila has been unwell ever since then, very unwell.'

'And Teddy? What did she tell the police about him?'

'They called a halt then, as she was getting tired. They're going to see her again when the doctors give permission. They want to ask her about that other child as well, the one who died at the party. However, when we spoke alone she assured me that what happened to Teddy was nothing to do with her. She swore on her dead child that she had no part in that and I believe her.'

Swift could imagine the drama of the scene at the hospital bed. 'Has Tim seen Sheila?'

'He came to the hospital, yes. He wouldn't speak to me. I believe he didn't stay long.'

'Well, that's something.'

'I suppose.'

'I'm following other enquiries about Teddy at the moment.'

'Very well. Frankly, he's the one child I'm not actively concerned about right now. I have to go, I have a doctor's appointment myself. I need something to help me sleep.'

Cedric swerved into the car park of Saffron House as the conversation ended, narrowly avoiding a low wall.

'That sounded interesting,' he said. 'Was it about the Druid boy who was attacked?'

'It was. Interesting doesn't start to cover it, my friend.' He ticked off on his fingers. 'Father leaves family for sister-in-law; abandoned wife sinks into medicated depression; eldest daughter rules house and conceals a pregnancy; brother Teddy is coerced into assisting her with giving birth; baby dies and she keeps it in a box in the loft; sister and brother argue about revealing the death; the gender-uncertain, Druidically inclined Teddy ends up brain-damaged in Epping Forest; youngest son takes to anger and drugs; throw another bizarre family belonging to a strict religious sect into the mix and stir.'

Cedric scratched his head. 'Do you ever wish you'd become a librarian, dear boy?'

Swift laughed. 'Only occasionally, in the early hours. I believe I am about to find out who attacked Teddy. There's a gut feeling a detective gets when a case is coming together, however slowly. Untying knots is a satisfying activity.'

'Well, all I can say is that it makes my little difficulties with Oliver seem like small potatoes. Look, we're early and Kris is already here!'

She was waving to them from inside the porch, a cup of coffee in her hand. She came out and greeted them on the steps.

'You see, I made a very special effort not to be late because I know how much you don't approve of tardiness. That's a new word in my vocabulary by the way, and I like it.'

She wore a half cap, shaped like a crescent and made of black and white fabric and netting. Swift adjusted it and kissed her.

'I appreciate the lack of tardiness and I admire the hat/cap/creation on your head.'

Mary and Simone arrived with the registrar who was to conduct the service, a woman called Debbie. Over coffee, they ran through the order of events. Debbie explained some of the phrases that had to be included in the ceremony to satisfy legal requirements. Mary had a copy of the service they had chosen. There was going to be a male pianist and female vocalist who would play the couple in with *Your Song* and finish with *All You Need Is Love*. For readings, Simone had chosen *Love and Friendship* by Emily Bronte and Mary had selected *Scaffolding* by Seamus Heaney. Harvey, Simone's brother, emerged from the kitchen to confirm that the meal would be a mixture of canapes and crostini, followed by mustard-glazed roast beef or asparagus, lemon and ricotta tart with a cupcakes assortment to finish. Cedric had a long-standing acquaintance with a jazz quartet called The Mouldy Figs, who had played for his eightieth birthday. He explained that their name was a term used in some quarters to deride those who liked traditional jazz. They were going to do a set after the meal.

Simone sat shaking her hair out frequently. She double-checked everything that was said, or interrupted before the speaker had finished. Swift suppressed his irritation and smiled at Mary. She was looking excited and strained. She gave him a thumbs-up as Debbie confirmed that everything was satisfactory from her point of view.

'Well,' Mary said, relieved. 'I think that's everything. Have you written your very brief speech, Ty?'

'Yes,' he lied. 'Just need to polish it up. No more than five minutes, as requested.'

'You can practise it on me,' Kris told him. 'What are you wearing?' she asked Mary and Simone.

Swift half listened as they spoke of their outfits, table decorations and their honeymoon in Siena. His thoughts had turned to Teddy Bartlett. The boy must have been hugely distressed by his sister's secret pregnancy and then the baby's death. A baby he had helped bring into the world, but who would have been abandoned if he had lived. The pressure of keeping that knowledge to himself for months on end would have weighed on him. No wonder he had felt as if he was living in a miserable world and wanted to escape it. Then there was Sheila, interring her baby in a box, making regular trips to the loft to grieve over the corpse, tending the bones. The disintegration of the Bartlett family was awful. Teddy's note now made complete sense — almost. His mother had been using Tim as an emotional crutch and Sheila had used him. But who had he been seeking as his companion in his new, free life? Swift was now convinced, from what he knew of them, that neither Sheila nor Joshua had been responsible for Teddy's attack. But he was sure that the answer lay somewhere with the Saltbys. The mother or the father, then, had found some way of luring Teddy to Low Copsley. He made a decision. He knew it would put the cat amongst the pigeons but he had to clear a path through their evasions. He would visit Steven Saltby.

Kris nudged him. 'Where have you gone to?'

'Sorry. I was thinking about this case I'm working on.' He looked at her. 'Maybe when the wedding is over and I've finished this piece of work, we could have a short break somewhere?'

'That would be wonderful.'

'Where would you like to go?'

'Bath! There are some vintage shops there I'd love to look in.'

'It's a deal.'

He took her hand and kissed it. Her fingers were often chilly — because of all the sitting still and sewing, she said. He cupped both her hands in his and rubbed them, then tucked the nearest into his pocket, where she liked to nestle and warm it.

* * *

The morning was murky, the air thick and stagnant as he walked to the Saltby home. The temperature had dropped to freezing overnight and he had dug out his black wool cap with ear flaps. He hoped that Mary would have blue skies for her wedding in two days' time, one of those cold but sunny winter days that cheered the spirits. He turned in at the gate of the small terraced house, betting that Steven Saltby would be at home on his own at this time of day. There was a ramp up to the front door and he stood by the side of it with his finger on the bell.

After a long minute he heard a slam, a security chain being attached and the latch moving. The door opened a couple of inches. Steven Saltby was sideways on in his wheelchair, staring out at him.

'Yes?'

'Good morning. Mr Steven Saltby?'

'Yes. Who are you?'

'My name is Tyrone Swift. I'm a private investigator looking into an attack that happened some years ago. I've spoken to your daughter, your son and your wife and now I'd like to talk to you. You'll probably recall seeing me at your church a short time ago.'

There was a silence while Saltby frowned and looked him up and down. 'I've never heard of you. Don't remember seeing you.' The voice was deep and flat. Uncompromising.

'I believe your family haven't mentioned me or the information they've given me because they thought you would be upset. I do think that as the head of the family, you should be involved or at least allowed to make your own decisions on the matter. It's a complicated situation, you see, and I'd appreciate your views.' Appealing to status usually helped in these situations.

A longer silence. 'Have you got some kind of ID?'

'Of course. I carry a card with my photo.'

'Let's see it then.'

Swift held it out as instructed, pleased that these security precautions indicated that Saltby was alone. Saltby raised a pair of glasses on a string around his neck and scrutinised it, then looked hard again at Swift.

'You can come in.'

He reached up with a grunt to undo the chain and moved his wheelchair backwards and forwards until he could turn back into the house. The effort was obviously painful. Swift thought how much easier it would be for him if there was an intercom system with a door release, but he presumed that The Select Flock would abjure such technology. He followed Saltby along the hallway and into a combined sitting/dining room. Saltby positioned himself by a bay window and indicated a straight-backed chair with no arms.

The room was plainly furnished with dark cream walls. It was spotless, drab and also cold, with a boarded-in fireplace. There was one free-standing electric heater, unplugged. The floor was covered in a thin hessian carpet and the only decoration was a huge wooden cross on one wall. A chipped pine coffee table was beside Saltby's wheelchair, with what looked like a well-used prayer book on top. A small crucifix lay across it. Swift couldn't help thinking of Teddy and Judith upstairs in this joyless place, laughing and miming to songs and Joshua sneaking into his second-hand women's finery, his mouth dry with self-hatred and longing.

Saltby was looking at him impassively. His deep-set, almost black eyes were unreadable. Up close, his thick, greyish, heavily lined skin looked even more like an elephant's hide. The grey ribbed fleece he was wearing added to the impression. His mouth was disconcertingly at odds with the rest of his face, a feminine-looking cupid's bow. He seemed like a man who took no prisoners, so Swift decided to adopt the same approach. He stared back and told Saltby about Teddy and Judith's friendship, Joshua's involvement at Cyberia, the attack on Teddy and Dorcas Saltby's knowledge of what had happened. He included the details about Joshua's dressing up. The man barely blinked.

'Teddy's family want to know who attacked him. I believe that his attack is linked to your family. Both your son and your wife lied to me initially and I think that lies are still being told.'

Saltby shifted in his chair and adjusted the footrest. 'That's quite a story you've come here with.'

'Facts. Those are facts.'

'If you say so. You think I'm involved?'

'You tell me.'

There was a silence. Saltby touched the crucifix. The faint drone of a vacuum cleaner sounded from next door. When Saltby spoke, his voice was stony with hostility.

'So you think I would sit here in the knowledge that my son is a pernicious deviant and my wife a foul liar and perhaps they are also criminals? You think I wouldn't have denounced them and had them expelled from our congregation and my home? You don't know me, Mr Swift.'

Swift thought he was telling the truth. He was an extreme, merciless man who would give no quarter to weakness. He was a father who was capable of telling his daughter that she was no longer his child. Thank goodness, Judith had escaped and found another life.

'Maybe you are telling the truth, Mr Saltby. All I know is that there is a web of deceit within your family.'

'You are sure that these things you have told me about, these unspeakable, disgusting events are all true?'

'Yes. Your own family have given me most of the information.'

'Then they are an abomination in the Lord's eyes. I know that my daughter is. She was lost many years ago. But now I find that my wife and son have trodden the same path. *"May they be blotted out of the book of life and not be listed with the righteous."* There is shame upon this house. The Lord must have some reason to punish us.'

He took up the crucifix, bowed his head and started muttering a prayer or biblical imprecation. The words sounded harsh. Swift didn't want to lose his advantage and decided to try another tack. He broke in, raising his voice.

'When you had your accident, did you receive compensation?'

Saltby kissed the crucifix and held it to his chest, a protective talisman. For the first time, he looked taken aback. 'Yes.'

'What did you do with it?'

'What business is that of yours?'

'In April 2011, someone made an anonymous donation of twenty thousand pounds to Teddy Bartlett, for his welfare. They put an unsigned note with the money. I believe it was blood money, guilt money. You'll see where I'm going with this, as it was not long after your accident.'

Saltby rested his chin in his hand. 'My compensation was paid into a church account, to do the Lord's work.'

Swift could almost see his thoughts churning. The next question was crucial and Saltby would know it.

'Who can sign off on the account or make withdrawals?'

A look of relief and a glint of malice appeared on Saltby's face. 'I am one of the signatories for the account. The other is Graham Manchester. Either of us can authorise expenditure.'

'Your wife's cousin?'

'Yes. He has been church treasurer for many years. He is an accountant. Well, more of a jumped-up office boy really, as far as I can make out.'

'Who keeps the records?'

'He does, at his home.'

'You could presumably contact your bank and check transactions for April 2011?'

Saltby shifted his legs, placing his hands below each knee and repositioning them.

'I could do that, but why should I?'

'Oh, Mr Saltby. You're an intelligent man. Surely you would like to know if church funds have been misspent on Teddy Bartlett. And if they have, there is then the bigger question as to why. Someone, or more than one person, has been pulling the wool over your eyes for years.'

'Why have they done these things? This falsehood and deviancy?' Saltby looked upwards, whispering. He was trembling, the shock of what he had heard finally hitting home.

Swift assumed he was addressing a higher authority but he took the liberty of answering. 'Perhaps because they're human and frail. I don't know that much about the Lord these days but isn't he supposed to understand sinners?'

Saltby slapped his palms down on the sides of his chair. 'They think because I'm a cripple I can be fooled. I may need to be pushed around but I'm no pushover. If there is cancer in my home and in my church, I will cut it out remorselessly.'

Swift was expecting another Old Testament quote but Saltby wheeled himself to the telephone, an old-fashioned wall-mounted model, and took a notebook and pen from the shelf beneath it. He rang his bank and went through several laborious minutes of identifying himself. He then asked the help desk to look through the account for Hope Chapel around April 2011 and advise him of money spent. He listened, making notes, and rang off abruptly. He sat with his back to Swift, tapping the pen against the paper, then returned to his position by the window. Swift remained still, waiting.

'No large amount of money was withdrawn around that time. Two hundred and fifty pounds was spent between February and May 2011 on general maintenance. At least theft is not one of the evils that has been committed.'

Swift felt a pang of frustration and disappointment. Saltby had slumped a little in his chair and was underlining in the notebook, leaning so heavily on the pen that it tore the paper.

'There are still more questions to be asked, Mr Saltby.'

Saltby nodded and gestured at the window. 'Well, here's my son. We can start with him.'

There was the sound of a key in the lock and a draught of icy air.

'Hello!' Joshua Saltby called and appeared in the doorway, dressed in work clothes — jeans and a quilted jacket. A lock of hair fell over his forehead. Out of his sombre suit, he looked younger. He froze when he saw Swift.

'What are you doing here?'

His father drew himself up ramrod straight in his chair. 'Come in and close the door.'

He did as he was told, standing just inside the door, hands by his side. In his father's presence he was rapidly diminished, more boy than pastor of his flock.

'Mr Swift has been explaining a series of events to me,' his father continued. 'A tale of sin and perversion and betrayal of the foulest kind. I have harboured serpents under my roof.'

Joshua Saltby blanched and swayed. 'What have you done?' he said to Swift.

'He has come here with the truth,' his father said grimly. 'The truth has had to proceed from the tongue of a non-believer. Or are you going to deny corruption and evil? Well, are you? Answer me!'

Joshua flinched. 'I won't deny it.'

'No, I thought not. That I should witness such a day! I have nursed a nest of vipers in my bosom. I stood aside for you. I could have been pastor but I refused. I helped raise you to the highest position of responsibility in our congregation, a place of trust and leadership and how do you replay me?'

His son put the heels of his hands over his eyes, shaking his head. His body was trembling.

'Maybe you should sit down, Joshua,' Swift said. 'I'm sorry that I've had to reveal these things but I have to find out the truth of what happened to Teddy.'

'Let him stand!' Saltby shouted. 'Let him stand like the wicked man that he is! Let him stand before the Lord!'

Joshua clasped his hands together. 'I've told you that I had nothing to do with Teddy's death and that is the truth. I could never have harmed him.'

Saltby let out a cry like an animal in pain. Joshua bent his head, whispering 'sorry.'

'Your mother is no better than you. She is a worse sinner. She has allowed both her children to carry out iniquitous deeds and go unpunished.' Saltby moved his chair forward. 'At least Manchester didn't embezzle church funds to give to this Bartlett deviant. That's a small mercy.'

Joshua looked up. 'Graham? What do you mean? He hasn't taken money.' His eyes were wild and strained and now his mask had dropped, agony was written on his face. 'Do you hear me, *Graham didn't take any money!*'

Swift turned towards him. Now he understood. 'The twenty thousand pounds that was donated anonymously for Teddy. I asked you about it and you said you knew nothing. I believe that was another lie.' He looked at the father. 'You know, I think we asked about the wrong account when you rang the bank. Presumably you have a business account?'

Saltby nodded. Joshua made a low moaning sound, like an animal in pain. Swift stood so that Joshua would not look like the accused in the dock.

'Joshua, you cared deeply about Teddy Bartlett. I think he is probably the only person you have ever had those feelings for, or allowed yourself to. You brooded about what had happened to him. Did you give that money to Mayfields for Teddy? If you did, I think that ultimately it was a good thing to have done, a decent thing. You might as well tell me now. No more secrets.'

The young man tensed and Swift thought he might run but then he slumped back against the wall. He closed his eyes as he spoke.

'Yes. I gave the money for Teddy.'

His father snorted. 'Where would you get money like that? Well? Tell me! Or do I know before you open your mouth?'

His son swallowed and wiped a tear from his cheek. Swift looked away. It was difficult to watch a man disintegrate so completely.

'I took it from the business account. I'd been thinking about it for some time, how I might do it. It was when you were still ill after your accident and I was looking after everything. I knew you wouldn't notice. I moved some money around. We could afford it. I felt . . . I felt it was the least I could do for him. I felt overwhelming guilt because I encouraged him in his sin and I thought maybe he had fallen into bad company. I hope it's helped him in some way.'

'Traitor and liar,' Saltby whispered. 'Did your mother know about this?'

'No! I swear she knew nothing about the money.'

'I can't bear to look at you any longer. You're no son of mine. Get out of my sight.'

Joshua turned to the door, tears now running down his face.

'Wait a minute,' Swift said, addressing him. 'I'm going now. I do know what I've done by coming here, Joshua, but I had to. I'm sorry for you but I'm sorrier for Teddy. I wish you'd got away from here, like Judith. I need to speak to your mother again. I'm going to ring her to tell her I've been here. To warn her.' He turned to Saltby. 'If you harm your wife in any way, I'll make sure your own kind of biblical wrath is brought down on your head.'

He left the house in a dense, awful silence. Outside, he immediately rang Dorcas Saltby at her office. When he was put through, he told her what had happened.

'I wanted to prepare you. As I said to your son, I'm sorry I had to do this but I think there are still things you're not telling me. I have a duty to a troubled family who want to know who attacked their son and brother. I need to speak to you again.'

There was the sound of her ragged breathing, then the line went dead. She may not have been the source of the

money for Teddy but she was somehow at the core of
what had taken place.

.

Chapter 14

Swift rang Dorcas Saltby and the family home several times the following day but got no reply. Her workplace informed him she was off sick with flu. He looked up Graham Manchester and found he was ex-directory but tracked him to an address in Alexandra Palace. He decided that he had better concentrate on preparing for Mary's wedding and resume his investigation afterwards. Kris was too busy with several new orders, including four evening dresses, to see him, so he read his completed speech to her over the phone.

'It's great,' she said. 'Short, as they wanted, but from your heart. I like the bit about Mary putting up with you undoing her pigtails when you were little.'

'She's always been too kind-hearted. Have I been diplomatic about Simone?'

'Very. Like when you said that they're devoted to each other.'

'Good. That was all I was worried about. I think I've read too many stories about best men who've made terrible gaffes. Are your fingers worn to the bone with sewing?'

'The machine's hot, I can tell you that. I just have to make a few final touches to my outfit for tomorrow. I'm excited! Have you seen a weather forecast? I've not looked up today.'

'Rain early but clearing to a cold, fine day in the south. Perfect.'

'Well, see you there in your velvet jacket, Mr Best Man. *Powodzenia!* That's Polish for good luck.'

* * *

Swift had persuaded Cedric to let him drive to Kew so that he wouldn't turn up with all his muscles knotted. The ceremony was due to start at 11.30 and they arrived at 10.45, in time for coffee. Mary and Simone were already there, in shift dresses and shoes that made them a mirror image of the other. Mary's dress was cream with a plum bodice and plum shoes — Simone's plum with a cream bodice and cream shoes. Simone wasn't yet showing any sign of pregnancy but now and again she placed her hand on her abdomen. They were talking to Joyce, Swift's stepmother, who was dressed in a tangerine suit with a broad-brimmed apricot boater which collided with Swift's nose when she kissed him. As usual, her conversation consisted mainly of questions and exclamations.

'Oops!' she laughed. Her foundation was so thick that he stuck to her slightly when she grasped him. 'Don't these two look lovely? And you, so distinguished! I was just saying I hope we will all be attending your wedding one day soon. I hear you have a young lady! Is she here?'

'Not yet, she'll be here any minute. Her name is Kris. Mary and Simone, you look wonderful.'

He kissed them both and there was only a tiny frisson of tension when his cheek touched Simone's. He took Mary's hand.

'Okay there on your big day?'

'Fine. You look terrific. Well done, Kris!'

'Yes.' He glanced at his watch. It was almost 11 a.m. 'She should be here by now.'

'How is she travelling?'

'By train, then cab. She had a crucial fitting for a customer early this morning, otherwise she could have come in the car with us.'

'Don't worry, there's plenty of time.'

Cedric had gone to check that the wines were in order and to greet The Mouldy Figs who were unpacking their instruments. Mary entrusted the rings to Swift, who tucked them carefully into the inside pocket of his jacket. Joyce started telling him about the latest Gilbert and Sullivan production at her local church hall. He listened with half an ear to details of *The Pirates of Penzance* while gazing anxiously towards the main door of the hotel. At 11.20 he peeled away from Joyce and rang Kris. Her phone went to answer and he left a terse message, asking her to ring him if she was running late. Debbie, the registrar, had arrived and vanished with Mary and Simone. Cedric started asking people to move into the salon where the ceremony was to take place. He saw Swift's darkened brow.

'Are you all right, dear boy?'

'Kris isn't here and she's not answering her phone.'

'Oh dear. We do need to go in.'

'I know. For goodness sake! You'd think she be on time today, of all days!' He felt a headache forming across his temples.

'Maybe there's some major delay beyond her control and she can't get a phone signal.'

'Maybe. Well, I have to go in.'

'Yes, you're needed right away. Tell you what, I'll loiter at the back and keep an eye out. When Kris arrives I'll smuggle her in quietly.'

'Thanks, I appreciate it.'

The service ran smoothly. Swift wanted to glance around to see if Kris had arrived but kept his gaze straight ahead, not wishing to cause a distraction. He handed the rings over cleanly, watching Mary smile, and led the applause at the end. As the couple walked back down the room, he turned and looked at Cedric, who was standing by the door with confetti. Cedric shook his head and gave a little shrug.

Swift stepped outside and checked his phone. There were no messages or missed calls. He rang Kris again and left another message, unable to keep the annoyance from his voice. How could anyone be so late for such an important event? He accepted a glass of champagne and decided that he would forget about Kris until after the wedding breakfast. He found Mary and apologised to her for Kris's bad manners.

'Don't worry,' she said, sipping champagne and patting his arm. 'There must be some major hitch. You know what transport in London can be like. She'll be here. Didn't that go amazingly well?'

'It did. You did great.'

He sat through the meal, barely tasting the food, distracted by the empty seat opposite him. He was aware of elegant china and snowy linen, the musical ring of crystal as toasts were made, the cheerful hum of conversation. He talked to the man on his left and the woman on his right but couldn't recall their names or who they were related to. Whenever the door opened he looked towards it, but no Kris. Every ten minutes or so he sneaked his phone from his pocket but there was no call, no message. He managed to concentrate enough to deliver his speech competently, but was relieved when it was done. Joyce buttonholed him as people moved towards the salon again for music and cakes.

'Ty dear, what's happened to your friend?'

'I have no idea. I haven't heard from her.'

'Oh dear, I am sorry. I hope she hasn't had an accident!'

Joyce smoothed his jacket unnecessarily and he stepped back. He had started to worry along similar lines.

He checked the main news and travel websites but couldn't see anything about delays or accidents. He rang Kris again with no success. His head was now throbbing, a mix of anxiety and champagne. The Mouldy Figs had started playing, the clarinet leading on *It Had to Be You*. The sweet notes didn't chime with his mood. It was now nearly 3 p.m. She should have been here by his side in her beautiful dress, sharing the happiness, dancing. The wine he had drunk was bitter in his throat. He had to do something. He looked into the salon. Mary and Simone were dancing, with others gradually joining in. He beckoned to Cedric who was glazed with champagne, his tie askew.

'Can you give my apologies to Mary and Simone? I can't raise Kris at all and I'm worried about her. I'm going to go to her flat in case she's ill.'

'Have you got a key?'

'No, but the woman who owns it lives on the ground floor, so I'm hoping to find her if Kris doesn't answer the bell.'

'I'm so sorry, dear boy. I do hope Kris is all right. Don't worry, I'll let the brides know. You've done your bit. Let us know how she is. Do you want to take the car?'

'I'd better not. I've had a fair amount to drink. And I'll probably be quicker by train and tube, heading into Friday rush hour. I'll phone you. You do have your phone switched on?'

Cedric checked. 'Ah, good point, no. There. I'd switched it off for the service but all go now. Obviously, I'll call you if she turns up.'

* * *

It was early evening by the time he reached Kennington. Kris still wasn't answering her phone and when he rang her bell there was no reply. There was no light in the top front window, where her living room was and the curtains were pulled back. The bell for the ground floor flat showed the name Burns. He pressed it, taking out his ID. A teenage boy answered, eating a packet of crisps.

'Hi, is your mum in?'

'Not back from work yet. Who's asking?'

'My friend Kris Jelen lives in the top flat. I'm worried about her because I can't contact her. Have you seen her today?'

'Nope, been at school.'

'I think your mum has a key to her flat. This is my ID. I'm a private detective.'

'Wow! You'll have to talk to my mum.'

The pickled onion smell from the crisps was revolting.

'What time does she get home?'

'Any time soon.'

'Have you got a number I can ring her on?'

The boy took a phone from his back pocket, scrolled down the screen and pressed a number with a greasy thumb. 'Hi, Mum, there's a bloke here says he wants to get in the top flat. Says he's a detective. What? I dunno.'

Swift mimed being allowed to speak. The boy handed his phone over and fished around in the bottom of the crisp packet, dabbing up crumbs and licking his fingers. Swift explained the situation.

'Have you seen or heard Kris today?' he asked.

'No. I saw her in the hallway yesterday morning. She seemed fine. Listen, I'm about five minutes away. Hang on and I'll be there. Can you put my son back on?'

The boy listened, grunted into the phone and shrugged.

'She says I can't let you in till she gets here.'

'Okay. You go back in if you want and close the door. I'll wait here.'

The boy blew into the crisp packet as he turned away, exploding it with his fist. Swift tried Kris's number again as he waited, not expecting a response. The sky was growing leaden with purple clouds that reminded him of the colour of Mary and Simone's dresses. He walked up and down the pavement, growing more fearful with each passing minute. Finally a woman holding two bags of shopping came towards him.

'Ms Burns?'

'Yes, Martha Burns. Are you Mr Swift?'

'That's right. Here's my ID. I wouldn't ask you to let me into Kris's flat without good reason.'

'Okay. Let me put these bags inside and get the key. I think I should come up with you.'

'Yes, of course.'

He was grateful that she seemed calm and sensible. She led him up the stairs to Kris's flat and knocked loudly on the door.

'Kris, Kris! It's Martha, are you there?'

There was no sound from within. She turned to him, biting her lip, looking worried. He banged on the door and called Kris's name several times. He rang her phone and heard the familiar call tune from inside the flat.

Martha breathed, 'Oh.'

'I think you should let me open the door and go in first,' he told her.

She handed him the key. He stepped through the door and sensed that familiar, strange hush in the atmosphere of a place when something was wrong. The Polish radio station that Kris tuned into on her laptop sounded faintly from the living room.

'Please wait here,' he said to Martha, who nodded, her hand to her mouth. He walked along the hallway, calling Kris's name softly. The door to the living room was ajar and he saw her feet, one pointed sideways, the other upwards in the soft black ballet pumps she wore at home. She was wearing her blue and white striped dressing gown and lying on her back near the sewing machine, amidst a tumble of patterned materials and netting. A strip of thick damask was knotted tightly into her neck. Dark red and mauve marks suffused the skin around it. She stared

207

sightlessly at the ceiling. He knelt beside her and touched her arm, then an ankle. They were stiff and cold. She had gone away. There was a terrible absence.

'Mr Swift?' Martha Burns had stepped into the hall.

He raised himself, took a breath and stood in the doorway. 'Kris is dead. She's been murdered. I'm going to ring the police. Don't come in any further.'

She gaped at him. 'What can I do?'

'Nothing. Let the police in. I'll stay here. Don't say anything, not even to your son.'

She turned and ran downstairs. Swift rang emergency services. Then he gazed again at the living room. There had been a struggle. A box of pins had spilled across the carpet and a bolt of shiny cloth had been knocked over. A couple of pattern books lay scattered beside it with some scissors and a spool of white thread. There had been no sign of forced entry at her door. She must have let her killer in. He knew that Kris liked a hot bath around nine o'clock when she was in for the evening. Afterwards she would put her dressing gown on and continue working at her sewing machine, listening to background music from home. The stiffness of her limbs indicated that she had died sometime the previous night. Polskie Radio continued playing from her laptop, a high pitched jingle, then a fast, merry pop tune.

He knelt by her side again, saying her name. Her hair was clipped back so that it wouldn't fall in her eyes when she was machining. He had been angry with her for being late. In his last message on her phone his voice had been cutting. He made a smoothing motion over her head, without touching. Minutes passed. He hoped she had died quickly.

Her dark blue and aquamarine wedding outfit was on a hanger, pressed and ready to wear, her navy shoes beneath it. He knew he should phone Cedric but couldn't bring himself to make the call yet. He shouldn't touch anything but he moved to the elegant dress and rested his face against the cool, thick satin of the full skirt. He closed his eyes, waiting for the police as the inconsequential music played on.

* * *

As he reached home, his phone rang. It was Mary.

'Oh Ty, what can I say? Cedric told me. Come round and we can talk properly.'

'Thanks, but I won't. It's very late and I know you've got an early flight in the morning. I'm in a cab, on the way home.'

'I could come to you.'

'No, that's okay, Mary. I want to be on my own. Your day has been overshadowed enough as it is.'

'That doesn't matter. What have the police said?'

'Not much. Kris was strangled and there's no sign of forced entry. Judging by rigor, I think it happened late last night. I have to talk to them again tomorrow. Naturally, they wanted to know where I was last night so I told them I was with Cedric in his flat having supper and playing dominoes with him and Milo from eight until gone midnight yesterday.'

'What about Kris's family?'

'The police are going to locate them. Her parents live in Lodz. She had a brother in New York.'

'Ty, if you want me to stay around we can postpone the honeymoon . . .'

'Absolutely not, Mary. I'm okay. I want you to go away and enjoy yourselves. Please don't contact me until you get back. There's no need and no point.'

'Yes, all right, I know. I know you won't want fuss. It's just that, you know, there was Ruth and now this happening to Kris. Grief can sneak up on you. Not everything can be resolved in a rowing boat.'

'Yes, I know. It will help me to know that you're happy. I'm going to sign off now. Ring me when you get back.'

She knew better than to try and talk to him further and said goodnight. Back home, Swift fetched two bottles of red wine, opened one and turned on a single lamp in the living room. He downed a glass quickly and refilled. He sat in silence, staring at the wall. Cedric tapped on the door after a while, holding a bottle of whisky.

'Come in,' Swift said. 'I've got wine going if you want a glass of that.'

'I'll have some of this stuff.'

Cedric fetched a glass and poured amber liquid. They sat opposite each other, both still wearing their wedding outfits. Cedric loosened his tie and stared down at his drink for a while.

'Was this a random attack, Ty?'

'I suppose so. I don't know as yet, but judging by the way I found her, I don't think Kris was raped.'

'I'm so, so sorry.'

Swift didn't reply, just nodded and drank. Outside, a dog barked and a car's brakes squealed.

'Not the wedding day Mary and Simone were hoping for,' Swift said eventually.

'No.'

'I was angry with her. I left a sharp message on her phone the second time I called, saying not to bother coming if she couldn't be on time.'

'You didn't know. Don't blame yourself for that.'

'I really liked her.'

'I could tell.'

They sat in silence a while longer. Swift opened the second bottle.

'Can I get you anything, my dear?' Cedric asked. 'A sandwich? It's a long time since we ate.'

'No thanks. I'm going to get very drunk and then I might sleep. You head off to bed. It was a beautiful dress she was going to wear, classy. She must have spent hours on it.'

'I can imagine.' Cedric rose and touched Swift's shoulder lightly as he left.

Swift made his way quickly through the second bottle of wine, glad of its numbing powers. He woke at six, sprawled on the sofa, his velvet jacket twisted around him. His head was thumping, his mouth parched. He thought about getting a glass of water but lay instead staring at the floorboards. Moving his limbs seemed like an enormous challenge. His last words to her had been unkind, even if she had never heard them. The last thing she had said to him was good luck.

* * *

Kris's parents were at the police station, two glazed-looking people in their fifties. Her father's eyes were reddened with tears, her mother's dry with anguish. They spoke little English, and an interpreter had been provided, a young man who sat on the edge of his seat, alert and watchful. It was hard, communicating grief through a third party in the sterile, airless little room with worn fabric chairs. Two pot plants languished on the narrow window ledge and there was a burn mark on the carpet. Swift explained that he had known Kris for a while and they had become close. He talked about the wedding and the dress she had made. Her mother took his hand and held on to it throughout the meeting, as if it were a lifebelt. Her fingers were cool and he thought of Kris's chilly hands between his.

'I'm so sorry,' he said. 'She was talented and lovely.'

The interpreter spoke and they both nodded. Her father was crying again, into a large hanky. Her mother cleared her throat and spoke. Her eyes held a pleading look, as if she hoped he could explain the horror, make some sense of it.

'Mrs Jelen says Krystyna had talked about you in emails. She sounded happy. She was hoping to take you to visit Lodz one day. Mrs Jelen asks who could have done this, who could have wanted to harm Krystyna?'

'I don't know,' Swift said helplessly. 'I can assure them that the police will find whoever did it. Please ask them if there's anything they need, anything I can help with.'

The interpreter spoke to them. 'They say thank you but they are alright. They just want to see their daughter's home, get an idea of her life here. They are going to be taken there this afternoon.'

'Tell them there is a lovely dress there that Kris had made to wear to the wedding we were attending. They might want to take it home with them. Please say as well that Kris was happy. Her business was doing really well, she liked her flat and her life here.'

Mrs Jelen listened, while her husband sobbed. She nodded at Swift, then turned to her husband, took the hanky from him and dabbed at his eyes. He drew himself up and spoke, his voice catching.

'Mr Jelen asks if you know when Krystyna's body will be released to them. They wish to arrange to take her home to Lodz for burial.'

'I don't know. Once the police have all the information they need, they will agree to the release. It's best to talk to their family liaison officer about that.'

Mrs Jelen kissed his hand as he left and stroked his arm as if he were the one who had lost a child. Her generosity touched him. He went to the men's cloakroom and splashed his face with cold water, holding his eyes open. He found the DI in charge of the enquiry, an Alexa Markham, and spoke to her briefly. She said that they were checking a fingerprint that had been found on the corner of the chair by the sewing machine. Whoever had been in there had attempted to clean away any traces, but she was hoping that the one unidentified print might give a lead. She confirmed that there had been no sexual assault. That was some small comfort.

'It might have been a burglary gone wrong,' Alexa Markham told him. 'We haven't found Ms Jelen's purse or wallet and her bag had been thrown behind the sofa. The landlady's son said he might have left the front door ajar when he nipped out for a snack around half nine that evening. That would fit with the timescale for Ms Jelen's death so I'm working on the premise that the perp had access to get up to her flat and she opened the door.'

Swift rubbed his jaw. He was aching with sadness.

'Presumably you're going to contact her customers? Maybe she came up against someone who wished her ill.'

'Yes. We're going to focus on the male customers first. There are only two. You said in your statement that you don't know of anyone else we should look at?'

'No. We'd been seeing each other for just a couple of months. Kris said she'd been too busy working since she came here to make many friends. There are just the two women I mentioned, that she spoke about, but I hadn't met them yet.'

'Okay. We're still door-knocking but so far no one in the area saw or heard anything. Early days, though. I'm sorry for your loss and that your cousin's wedding has been tainted by this. I met Mary once, at a conference. She's an inspiring speaker.' .

'It should have been such a happy occasion. Kris was looking forward to it immensely.'

* * *

It was a bitter day, the wind slicing in from the east. The low sky was filled with charcoal-smudged clouds. Swift walked aimlessly for a while, hardly noticing where he was heading. He wanted to go and knock on doors near Kris's flat himself, do something to help find her killer but he knew that he needed to leave it to the Met for now. If he interfered at this stage, he might confuse any witnesses, muddy the scene. He stopped for a coffee. He was hungry but couldn't eat. The barista placed a round of shortbread on the saucer and Swift snapped at him, asking for it to be removed. The young man looked taken aback at his brusqueness.

He sat in a quiet corner, pushing images of Kris and her parents from his mind. It was best to keep busy and focus on Teddy. Activity helped keep sorrow at bay during the day. He rang the Saltby's house and heard Steven Saltby's flinty tones.

'I want to speak to your wife again. Is she there? Her workplace says she has flu.'

'She's gone. I told her to get out and take her devil's spawn with her.'

'You mean Joshua?'

'Yes.'

'Where have they gone?'

'I don't know and I don't want to know.'

'When did they go?'

'The evening you were here. That's it. I don't want to have any more conversations about them.'

The line went dead. Swift wondered briefly how a man in a wheelchair was going to cope on his own without a handmaiden but didn't let it bother him. If Dorcas Saltby and Graham Manchester were as close as siblings, she and Joshua might well be staying with him. He decided to head to Alexandra Palace. He was feeling too drained to take public transport so he hailed a taxi. He closed his eyes briefly as it weaved through the afternoon traffic. He couldn't bear to think of Kris lying cold and alone. She had hated the cold so much. He forced his eyes open and looked out of the window at life spinning onwards.

Graham Manchester's house was in a small new development of box-like dwellings. They were detached, but only just. The show home was still for sale. Freshly planted spindly trees and tiny shrubs struggled upwards in the chilly soil. There was a raw smell of recently turned earth mixed with the burnt aroma of tarmac. He rang the bell of Manchester's house but there was no answer. He rang again, then looked through the front window into an empty living room. He walked past a dustbin and around the narrow passage at the side of the house to an unlocked metal gate and through to the back. There was a tiny square of patio and an equally small lawn. Through French windows he could see a kitchen cum dining area. A couple of mugs and a saucepan stood on a worktop and three chairs were pulled out at angles from the table. There was no sign of anyone. He returned to the front and rang the bell again, then quickly looked upwards. It was a trick that often worked and it did on this occasion. He saw Joshua Saltby's pale face fleetingly at a bedroom window before he stepped back out of sight.

Swift rang the bell once more and rattled the letter box, shouting through it.

'Joshua, I know you're in there. I've just seen you upstairs. I want to talk to your mother. I'm not going away until you speak to me. Is your mother there?'

He waited, then yelled again. 'Joshua! Come on, I don't bite. Just come to the door, will you?' He banged on the wood with his fist. 'The neighbours will start complaining soon. Come on.'

He waited, then banged again and rang the bell, keeping his finger on it. He saw a blurred figure through the frosted glass, coming down the stairs. Saltby opened the door. He looked thinner, shabby and exhausted, in crumpled pyjamas and bare feet. His hair lay flat against his scalp. His eyes were bruised-looking and vacant. There was a strong, rancid smell of body odour. The contrast to the smart, assured pastor could not have been more marked. He stared at Swift, swaying slightly. He spoke in a whisper.

'What have you come here for?'

'I want to speak to your mother.'

'She's not here.'

'Where is she?'

215

He shook his head, swaying again. 'Don't know.' He licked his lips. His tongue looked dry and coated. 'I've got a terrible headache. I don't feel too well. Sort of dizzy . . .'

He turned away and stumbled, slipping down to the floor. He made no effort to get up. Swift stepped in beside him and shut the door. The house was unbearably hot and stifling. He bent down to Saltby, who was lying on his side and shivering in the heat. He felt his pulse. It was weak.

'Joshua, have you taken something?'

'Thirsty.'

Swift fetched a glass of water and helped Saltby to sit up against the wall.

'Drink this slowly.'

Swift put the glass into his hand and sat opposite him, watching him drink, gulping as if it hurt his throat. Then he helped him up and supported him into the living room and sat him on a sofa. He was already responding to the liquid, holding his head up. Swift brought him more water and waited while he finished it.

'Have you taken something?'

Saltby rubbed his temples. 'He gave me sleeping tablets. Diazepam.'

'Who? Graham?'

'Yes. Made me take them. He said he'd hurt me if I didn't.'

'When was this?'

Saltby looked around, rubbing his throat. 'What day is it today?'

'Monday.'

'Thursday, I think.'

Swift could feel sweat slicking his forehead. He took his jacket off. 'Stay there. I'm going to fetch you a blanket and turn the heating down.'

He switched a thermostat on the wall by the stairs from thirty to fifteen degrees and ran up to the landing. He headed to the front bedroom. It was hot and smelled sour. There was a pool of vomit on the carpet by the single bed.

He took the duvet and checked the room and the bathroom cabinet, making sure that there were no more sleeping tablets lying around.

Downstairs, he placed the duvet over Saltby.

'Have you got any painkillers? My head is thumping.'

Swift felt his pulse again. It was stronger. 'When did you last eat and drink?'

'Ahmm, not sure. Days ago. I've been awake for a while but I didn't want to get up. Couldn't.'

'Okay. I'm going to get you something to eat. Then after that you can have painkillers. You understand?'

Saltby nodded, closed his eyes and rested his head on the cushion. In the kitchen Swift found sliced bread and made toast with honey for them both and two large mugs of tea. He was running on empty himself. They sat in silence as they ate. Saltby was gradually looking more alert but when he had finished he started crying silently. Swift cleared away the empty dishes, refilled Saltby's mug and gave it to him with a couple of painkillers he found in a kitchen drawer.

'Thanks. Sorry about this.' Saltby pressed his hands into his eyes and pushed the duvet down.

'Are you feeling stronger?'

'A bit.'

'You were dehydrated and hungry. Did your mother and Manchester leave here on Thursday?'

'I think so.'

'Why did he give you sleeping tablets? To buy them time?'

Saltby nodded and yawned. His eyes still leaked tears.

'Drink that tea. You need to give me answers, Joshua. Try and concentrate. Your father threw you and your mother out last Wednesday and you came here. What happened then?'

Saltby sipped the tea, staring miserably ahead. He spoke dully.

'When I was little, we had a story in school about some animals who went to tell the king the sky was falling. That's how I feel, as if the sky has fallen. Everything is in ruins.'

Swift felt an echoing tug of pain. 'Just tell me, Joshua. If the sky has fallen, the worst has already happened.'

'I need the bathroom.'

'Okay, but don't lock the door in case you feel unwell again.'

He walked around the tiny living room while Saltby was in the bathroom. It was bright and clean because of its newness but the furniture was worn and the only decoration was the same large cross that he had seen at the Saltbys'. A heavy bible lay on a chair. Apart from knowing they were religious, you'd have no clue about the person who lived here. Saltby returned, the front of his hair damp from where he had washed his face. He took the duvet and wrapped it around his shoulders, hugging it like a child with a comforter. Swift sat and waited.

'My mother was in a bad way when we got here. I thought she was having a breakdown. I was . . . I don't know, stunned, I suppose. Graham was furious with me when she told him I'd given the money to Teddy Bartlett. She was too. She said I'd betrayed her. She'd done everything to protect me and I'd gone behind her back yet again, so many years later. I tried to explain about how I'd felt but the more I talked about Teddy, the angrier she got. I've never seen her that way.' He pulled his feet up under the duvet, seeming more childlike by the minute.

'I suppose she felt that her world had been blown apart.'

'She said . . . she said that she had made a pact with the devil himself to protect me and all I did was shame her. Graham was ranting at me as well, saying terrible sacrifices had been made for me. I was frightened. I'd have left then but I had nowhere to go. I couldn't even go to the chapel because Graham had the keys. Can I have some more water?'

Swift brought another glass to him. He was still pallid but the shaking had stopped. He drank, and wiped his lips.

'I tried to defend myself, saying I'd done my best as pastor, to be the son she wanted and make up for my sin. I said it had been a constant struggle, suppressing those desires. I couldn't even confess the awful truth of it, the countless days I've stood, looking at women's clothes in shop windows. The times I've looked away or literally run when a man has given me a certain glance, the longings and dreams I've battled with. They could tell, I suppose, smell it on me like some awful, sulphurous stench. I've lived my life feeling as if unseen forces are pulling me in different directions. My mother howled then. She smacked me across the face. Then she told me. Graham attacked Teddy. He thought he'd killed him. He intended to. Oh God, this is so awful!'

'Go on, tell me everything she said.'

He took a breath, held it for a moment. 'She said what was she supposed to do? She had a son and daughter who were both deviants. We were the ones at fault but she would be blamed. She was terrified that our father would find out. She prayed on her knees day and night but no answer came. Graham found her in tears in chapel so she told him what had been going on. They agreed that the only thing to do was rid the world of the sinful boy who had brought her children so low. As long as he was around, spreading his evil and temptation, the family was at risk of further iniquity. The Select Flock would be tainted if what had been happening ever got out. With him gone, we could all be on the true path again. She used the computer at work to contact Teddy on the website I'd told her about. She pretended to be a practising Druid and a . . . a pervert like him. She got him chatting. She and Graham read up about the kinds of things to say. She said she was seventeen. She spun him a sob story about being unhappy at home and wanting to leave. He was hungry for the claptrap she fed him, he swallowed it all. They agreed to meet in Epping Forest, conduct a cleansing ritual and seek a new life. Graham was there waiting for him. They thought he was dead. She said they'd done all this for me and all I could do was creep about behind her back, giving our money to that boy who blighted our lives! She tried to make me kneel, said I should be going down on my knees to Graham to thank him for what he did . . .'

He closed his eyes, took another breath. Swift waited.

'Graham started in then, telling Mum not to upset herself. He said he'd do it all again, to cut the worm of darkness from our midst and keep Mum safe. He told me if he'd known that I was still a worm in their midst he'd have dealt with me too. Then he said I wasn't fit to wipe my mother's shoes, let alone be their pastor.' Saltby hammered his fists against his temples. 'He was right. I'm not fit,' he said dully. He laughed suddenly, a hysterical sound. 'Do you remember I said I'd given Teddy the money because I worried that he had come to harm because he'd fallen into bad company? Such irony! What did we do to him? I lied about who I was and then my own mother did the same.'

Swift looked at him. Hopeful, confused, gullible Teddy. He hadn't stood a chance with the bait that had been laid so carefully.

'Have you any idea where they've gone?'

'No. Graham made me take the tablets. He said I couldn't be trusted not to betray them. My mother said I'd never see her again.'

'Have they got family anywhere? Are there places they went on holiday?'

'We never had holidays. Mum hasn't got a passport. There's no family that I know of. My mother is as good as a murderer and all because of me. I wish Graham had given me enough tablets to kill me.' He drew his knees up to his chest and wrapped his arms around his head.

Swift couldn't summon much sympathy. 'You have to face this now and deal with it. It's the least you can do for Teddy. I'm going to ring the police. They'll need to speak to you. Do you understand?' He raised his voice. 'Joshua, look at me!'

Saltby looked up and nodded.

'Good. I think you should have a shower and get dressed while I make some calls.'

Swift went out to the patio and phoned Archie Lorrimer's mobile. The sky above was now a cheerless knife grey. After his call to the police he saw that he'd received an email from a hotel in Bath. He had sent them a query about a double room in January, planning his trip with Kris as a New Year treat. He deleted it without reading the message.

Chapter 15

Swift's new boat had arrived. It was made of super carbon and gel-coated, a much superior model to his previous one. He had made it ready and taken it for a first trip on the river. It was a raw, still day, most of the trees now bare. The river banks looked stripped and bleak. The season suited his mood. He sculled for miles, stopping only for water and some fruit and once to look at a small flock of ringed plover through his binoculars. It was a lovely craft, well balanced in the water, yet he could take little pleasure from it. Memories of Kris kept ambushing him, the little caps she wore tilted on her hair, the way she blew her fringe back, the enthusiasm with which she demolished puddings. She had been so full of infectious vitality, so full of plans. Although they had only been lovers for a short while, he had thought the relationship could deepen, become long-term.

He shook himself and thought of the Bartletts. DI Lorrimer had told him that Sheila had confessed to suffocating Clara, the baby found dead after the party. She had heard her crying, she said. When she picked her up and tried to comfort her, she wouldn't stop. She had panicked and held a pillow over her face. Lorrimer said that given the events that had taken place with her own baby the year before, she had probably been suffering postnatal depression. That would certainly be taken into account at any trial. Joshua Saltby had been interviewed about his association with Teddy and a search for his mother and Manchester was underway.

'He's a deeply troubled man, all over the place emotionally,' Lorrimer had said. 'He's staying in a seedy bed and breakfast, says he can't bear to be at Manchester's, and obviously the family home is a no-go area. He said he'd like to get in touch with his sister and asked if you could find out if she'll talk to him.'

'I can contact her and see. I'll phone her.'

Swift had met with Rowan Bartlett, to update him about Teddy. There was a *Sold* sign outside the house and the place had been cleaned. Bartlett himself was also looking smarter. He seemed bemused, rather than angered or upset, by the details of how his son had been lured to Epping Forest.

'How can these people have called themselves religious and carried out such a terrible crime? It's hard to take in. And this . . . this Graham Manchester is a church-goer?'

'Yes. The whole family are deeply religious. Crimes are committed in the name of religion, unfortunately. You can read about that every day.'

'Poor Teddy. Poor boy. To have his hopes crushed . . ?'

'Dorcas Saltby and Manchester were very clever in the way they went about contacting him. Fury, fear and desperation made her cunning. She saw Teddy as a menace to her family and her church, as did Manchester when she told him. If Teddy was removed, the status quo could be re-established and temptation removed from Joshua and Judith.'

'I'm glad you got to the truth of it. But my goodness, such awful people! How unfortunate for Teddy that he got mixed up with the daughter.'

'For what it's worth, they were very fond of each other. I think Judith provided some stability and refuge for Teddy at a difficult time.'

'Yes. He must have suffered, knowing what he did about Sheila. She's been remanded to a psychiatric unit until her trial. I'm not sure she will ever recover, especially as she won't be able to work in nursing again. I've informed her about Teddy. She's having medication at present, so I'm not sure how much has sunk in.' He winced. 'In fact, they've asked me not to visit again for a while. She gets upset when she sees me.'

'Have you told Tim about Teddy?'

'I emailed him, about Teddy and Sheila. He hasn't replied. I can only do so much.'

Two sons lost to him and his daughter tidied away. Swift watched him make coffee and open some biscuits. He seemed to have no trouble carrying on, making plans.

'I have a buyer for the house,' he said brightly. 'Sold it within twenty-four hours of putting it on the market. I hope it will be a happier place for the new owner.'

'Where are you moving to?'

'Cornwall, I think, somewhere by the sea.'

'A long way from London. You won't be seeing much of your children, then.'

Bartlett shrugged. 'I don't think that will matter to them. I can visit London as and when. Tim and Sheila don't want my company and Teddy is unaware. I can't see there's anything more I can do for them now.'

You could try being around and being a father, digging in for the long haul, Swift thought, *but then why break the habit of a lifetime?*

'Do you think the police will find this Graham Manchester and the Saltby woman?' Bartlett asked.

'Probably. They can't have left the country, as she has no passport. It might take time, depending on how well they can cover their tracks.'

At the front door, Bartlett had said, 'At least I did this for Teddy, found out who attacked him. Some small comfort.'

Swift had just reached the river bank by his rowing club when his phone rang. It was Alexa Markham.

'Hello, DI Markham.'

'Mr Swift, hello. Where are you at the moment?' She sounded terse.

'I've just been rowing on the river, about to leave my boat. Have you got news?'

'Yes. Listen, I'm coming over to your home, so head back there now. I'll see you in about half an hour.'

'What's the matter?'

She paused. 'There's some news about Kris Jelen. I do need to see you in person. I have to go now.'

She had gone before he could ask any more. A personal visit at home from a DI. Something significant had happened. He felt a sudden nausea. He stowed his boat rapidly and ran home. Indoors he towelled his face and head and paced, looking out of the window. His tracksuit bottoms and fleece top were sweaty but he didn't want to miss DI Markham's arrival. She was there within a few minutes and he opened the door before she rang the bell.

'I haven't had time to shower, you'll have to excuse me,' he said, showing her to a seat in the living room.

'No problem. Please, sit down. I've got some information for you that won't be easy to listen to.'

She had fine hair, drawn back into a neat bun and a pale, bland face but he knew the look in her eyes. It was the intent, steady gaze of the police officer who bears difficult news. He sat, still holding the towel.

'What is it?' he asked.

She adjusted her heavy rimmed glasses. 'We've charged a man with Kris Jelen's murder. He claims he didn't mean to kill her. I'm afraid you know him.'

'Who?'

'His name is Francis Howell.'

Swift stared at her. He felt as if time had stopped. Moisture dripped down the back of his neck.

'Yes, I know him. Go on,' he said.

She nodded, lacing her fingers together. 'We got a match from the fingerprint we found. Howell has been in prison before for petty crime, but I think you know that. We've also interviewed an Emlyn Taylor. He had previously employed Howell to carry out a campaign of harassment against you because you had been seeing his wife. You reported a series of incidents to your local police, although, it seems, not all of them. Howell admitted a knife attack on you which we have no previous details of.'

'Yes. I didn't report the attack because the harassing stopped. I spoke to Taylor on the phone after Howell broke in here and it stopped.'

'Right, okay. Obviously, it would have been better if you had informed the police about that assault. I'm afraid that after Emlyn Taylor agreed to call off Howell, he thought he had reason to take further action. He wanted Howell to find out if you had a partner and frighten her, torment her. Howell claims that he went to Kris's flat that night to scare her but she started shouting and coming at him and he panicked. Having sat for some time with him, I'm inclined to believe him. He's not the brightest and I can imagine him just reacting in the only way he knows, in that situation.'

Swift recalled the knife that Howell had wielded on the night he broke in. It was still in his kitchen drawer. He felt cold streaks of sweat on his skin. 'Why did Taylor want to start this again?'

DI Markham took a breath. It was clear that she was approaching the most difficult part of the visit.

'Mr Taylor informed us that Ruth, his wife, told him that he is not the father of the child she is expecting. She said that you are the father. She packed and left their home after a blazing row. He says he doesn't know where she has gone. After hearing this, he was beside himself. He got hold of Howell again, told him what had happened and sent him on another task. Howell found out that you were seeing Kris and went to her flat that evening. I'm so sorry.'

Swift pressed the towel against his face and blinked into it, marshalling control. He swallowed hard.

'Have Kris's parents been told all this?'

'Yes. It took a while for them to understand. They flew back to Poland this morning. Kris's body has been released and they've arranged for her to be returned to Lodz later today.'

Mrs Jelen wouldn't want to hold on to his hand or offer him comfort now, he thought. She was probably wishing her daughter had never met him.

'So,' he said slowly. 'Kris died because of me.'

DI Markham sat forward. 'You know that's not true. She died because a man called Francis Howell strangled her. Can I get you a glass of water?'

'No. it's okay. What about Taylor?'

'We're mulling over what to do about him and taking advice because of his illness. He'll probably be charged with encouraging a crime. You won't be surprised to hear he's got himself a top notch lawyer. He's on bail at present and at home.'

'And Ruth? Ruth doesn't know about her husband and Howell or Kris's death?'

'Not as far as I know.'

'If I'd come back to the police about Howell and Taylor, when I found Howell here and discovered what was going on, this might never have happened. Kris would still be alive.'

'It's hard to know. There's not much point tormenting yourself about *what ifs*. You've been in the force. You'll have said this kind of thing to grieving people yourself. I know it's different when you're involved, but it's still true. Given Taylor's state of mind when his wife gave him this news, he might still have gone after you indirectly. I would say that the man is warped in his thinking, mentally unwell. I don't know how much that might be related to his illness. He certainly sees himself as hard done by, a victim. He seemed to think his actions were justified. People behave in strange ways when they - believe the world's against them.' Her phone beeped and she glanced at it. 'Look, I have to go now. I'll need you to come and make a full statement about what happened previously with Howell and the background with Emlyn and Ruth Taylor.'

'Have you been in contact with Ruth?'

'I've tried but she's not answering her phone. Her family in Shropshire haven't heard from her. I shan't be pursuing her. She has no direct involvement with what's happened. I expect you'll try to reach her, given what I've told you.'

He sat after she had gone, pressing his towel against his face again. He tried to think about what he had been told, to sort it out in his mind but his head felt full of cotton wool. Two women, one dead, one probably alone and possibly frightened, and carrying his child. Life had imploded around him. He groaned and called out Kris's name. In his mind's eye he could see Howell forcing his way through her door when she opened it. He imagined her alarm. Howell would have started playing his new game, taunting her, telling her he knew where she lived now and she'd hear more from him. He might have mentioned Swift in that cocky way of his, might have asked her if she knew that her boyfriend had got another woman pregnant. Through her fear, she probably realised that he was the man who had previously attacked Swift.

Maybe Howell had strutted around the living room, throwing a few of her sewing implements on the floor to emphasise his control and knowledge of her life. She would have been incensed by such disrespect. That was probably when she summoned the courage to shout at him and that was when he panicked. She might have died, then, at the hands of that low life, knowing that Swift and Ruth's relationship was far from over and wondering if Swift already knew about the baby.

He forced himself to shower and shave, staring at his misery-filled eyes in the mirror. He had brought misfortune directly to Kris's door through his own careless actions. He knew that he would never put down the burden of that knowledge. As he picked up his razor, he saw a tiny tube of moisturiser tucked under the rim of the glass shelf and teased it out with his finger tip. It was Kris's. They hadn't yet got to the stage where they were leaving toiletries at each other's homes but he recalled the evening when she said she'd been given some freebies when she was shopping — shower gel, soap, a scented linen sachet. She had opened the tube of moisturiser for him to sniff and laughed when it made him sneeze. He undid the cap and inhaled the mild orange and honey scent. It was all he had to remind him of her. He stood there for a long time, the tube in his hand, his mind crowded with *what ifs*.

* * *

It was almost midnight. There was a gale blowing, whipping in from the river, the wind moaning in the chimney. Swift sat with a hot whisky laced with sugar and lemon. Mary and Cedric had just left. He had wanted to tell them both his news so that he could be honest with them and not have to repeat the painful details. They had brought a spicy takeaway and over the food he had told them about Ruth and how ultimately his ongoing relationship with her had impacted on Kris. They had been stunned but kind, not saying much. When he walked Mary to her car she linked arms with him, pulling him into her in a gesture he was glad of.

'We're both going to be parents, then,' she said.

'Yes, but you've gone about it more responsibly.'

'Oh, Ty. I know you hate it when life is messy but sometimes it just is. I do hope you get to speak to Ruth soon.'

He sipped his drink, hoping that Ruth was somewhere safe and warm. He had been hoping that she would contact him but had heard nothing from her. He had phoned her mother in Shropshire. She had been in tears, saying how worried she was and that Ruth hadn't been in touch and no one else in her family had had any contact. He had rung her closest friends and her work but heard the same messages. He rang Taylor's number but put the phone down before it was answered. He couldn't trust himself to speak to the man. His anger was too fierce, and what could he hope to achieve? There would only be a bitter exchange that would offer no resolution. He opened his laptop and wrote an email to her, choosing his words carefully:

> *Dear Ruth,*
> *I've been informed that you have left Emlyn and that you told him the baby you're expecting is yours and mine. No one has heard from you. Please get in touch with me. It doesn't matter if you don't want to see me or tell me where you are. I just want to speak to you and know that you are safe and well. I would like to be part of our baby's life. I am worried about you and I do have responsibilities towards you and our child.*
> *Please, Ruth, reply to this email.*

He pressed *send* and poured another whisky. He was drinking too much but he needed the numbness. He was tired but too fretful to sleep. When he did sleep his dreams were haunted by blurred images of Kris and Ruth or at times of a woman who looked like Kris but spoke with Ruth's voice. The previous night, he had had a nightmare in which he was searching for a lost baby. He could hear its cries but even though he was looking desperately, its sobs grew ever fainter. He lay on the sofa, listening to Nina Simone, sipping his drink, hoping to hear the ping of an email arriving.

* * *

Judith Saltby had agreed to meet her brother. When Swift phoned her, she listened in silence as he detailed the events leading to Teddy's injuries, her father's reactions and Joshua's present situation. He was able to tell her that just that morning, her mother and Graham Manchester had been arrested in Aberdeen, attempting to board a ferry to Shetland.

'My God,' she said at last, 'I pity Joshua. What a life he has been living. A family can exist under the same roof and have no idea of what's happening to each other. And my mother and Graham, they'll go to prison?'

'Inevitably.'

'Oh, this is appalling. I'm holding on to Samuel here. This makes me feel that I never want to let him out of my sight.'

He pictured her with the child, cupping her hand protectively around his vulnerable head.

'Did you say Joshua has nowhere to live?' she continued.

'That's right. He's in a bad way. He feels overwhelming guilt. I think he might consider self-harm.'

'I'm not surprised. This is a lot to take in. I need to think. I'll speak to my husband, then I'll ring you back.'

231

Swift had reflected on her comment about her family, thinking it applied equally to the Bartletts. When she phoned him back, Judith said that she would like to invite Joshua to stay for a couple of days. They had a spare room and it sounded as if he needed a refuge.

Swift offered to drive Joshua Saltby to Cambridge. The man was in pieces, a bewildered, sickly figure, unshaven. On seeing him in his small room in the B & B, sitting hunched on a chair, Swift had been moved. He looked as if he should be in a hospital bed. He didn't think Joshua could make it to his sister's on his own and he worried about what might happen to him if he was left alone. There had been enough damage and despair in the Saltby family without a suicide.

Joshua sat beside him in the car, knotting and unknotting the tassels of a wool scarf. Most of the journey passed in silence. Swift stopped once and bought two coffees and croissants.

'Try to eat,' he told Joshua gently, watching the tremor in his hands.

'My throat closes when I try.'

'I know, but take tiny bites. And at least drink all the latte, the milk will sustain you.'

Joshua managed a couple of bites of the croissant and sipped most of the coffee.

'Your sister Judith is a good woman,' Swift said. 'As in genuine goodness. This is a huge gesture she is making, inviting you back into her life after you rejected her. You need to be careful with her.'

'Yes, I know,' he whispered. 'I didn't think she would want to see me. I don't know what I can say to her after all that's happened, all we did to her . . . what on earth can I say?' He touched Swift's arm, giving him an imploring look.

'You could start with sorry and take it from there.'

Joshua nodded. He slept for the rest of the journey, an uneasy, restless slumber, his head twitching. Swift saw

232

him in to the house and watched as Judith put her hand out and shook her brother's. She was clearly alarmed at his appearance and sat him in the living room, where Samuel was lying on a rug in a nest of soft toys. Swift refused a drink, saying he wouldn't stay. The truth was, he couldn't bear to watch Judith with her baby and witness the warm glow that enveloped them.

'You did the job you were employed to do, then,' Judith said to him at the door.

'Yes, and more. I'm sorry about your mother and Graham and the shock of all of this. I hope it goes well for you and Joshua. I think he can only benefit from being in your home with you. He needs to see the possibility of another life.'

'Thank you. We'll take it slowly. The Select Flock is a difficult burden to lay down but at least I know something about how to try. Small steps.'

* * *

As Swift neared London, he realised that he wanted to return to Low Copsley and visit The Yew Grove once more. He wasn't sure why. Perhaps it was to seek the profound silence and bring Teddy's story full circle. He retraced the route to the village, parked in the same spot and set off along the path. It was soft and muddy after the recent rain. The spongy earth sucked at his boots. Looking at the fretful dark clouds overhead, he thought it might pour again soon and quickened his pace. A cloudburst came as he reached the yew trees and hurried under them. The water barely penetrated their weighty branches. He sat on the ground against a tree trunk. The hazy light was restful. The sound of the deluge hissing against the leaves above was powerful and soothing. Mary, he knew, had an app on her phone which played sounds of falling rain. On frantic days she sat for a few minutes in her car and listened. She said it lowered her blood pressure.

He thought how wonderful it would be to believe in an Otherworld, a place where Kris would be in a state of transformation. He spoke her name, called to her, told her he was sorry, so sorry. His head bowed, he wept. Slowly he surrendered to the hypnotic pulsing of the raindrops and listened to his own soft breathing. His mind emptied for the first time in days. He dozed for a few minutes and woke when his phone buzzed. It was an email from Ruth:

> *Ty, I understand why you've contacted me. We are expecting a girl and she is doing fine. I left Emlyn because I couldn't take his anger any longer and I couldn't continue to deceive him about the baby. I can't regret that you're the father but I feel confused and overwhelmed. I don't know what I want to do. I'm okay. I need to be on my own for now, no fuss. I will let my family know I'm alright. I know I've been selfish, leaving them to worry. Please don't contact me again or try to find me and please don't fret. I'll get in touch again as and when. Sorry, but that's all I can say for now. R.*

He read it several times. It brought him little consolation, except the knowledge that she was safe. She could be anywhere in the world. He put his phone in his pocket and looked around the grove where Teddy's tragedy and the solstice celebration with its promise of light and life coexisted. The ancient beliefs celebrated the wheel of the year here, where Teddy's blood had flowed. This was where the Druids greeted the earth's relentless movement towards renewal. The long-lived yews would have witnessed it all.

He watched a squirrel dart along a tree trunk, seeking winter stores, preparing for the frosts to come.

He thought: *I have a daughter.*

THE END

Thank you for reading this book. If you enjoyed it please leave feedback on Amazon, and if there is anything we missed or you have a question about then please get in touch. The author and publishing team appreciate your feedback and time reading this book.

Our email is office@joffebooks.com

www.joffebooks.com

ALSO BY GRETTA MULROONEY

ARABY
MARBLE HEART
OUT OF THE BLUE
COMING OF AGE
THE LADY VANISHED

Printed in Germany
by Amazon Distribution
GmbH, Leipzig